GREEN BROTHERHOOD TRILOGY #1

THE GREEN BROTHERHOOD: SEAL TEAM XII

DEBRA PARMLEY

FINDING BRYCE

For my readers, with infinite love and gratitude.

1

Virginia Beach

"See you guys at Chicks?" Matthew Hunt "Matt" had opened the door, leaned in, and addressed Diesel and R.T. as they sat at two tables filling out paperwork.

"It's Kik's birthday," he reminded them.

Chicks Oyster Bar Marina was the favored place for SEAL Team Twelve to hang out when they were free to grab a beer and a bite to eat. Many celebrations through the years had been held there, from birthdays, to bachelor parties, and funeral wakes.

"Yeah," Tanner "Diesel" Taylor replied, then he held up the form he was filling out. "When these are done." He laid the paper down again and looked directly at Matt. "That was a clean op. Seems like there ought to be less paperwork instead of more, since we acquired the package and never had to fire one round."

Matt gave a nod, to acknowledge the comment and then said. "You're close to done. See you there."

A mostly by the book, no nonsense sort of man, dealing with what is, was his way. Matt wasn't likely to engage in any kind of discussion about how things ought to be.

Diesel didn't usually complain about things, but he wasn't in his usual mood today. He filled out one more line and then pushed the form across the table to his buddy, Reed "Railroad" Tindall. "We ought to be out running maneuvers, not stuck here in the office doing paperwork."

Reed hated that nickname and was stuck with it, but Diesel had his own nickname for his buddy, and called him R.T. 'Short for railroad tracks' is what he said if anyone asked.

Tanner didn't mind his nickname one bit. Tanner "Diesel" Taylor earned his nickname the first week of basic, when he showed up with grease stains under his fingernails.

Working at his dad's repair shop every week during high school, he'd despaired of his hands, and how the pretty girls would turn him down for dates, thinking his hands were dirty. They didn't know a mechanic could scrub and scrub his hands, and still have stains.

Although it didn't take long for his Navy and SEAL training to wash away those stains, the nickname stuck, along with his ability to repair just about any kind of engine, even in the dark.

In his mind, it was just another skill, but as he'd only followed in his father's footsteps for one year after high school, he was as proud of carrying on his father's legacy into the armed force, as he was of carrying the name.

All the men in his father's side of the family had been mechanics, and his grandfather, and great grandfather had served in the Army during World Wars I and II, which was where they'd learned the ability to work on engines in the dark.

It wasn't that he hadn't wanted to follow in their footsteps even down to their military service, it was that he'd wanted to do more.

Serving as a SEAL was more. Much more.

And he loved every minute of it.

After SEAL training, Diesel never had trouble getting dates again. He was now a lady magnet. Just one of the things his latest girlfriend had more than a little trouble with.

Last night, Kari had broken up with him again, which meant he was free to see whoever he wanted to see.

Diesel watched as R.T. pulled that damn letter out of his pocket again, and with a sad expression, prepared to read the letter again.

"Hey man, you're not going to read that letter again, are you?" Diesel could've repeated most of the letter, having heard it often enough.

"I just don't understand why Becky called it off. She never explained, and she won't answer my phone calls." R.T. bent his head to the letter.

Damn. Dear John letters ought to be written in disappearing ink, or on exploding paper.

Diesel kept his thoughts to himself, but shook his head. Watching R.T, he got an idea.

"Hey. Saturday night. Got plans?"

"Nope." R.T, kept reading." Got laundry."

"You've got plans now." Diesel said. "You can do laundry some other time."

R.T. raised his head, and looked at Diesel.

Good. I got his attention away from that letter.

"Picture lots of chicks in skimpy Halloween costumes," Diesel said.

R.T. groaned. "Costumes?"

"Yeah. Costumes. Don't worry. This will be fun. Costume party is a masquerade."

"I don't have a costume, and there's not enough time to put one together."

"Got you covered. I know a place that rents them, and they're open tonight."

"I don't know, man. I ought to try calling Becky again."

"Come on. This party is a much better time than doing laundry, and crying into your beer. Gonna be plenty of ladies at this party. You know how chicks dig costumes."

"Yeah." R.T. had to admit they did. "Thanks Diesel."

Diesel nodded. "Welcome."

R.T. put the letter away, before picking up the pen again, to finish his task.

It didn't take them long to finish. Then they went home to change clothes, with a plan to meet up at the bar.

After they'd arrived at Chicks, before the other guys arrived, they went to sit out on the deck, and startled a seagull who'd perched on the railing hoping to find food.

The seagull was often there, in that spot. So often, that tourists coming to the marina had started feeding it. Now it came every night, expecting to find food.

The waitress who appeared soon after, to take their orders, had named the bird Fred. She claimed "Fred just wants to be fed."

"What'll you have, guys?" Sheri asked, with a wide smile, between two dimples.

The little waitress was an adorable bundle of energy, and currently dating an airline pilot, who was gone not quite as often as a SEAL would be.

"When are you going to trade that boyfriend in, for a real SEAL?" Diesel teased, already knowing what her answer would be.

"You guys are gone too often, and too long," she said, with a shake of her head, and a laugh.

All the guys teased her this way, and Diesel knew she liked it, though her answer was always the same.

Diesel thought her answer was a lot of hooey. Commercial pilots were gone a lot too, and a woman who could handle that, could handle dating a SEAL.

Women who couldn't, likely wouldn't be able to handle their man being on the road, for any job.

Some women needed more maintenance, just like some cars.

Kari was one of those women. But he and Kari were through.

Diesel enjoyed watching the boats dock at the Marina, which took his mind off Kari just like knocking back a few beers with the guys would take R.T.'s mind off that damn letter.

Cutter, and Matt joined them, and took seats.

"I'll buy a round," "Cutter" Antonius (Tony) Cuttino said.

"What are we celebrating?" R.T. asked.

"My winning at the casino last weekend," Cutter said.

"You have Italian connections?" Sheri asked with a giggle.

The guys knew Cutter had cousins with connections to a casino in New Jersey. When he went home to visit his grandmother, he'd visit the casino and come back with his wins.

"Did you bring me back any cannoli?" Sheri asked.

Last time he'd brought back cannoli his grandma had made.

"Not this time," he said. "Next time, cannoli for you, sweet." He gave her a wink.

She blushed and smiled.

The men placed their beer orders, and she hurried to the bar for their drinks.

"Any of you guys going to the costume party Saturday?" Diesel asked.

"Yeah," Matt said. "I'm gonna go as an IRS auditor."

"Really, man?" R.T. said. "What kind of costume is that?"

"An easy one. Just wear a suit and tie, and carry a calculator," Matt shrugged. "I even got business cards made up to hand out." He reached into his pocket, pulled one out, and handed it to R.T. "I'm here to audit your tax records," he said.

R.T. took the card, and glanced down at it. "That would scare the hell out of a lot of people," he said.

"You are so weird," Diesel shook his head.

"It's simple, cheap, and easy, and I'll have fun with it," Matt said with a shrug.

"That's what costume parties are for," Diesel nodded. "Having fun."

Just after Sheri delivered the beers, Rich, Osprey, and Enrique "Kik" Garcia joined them on the deck, and more beers were ordered.

"Add on some onion rings," Diesel said.

Sheri nodded, and headed for the kitchen.

"You going to the costume party, Rich?" Diesel asked.

"Nah. Costume parties aren't my thing," Richard "Rich" Irvine said.

One of the oldest members of the group, he'd turned down most invites to socialize, since getting back in touch with an old girlfriend from high school at his high school reunion. Now he spent most of his free time with her, trying to get out of the friend zone. She was hesitant about dating a SEAL.

All but Rich would attend the costume party.

Osprey was going as Robin Hood, and would carry a primitive bow he hunted with for fun, and Kik was going as Superman.

"Superman?" R.T. said. "I would've thought you'd want to go as Zorro, or something like that."

"Why, because I'm Latino?" Kik shook his head. He

smoothed his hair back with one hand, and then, reaching for a small section of his bangs, pulled it down, and made it curl. "I got the perfect hair. See? Superman."

All the guys laughed.

"Yeah, man," R.T. said. "I see it."

More SEAL brothers came in the door, which more than doubled the size of their gathering. The entire group was at Chicks tonight. All twenty SEALs.

Diesel glanced around the room. These twenty men were his brothers, and any one of them would have laid down his life for the other.

The Green Brotherhood was like no other, and he took a moment to take the sight of all his brothers in, creating a memory to savor in years to come.

The noise level in the bar rose, but the SEALs weren't the ones shouting and being rowdy.

They kept to themselves, and women in the bar were drawn to the strong silent warriors, like moths to flame. There was clearly something different about these men, the way they carried themselves, and the way they communicated amongst each other, often nonverbally, which set them apart. They exuded a quiet confidence, and their eyes were always taking in their surroundings with a quiet intelligence.

Craig McDonald "Big Mac" showed his Scots Irish heritage, by the multitude of freckles across his nose and cheeks, despite his deeply tanned face. It hid his ruddy complexion, and helped him blend in on their missions. Jet-black hair from his Irish mother saved him from having his fathers red hair, and allowed him to be picked for this special team.

To be on Team Twelve, you had to have dark hair as the team was often sent to South America, and needed to blend in. Blondes and redheads would stand out too much to be included. As a result, the men on Team Twelve could all be described as tall, dark, and handsome.

Blending in, in South America, was something Team Twelve did quite well.

Martin Lopez, the second Hispanic American on the team, was fluent in three languages, English, Spanish, and Portuguese. He was their go to man when it came to native dialects.

Chris Fenner "Fen" had almost gone to college on a chemistry scholarship, but he'd also wanted to become a SEAL. He was their best man with explosives, and a bit of a MacGyver, given his aptitude in chemistry.

He often said it was as much knowing what not to put together with another thing, as it was what to put together. He was also a pretty good cook, which he claimed also had to do with chemistry.

Daniel "Tractor" Edwards grew up on a hay farm, and would have been a fourth-generation farmer, if he'd stayed home on the farm instead of joining the SEALs.

His father had a John Deere collection that men traveled miles to see. Daniel had made the mistake of talking about it too often, early in his training, was handed the nickname "Tractor" and it stuck.

His best buddy in training told him it could've been worse; they could've saddled him with "Farm-boy."

Adam "DaVinci" Burgess was always drawing and doodling, with a pen, or pencil. Tonight, he was already drawing on his cocktail napkin before he'd finished his first beer.

It would have been easy to sit and watch him, instead of focusing on the hot young woman standing nearby, hoping for attention.

Thomas (Tom) Campbell "Soupman" got his nickname after explaining the way to spell his last name, was "Like the soup, man." Once the nickname stuck it was stuck good.

Scott Roberts, "Casper" was like a ghost. He could enter a room and then leave it, without anyone knowing he'd been there.

James Slater "Slim Jim" was a skinny man with toned muscles. His metabolism was so high, he could eat anything and not gain one pound of weight.

Sawyer "Pipes" Ferguson played the bagpipes with the local Scottish group, and sometimes wore a kilt, if performing with the group for weddings or funeral services.

Sam Valente, an Italian American known as "Sammie the Conductor" because of the expressive way he used his hands when he talked, was gesturing animatedly tonight, something he did when he'd drank enough beer.

Peter "Buzz" Horne had a weird snore that sounded like a low buzz.

Jocko "Numbers" Lewis was so good with numbers, they didn't need a calculator when he was around.

And Jake Summers "Oscar" could act any part, and make it believable.

But really, all these men were actors capable of blending in, making anyone believe they were who they pretended to be, and doing what it took to complete a mission.

They were a special team of Navy SEALs, one that few outside the SEAL Teams had ever heard of.

Tonight, they were all at the bar, because it was the rotation of their cycle to have them back in Virginia, before they cycled out again into the next phase. And it just happened to be Kik's birthday.

The beer was flowing, the noise level was rising, and if the good time Kik seemed to be having was any indication, he was going to have a huge hangover tomorrow.

Ordinarily, had he been back home with his family,

there would have been a large family party, with a barbecued goat, music, and beer. After he joined the SEAL team, he'd continued to invite every one of his brothers to celebrate his birthday, and if they were available, they would join in.

Kik was having the time of his life tonight.

All the men trained hard, worked hard, and partied hard.

By the end of the evening, they made sure Kik made it home safe, as he was in no shape to drive, and the bar emptied out, the only occupant left on the patio, a lone seagull with the nickname of Fred, who had returned, hoping for leftovers to eat.

~

"Come on Pippa, this is the best party of the year, and everyone will be in costume," Cheryl said. "No one will know who you are. It's the perfect chance."

It was only the tenth time Cheryl had asked her to go to the Halloween party.

Finally, tired of being bugged about it, Pippa said, "Okay, I'll go."

"Great!" Cheryl's eyes widened, and she grabbed both of Pippa's hands, squeezing tight as she bounced on her heels. "You're going to be so glad you changed your mind. We're going to have a blast."

For once, Pippa would take a page from her mother's diary, and live in the moment.

As her mother had said, "Joyce, my dear, you haven't yet learned that life must be grasped in the moment."

Joyce Pippalousa Smith never gave out her birth name. Her full middle name had always been an embarrassment to her, though she did like her daddy's nickname for her.

He was the only one to call her "Pippa", and she missed him dearly. Her mother had always called her Joyce.

After her mother had made her announcement, she'd gone sailing off to Hawaii with a new man, who kept a boat at his summer home. "Waiting just gives you more likelihood you'll miss out. Your father may be dead, but I'm not."

Her mother was the kind of woman who couldn't stand to be alone, and one of her friends had been waiting in the wings, ready to date her.

Thinking back to the huge blow-up Pippa and her younger sister, Jeanie Magic Smith, had with their mother the day before their mother left town, made Pippa wonder where her mother was now, and reminded her, she needed to call Jeanie this weekend, and get caught up.

Mother could be anywhere. I have no idea how to reach her at sea. I don't even have her new number.

But as Jeanie often said, 'The phone works both ways.' And her sister's number hadn't changed.

Though usually Pippa was the one who had to call her sister. Months could go by, if she didn't, before Jeanie got around to calling her.

For once, Pippa was going to take a page from her mother's book. She was going to live a little.

It had been a long time since she'd gone out and had fun, and she'd always loved costume parties and Halloween.

"Now, what are you gonna be?" Cheryl asked.

"I don't know. I haven't had time to think about it," Pippa said, her tone wry. She'd only agreed a second ago.

Cheryl waved a hand, and continued in her rapid-fire way; clearly thrilled Pippa was going. "We can go to the costume shop after we get off work."

"Okay," Pippa said.

A masquerade party seemed safe enough. It was unlikely that her ex would be there. She'd moved several states away from Stan Nitty, and hoped to never see him again.

~

After work, they headed to That Magical Place, a store which sold costumes, and decorations for Halloween.

"Do you have any sexy costumes for women?" Cheryl asked.

The clerk grinned. "Yes, we do. Follow me, and I'll show you. Do you have any themes in mind?"

"I looked up your selections online. I think I'd like to be a woodland fairy," Pippa said. "With wings, and pointed ears, and everything." Now that she was getting excited about going, why not go full-on fantasy?

"Oh, fun," Cheryl said. "I'm going as a sexy nurse. Maybe I can play nurse with one of those hot Navy SEALs tomorrow night. Is your costume going to be sexy?"

"Well..." Pippa considered the costume she remembered from the website. "It's short and shows a lot of leg, and a lot of cleavage. It's also cheap, which I need. I don't have much budget for a costume."

"Want me to help you with your makeup and hair?"

"Oh, would you? That would be awesome." Pippa knew Cheryl was good at doing hair and makeup.

"Yeah, I'll come over an hour before and help you get ready," Cheryl said.

"Thanks, Cheryl." As she did every day, Pippa thanked her instincts for bringing her here to Virginia. Her sister had been only too willing to give her safe harbor when she'd needed it, and she lived just an hour away.

"No problem, Miss Pipp."

Pippa wrinkled her nose. "You're not gonna call me that at the party, I hope."

"No, I'm not gonna call you at all, 'til we agree it's time to go home. We're gonna circulate as single ladies, so the men will be more likely to approach us," Cheryl winked.

"Oh, right," Pippa nodded. "Good thinking."

~

The next day, Pippa's cousin Louise called her at work and left a message for her to call back. Far from being a normal call, Louise would only have called if someone had died or something very big had happened. So as Pippa called Louise back, she held her breath. "Hey, Louise. What's happened?"

"This time it's good news, Pippa," Louise said. "You won't have to worry about Stan anymore. He's been sent to prison for three years. Felonious assault. He beat up a guy in a bar. That was bad enough. But then he went back and beat him some more. The guy was hurt bad, and they had to call an ambulance. Stan claimed it wasn't his fault, and the other guy did this and did that, but everything was caught on the bar's security cameras. And it didn't hurt that they had pictures of the bruises he left on your neck, or that you have a restraining order out on him, already on record. He's obviously a violent and dangerous man. I'm so glad he's been sent to prison and won't be out for a long time. I couldn't wait to tell you."

Pippa breathed a sigh of relief. Stress began to drain out of her body. "Oh, that is good news. He can't find me now, and suddenly show up on my doorstep to hurt me. Not while he's in prison. So, I'm safe. Finally. No more looking over my shoulder, worrying he might be the man in the baseball cap behind me. I'm safe, finally safe!"

She felt like dancing and spinning around the room.

"Yes, you are," Louise said. "Does this mean you'll come home, now?"

"I am home," Pippa said. "Virginia is my home now, and I just started taking a couple college classes."

"So, you're staying?"

"Yes." Pippa didn't say that she never wanted to move back to her hometown, but she surely felt that way. She'd escaped a horrible marriage, a depressing house, and a town, which lost more jobs every year, and she never wanted to go back.

There was no future there. Only the past. And the past was over and done. Finally.

"Well, all right. If that's what you want," Louise said. "I just want you to be happy."

"Oh, I am happy," Pippa said. "Happier than I've been in a very long time."

~

The night of the party, Pippa let Cheryl into her apartment, and they went straight into her bathroom, where she had a curling iron already plugged in. She wanted to look different tonight, and her long brown hair usually hung straight. Most days, she loved a wash-and-go kind of lifestyle and rarely wore makeup. But tonight, she wanted a little glamour—her hair curling, smoky-sparkling makeup, and fairy ears glued onto her ears.

Cheryl curled Pippa's hair until it had ringlets at the ends, which gave it a whole lot more body. Once she finished applying makeup to Pippa's face, Cheryl took gold glitter and sprinkled it in Pippa's hair and across her bared shoulders. Spaghetti straps held the silky fairy dress up, leaving a lot of skin bare. The way the dress was cut in back, there was no way to wear a bra with this one.

It was the most daring thing Pippa had ever worn in public.

"Might as well use it up," said Cheryl before sprinkling the rest of the vial of glitter down Pippa's cleavage.

Pippa felt the glitter whisper between her breasts. "Cheryl!" she said, laughing. "I don't need it everywhere."

"Oh, but I think you do," Cheryl said. "Keep him looking for the end of that glitter trail, and you'll have his attention for sure. Then he'll be hard at attention, and you'll have some real fun."

Pippa kept chuckling. "I'll bedazzle him with my cleavage."

"You know it." Cheryl winked and tossed the empty container into the trashcan. "Ready to go?"

"Yes, I just need my tiny purse."

"Here." Cheryl reached into her purse for two condoms and handed them to Pippa. "Be prepared, because those Navy boys are not always like boy scouts, and some of them really get around."

"Oh, right." They hadn't talked much about Pippa's former life, only that she'd divorced a man who was no good and that she was trying to make a new life without complications. She hadn't hinted at her ex's violent tendencies.

Cheryl, being a party girl, understood the "no complications" bit. She never dated a guy longer than six months. Said it got claustrophobic if they lingered any longer.

"Thanks. I hadn't thought to pick those up," Pippa said.

"Always keep one in your purse and some in your nightstand. Tonight's a chance for you to have fun without the hassle of a date. But if you need more than two of these, you're on your own, girlfriend."

Unable to stop a blush, Pippa shook her head. "I won't need more than two."

I'll be lucky to need one, she thought. It had been over a year since she'd had sex, and she missed it. In the good times, at the beginning of her marriage, before everything went terribly bad, sex had been good, with that rush of attraction that went straight to her core, lighting everything up, just like fairy lights. It had been magic.

I want that again, even if for just one night. This is a start. And no one will even know who I am. This is perfect.

2

———

Pippa watched the redheaded bartender as he mixed drinks and wondered what he was making. "Those look good," she said, pointing toward the colorful drinks. "What are they?"

"Hurricanes," he said, smiling.

"I can't believe you've never had a hurricane," Cheryl said. "They are so, so good. You should try one."

Pippa told the bartender, "I'll try a hurricane, please."

"Coming right up," he said and handed her a glass with a pineapple slice on the rim and a drink umbrella on it. "Enjoy your first hurricane."

She took a sip. "Ooh, these are good," she said. The drink was fruity and cold. It went down easily. "I think I'll stick with these tonight."

"Good choice," Cheryl said, eying a tall man across the room. "Have fun, Pipp. I'm off to try my luck."

"Good luck," she said, taking another sip and scanning the crowd. The house was packed with guests, everyone wearing masks. She loved the riot of color and the mysteriousness of the masks. She stood sipping and watching the crowd for a few moments, lost in thought.

She mused it was going to be hard to decide which guy

to try to approach. There were a lot of handsome, fit guys. But that's what Cheryl had predicted, living so near to a place where SEALs trained.

Her drink was half gone by the time she gathered the nerve to move. Crossing the room by weaving in and out of the crowd, she headed for a dark-haired pirate. She planned to ask him if he knew the way to the pirate treasure, but then he moved toward a woman and kissed her on the cheek.

Oh, too late, she thought. *I need to be faster. And maybe not pick a guy clear across the room.* She continued the internal pep talk, trying to work up her courage to ask one of the guys to dance.

She circulated, and soon, her drink was empty. She headed back to the bartender for a refill. The hurricanes were good, and the warmth of the room from all the people was making her thirsty.

Holding her now full glass, she decided to step outside onto the covered back porch and get some cooler air. The stars were out, and the night sky would be pretty.

She stood outside long enough to finish her drink as she counted the stars and listened to the people around her talking. As she turned to go back inside, to get another drink, she stumbled a little on the doormat.

She'd gotten tipsier than she'd expected. The hurricanes had snuck up on her. She couldn't remember the last time she'd allowed herself to relax at all, let alone drink.

And then he was there, coming through the front door, just as she stumbled and looked up. He was like a Greek God, with his tanned chest and washboard abs that made her want to run her fingers up and down them. And he moved with such smooth and controlled command. But no, as he got closer, she saw she'd mistaken his costume.

Instead of a Greek God, he was wearing a gladiator's outfit with a black mask.

For everyone who came to the front door without a mask, a black mask was handed to them before they were allowed inside. No mask, no entry. So, everyone who'd come without a mask was wearing the same black type of mask. Like he was. And the room was full of men wearing black masks. Yet in a room full of men wearing black masks, he stood out. Something about the way he stood, taking in the room, something about the way he moved made him stand out.

He spoke to the cowboy who'd entered with him and then they broke away from each other. He moved through the crowd and stopped halfway across the room to talk to a tall, thin man who wore a jester's costume. They both laughed about something.

She watched the gladiator's perfect white teeth flash beneath the mask, which contrasted with his tan. With an unobstructed view, still, she knew he was a good-looking man. Sipping her drink, she continued to watch him. She had yet to talk to anyone. Her shyness had gotten in the way, or her timing was always off when she made the attempt. But after finishing off that second drink, she felt much bolder.

Curious now, she thought to get close enough to hear his voice. Already she felt drawn to him, but she needed to hear his voice. She couldn't have explained why. It shouldn't have made any difference if they were only going to get together once, this night, then never see each other again. But it did matter.

As she neared, she heard him speak, his voice low, deep, and strong. Goose bumps prickled on her skin. She moved nearer.

He was talking about ghost tours with the other man and two women.

"I'd go for the historical aspect," he said. "I don't expect anyone would really see a ghost with that many people tramping through a room, and most people don't know how to be quiet." He laughed. "They'd scare the mice away."

"Not all of us have the training at being stealthy, like you SEALs," a woman wearing a saloon dancer's outfit said. Bursting out of the top half of her costume, her cleavage was getting plenty of attention from the men around her. "But you can sneak up on me any time."

"I'm not in the habit of sneaking up on women," he said. "Not my style."

What was his style? Pippa wondered. *Whatever it is, I'm sure I'd like it.*

His voice was doing funny things to her insides.

Listening to him is so nice I'd enjoy hearing him read the side of a cereal box.

When a large man nearly stepped on her foot, she moved backward and glanced up the next instant to find the gladiator was gone, heading to the dance floor with one of the women.

I'm just not having any luck, Pippa thought. Sighing, she headed to the bar for a third hurricane. *I must get better at this. Courage. I can do this. I will just go up to him and say...* Her thoughts froze.

The bartender handed her a refreshed drink.

She took a sip, her thoughts a jumble as she tried to think of what to do next.

I know what I'll do. I'll ask him to dance. Since he's dancing now, he obviously dances. I just must get back over there before he dances with someone else. Oh, how do men do this? The asking. It's much harder than I thought.

She made her way back to where he was dancing and

hovered beside a potted palm. The moment he'd finished, and the two moved apart, she went up to him, even though her stomach had started doing flips.

Taking her courage in both hands, she gave him a smile. "Hello," she said. "Would you like to dance with me?

Now that's what I like, Diesel thought as he looked down at the brown-haired woman with green eyes, wearing some kind of fairy costume. The glitter in her hair, across her shoulders, and down her cleavage, along with her question, made him want to smile.

A woman who knows what she wants and asks for it. Direct, and to the point. I like that.

"I would be honored," he said and held out his hand. He noted that if she moved closer, he'd see more of the glitter spilling down the inside her dress.

Diesel was six-feet-two, and this delightful creature couldn't have been more than five-five.

She moved closer to him and placed her soft hand in his. *Yes. A very good view.*

He pulled her close, and they moved to the music. "May I have your name?"

"I am the fairy of the green wood," she said. "I'm a woodland fairy, and I love nothing better than... wood."

He chuckled. *There are so many things I might say in response. Did she know the direction this conversation might take?* She'd said wood, not "the woods."

Testing her, he said, "Tell me more... about how you love... wood."

Her chest quivered with soft laughter. "I love wood so much I can't help but touch it," she said. "It's hard to keep my hands off rough bark."

The little green-eyed minx. How far would she take this? "Interesting," he said. "What do you do when you touch it?"

She swallowed, and then drew a deep breath that

caused the sparkles on her chest to shimmer. "Well, I run my hand up and down it," she said, sounding a little breathless. "I like to feel how hard it is, how strong and durable."

He pulled her close to him so she could feel his muscles beneath his gladiator costume.

Her eyes widened. "Mm," she said. "I like touching you."

He bent and whispered in her ear. "Something needs to be done. If I step away…"

"Don't step away," she said, her smile turning seductive. "Dance me out of this room and into another."

"As you command, fae enchantress."

He moved them through the main room and into the hallway. Then, away from the others, he tipped up her chin and said, in a low voice. "Tell me what you want."

Her lips pressed together then stretched into a slow whimsical grin. "I want to touch your bare skin," she said. "To feel your hard muscles, all over."

Her words were the sexiest he'd ever heard in his life. Truly, she was an enchantress, and he was about to have great sex here tonight. With an over-the-top flourish, he bowed. "You have but to ask," he said. "My wood is yours to command."

Giggling, a sound, which made her seem more adorable than seductress, made him laugh out loud.

She took him by the hand and led him down the hall. "I don't know this house or where to go," she said, and for the first time her voice sounded less than confident.

"Allow me." He pushed on one door, which was locked. "Come," he said. "We'll find a place." The third door he tried was unlocked, and the room was empty. He pulled her inside quick before anyone saw them and then closed and locked the door.

She looked up at him with wide green eyes beneath the

mask, and he thought for the first time that perhaps she was in over her head as he saw uncertainty.

Diesel didn't do uncertainty when it came to women and sex.

"Let's establish something here, before we return to the fantasy and play time," he said. "You want to have sex, yes?"

"Yes." She breathed the word out as if she were relieved.

Okay, so she's playing out her fantasy right now, but she did look as though she'd never done this before. As if she were unsure.

"I have protection," she said and reached for her bag.

She is an adorable creature, he thought. The mix of assertive seductress and shy, uncertain woman was fascinating. Her green eyes fascinated him; with their myriad of shades and emotions he'd seen since she'd said "hello".

He reached for the hem of his costume, pulled it up, and then tucked it into the belted waistband.

"Look what you've done to me with your fairy magic," he whispered, watching her eyes as they looked down and widened.

She looked up at him again and gave a quick nod.

Then she noticed the long white scar that ran down his right arm and ran her forefinger down the scar. Again, she looked up at him with those green take me now eyes peering out of her mask. "What is this from?" she asked.

"Long time ago. I was working in my dad's shop and a hot muffler fell on it."

"Oh, that had to hurt," she said.

"It did," he said. "But chicks dig scars." He winked at her. Then he took her by the hand.

He reached for and pulled the top of her fairy costume down, to bare her breasts and glitter spilled out everywhere.

"Magic fairy dust." He laughed. "I'd kiss them, but they're covered in glitter." He brushed at the glitter covering them, a light touch.

Her breath was changing, as were her eyes, the hazel green changing to more of a deeper green.

He let her go. "Lie down," he said.

She backed onto the bed.

He bent, hovered over her, watching her through his mask, watching as her eyes changed through each moment as he touched her, moving her closer to be ready to join with him. The masks forced them to focus on each other with an intensity neither had experienced before when making love.

Neither broke eye contact and they wordlessly connected, the masks giving the dream like quality to it all.

When she found her release, in her eyes he felt he'd glimpsed something rare, something he'd like to see again.

Pippa exhaled, spent. When she took her next breath, his scent lingered, making her want to snuggle next to him. Dancing close, touching his warm bare skin, and inhaling his scent had nearly done her in—before they'd even begun to remove clothing.

The chemistry between them was incredible.

When he spoke, his voice reached something deep inside her. From the start, she'd been a goner. That voice, combined with the gentle but intense passion of his love-making, was beyond anything she could've imagined.

If there is magic in the world, this is it.

Her thoughts drifted into that magic place, and her eyelids drifted downward.

Afterward, they lay together without speaking, sharing those final moments.

She didn't know what to say. This was beyond what she'd expected. This was deeper. Not a quickie. Their joining felt almost... sacred.

His hand reached for her mask before he bent to kiss her.

Her heart tripped. She stopped his hand with hers. "We

won't unmask," she said. "I want to remember us, just like this."

"All right," he said. "May I have your name now?"

Although it nearly killed her, she remembered why she'd wanted to keep this anonymous. This night had been magical, but she couldn't take the risk.

"Woodland fairy," she said, her voice firmer now. "And you are my gladiator."

He pulled away and clasped his fist to his chest. "I am your gladiator."

"Thank you for this," she said. "My fantasies came true."

"No, my enchantress," he replied. "Thank *you*."

They exchanged smiles.

She adjusted her fairy costume.

He dangled her panties from his finger, holding them out to her, teasing.

Feeling reckless, she tossed back her hair. "I can go without."

The thought made him groan. "Careful. Unless you want a repeat."

She wrinkled her nose at the panties. "They aren't very comfortable."

"Then don't wear them. Be comfortable. But also, be safe." He held out his hand. "Will you let me give you a ride home, to make sure you arrive safe?"

She shook her head. "I came with a co-worker. I'll ride home with her."

So much for figuring out where she lived. But she'd set the rules. He'd respect them. "I'll escort you back to the party."

Her hand was already on the door. "I'm good. No need to."

As he watched her go, he couldn't help disagreeing. There was *every* need to go with her.

Protective was his nature. But he was also good at surveillance. He'd watch until the women were safe in their car and heading home. She'd never know.

The moment he got in his car to follow her and removed his cell phone from the glove box he saw that Kira had been blowing up his phone with calls and texts. It was like the woman had a sixth sense when he was having a good time with another woman. Since they'd broken up, again, it was none of Kira's business who he was with tonight or what he was doing.

Ignoring the phone, he set it on the passenger seat and proceeded to follow his mystery woman at a distance.

All was going well until a semi-tractor trailer hit something and went sliding across the highway. All traffic behind the semi-tractor stopped.

Diesel stood on the floorboards of his car to see above his car, trying to glimpse past the wreck to the little blue Chevy he'd been following.

No sight of her. She'd driven on.

He didn't have her name or her number so he couldn't even call to make sure she got home safely. That bothered him.

Two days later, he had his duffel packed and was on his way out of the country, still wishing he knew how to contact her. He couldn't get the mystery woman out of his head.

There was just something about her...

I'll look for her when I get back. For now, I must focus on the mission.

~

"Maybe I should've given him my number," Pippa said, the corners of her mouth drooping.

Cheryl shrugged. "I think you did it just right. You had a

night of great sex with a hot guy, and no strings or complications, because he has no idea who you are."

She couldn't help feeling wistful. "He seemed very nice, and I don't mean just the hard body and great sex."

Cheryl flicked her fingers. "Focus on that hard body and the great sex and let the rest go."

Still, Pippa couldn't. "I mean, he seemed like the kind of guy you could introduce to your parents and might want to marry. I really liked him," Pippa said. "And there was something magical about our lovemaking."

Cheryl rolled her eyes. "That was the hurricanes talking. And the costumes, and the sleeping-with-a-complete-stranger fantasy. That's not real life, Pippa. You don't need complications right now. Not when you're trying to finish school. Having a man in your life just means having a guy *who wants your attention*. And then, when something goes wrong, and it always does, you'll have the heartbreak and drama of a breakup to deal with. Do you even have time for that?"

Cheryl made complete sense. However, Pippa's heart wouldn't be quiet.

Silly things, hearts. They get us into all sorts of trouble.

"Not really. You're right, I don't have time. And my track record with men isn't good. Getting to know him better might have ruined everything. No guy is that perfect," Pippa said, pouting her lips.

"Exactly. You needed to have sex with someone. You did that, and now you can move on. Think of it as a great night and a great memory and leave it there. No second guessing."

"Yeah, you're right... I guess," Pippa said.

"Now maybe you'll consider dating. Nothing serious, just going out maybe every other weekend. Have some fun. Stop staying in every night."

"No, I can't," Pippa said.

"You weren't afraid to have sex with a stranger. That's living bold, Pippa. But you're afraid to go out on a date. What are you so afraid of?"

Do I dare confide in her? Pippa watched Cheryl, pondering. *She's kept what I told her private so far. Maybe I can. She's the closest thing to a best friend that I have.*

"I was married once."

Cheryl settled back in her seat and looked at Pippa. "I knew there was something. What happened?"

"It was bad," Pippa said. "Not at first, but later. My dad passed six months after I married Stan Nitty and after he passed, the honeymoon period was over. It turned bad fast."

"Having your dad around gave you some protection."

"Yes and no," Pippa said. "Dad was a vocal kind of man, and he didn't put up with injustice, but he was a peace-loving newspaper reporter, who'd never fired a gun. He didn't like the fact Stan was fifteen years older than me, or the way he insisted everyone needed to stock up for doomsday. Stan made his own bullets."

"Wow," Cheryl said. "The two were complete opposites. So, what did you see in Stan?"

"He was charming at first. Always showing up with sweet words, flowers, bears."

"Bears?"

"I collected stuffed teddy bears. When he found out, he brought me one every week. He tried everything to charm me into going out with him and then to keep going out with him. Everything he does is extreme, and he wanted me, so he pursued me like he pursues everything. Full throttle."

"High school boys didn't stand a chance, competing for your attention against a grown man with experience," Cheryl said.

"True. I thought he wanted me more than they did. He said he'd do anything to win me and to make me his."

"So, you got married and things went south fast. What happened? Did he hurt you?"

Pippa nodded. "He's serving time now for felonious assault. Beat up a guy in a bar, but that wasn't good enough for him. He turned around and went back in and beat him again. They got it on tape and put him away."

"Wow. That's more than full throttle," Cheryl said. "He sounds like bad news. Real bad news. No wonder you're such a homebody and never go out."

"I'm not afraid to go out," Pippa said. "I just need to be cautious. Real cautious."

"That's why you never relax," Cheryl nodded. "You're always looking out windows or doors instead of giving your whole attention when someone is talking."

"It's not disinterest," Pippa said. "I'm still listening."

"Yeah, I get that now. I'm glad you told me."

"I am too."

"Is Pippa your real name?"

"Kind of. My parents met at a bluegrass festival and were inseparable from day one. They decided my middle name had to be part of the name of the festival where I was conceived."

"How cool."

"Not really. That's a lot to load onto a child. Brings on teasing, kids picking on you. It made me shy in school. I'd stick my nose in a book and try to pretend no one had just hurt my feelings."

"You found a way to run away to another world," Cheryl said. "In books."

"Yeah," Pippa nodded.

"So, what happened with you and Stan?"

"One New Year's Eve, Stan went out of his mind. He'd been drinking a lot and was very angry. He tried to choke me to death. Wrapped his hands around my neck and squeezed until I passed out. I was still in a daze, grieving my father and wasn't paying enough attention to Stan. He couldn't handle me not always giving him my full attention, so he turned mean."

"And he'd never done anything before that which let you know he might be dangerous?"

"There were signs," Pippa said. "I didn't want to believe he was that bad, that I was with the wrong guy. He tried to make me think the things he did were my fault."

"It was not your fault," Cheryl said.

"I know that now," Pippa said. "The first time Stan put a fist through the wall, I knew I needed a getaway plan."

"So, you made a plan and then when he went crazy you were ready and got out," Cheryl said.

"Not exactly," Pippa shook her head. "I knew I needed one but hadn't made one yet. It was like planning would mean I'd given up hope the marriage could ever be a good one. Sometimes he was nice to me. I was very confused back then and he knew exactly how to play me."

"Well, hell yeah, he had fifteen years of living experience on you to know how to manipulate and get his way," Cheryl said. "You married what, right out of high school?"

"Yeah." Pippa shrugged. "I was young and naïve."

"Virgin too, I bet."

"Oh yes." Pipped nodded. "That was very important to him. He talked about that a lot. Being the first and me being pure."

"Jeeze Louise. No wonder you're not used to going out with guys. He was your only until when?"

Pippa gave a blushing smile. "Until my gladiator."

"If anyone deserved a night of total fantasy fulfillment, it's you. Girlfriend, I don't even know what to say. I'm glad you got away from Stan Nitty and that you're okay now."

"Thanks Cheryl. I'm glad, too."

"So, after he choked you, then you had to leave."

Pippa nodded. "The night Stan lost his mind; he tore the bedroom door off the hinges and came after me. I knew then I had to run but then he had his hands around my neck, and I blacked out. The minute I woke up ready to run, I looked for him and he was still drunk and passed out on the living room couch, snoring. I had to get out of there while I still could, so I grabbed my purse and ran out the back door with only my purse and the clothes on my back."

"Damn. That had to be scary. You're a brave woman, Pippa Marks."

"I changed my name to Marks, legally. I got rid of Nitty, and I wanted a new name, one it would be easier to step away from my past with."

The restraining order she had against Stan was in her old name, and she didn't fully trust it to keep him away so there would be no point in getting a new one. That she had one made him very angry. He wasn't going to listen to a piece of paper. She wasn't even sure he'd listen to a policeman or a gun

Stan had always seemed like a force of nature. He was strong and tough minded and loved a challenge.

Likely a new restraining order would only make him come after her. And she was all the way across the country now, where she was much harder to find, and she was using a new name which she didn't want him to know.

"I'm guessing you're not from Virginia," Cheryl said. "You have that midwestern accent."

"I'm from Yellow Springs, Ohio. It's in between Dayton and Springfield Ohio."

"So, you came here and got a job in the grocery," Cheryl smiled. "I'm glad you did, or we wouldn't have met."

"I'm glad too." Pippa smiled.

"Now that I know, I won't keep pushing you to go out

with guys. Maybe what you need is one good guy instead of dating ones who could turn out to be losers."

"Yeah, but I'm in no hurry for that either. I need to finish my classes and get a better job. That, and work is keeping me busy."

Pippa was learning secretarial skills at the local community college and working at the grocery store while hoping her crazy ex would stay in Ohio and not show up in Virginia looking for her.

Though she'd been divorced for over a year, dating was the last thing on her mind. She didn't trust a new date to be the man he claimed to be. Once burned, twice shy. She wasn't sure she'd ever date again.

"I understand," Cheryl said. "Would you be up for a girl's night out every so often?"

"Yes, that sounds like fun."

"Cool beans," Cheryl said. "It will be. And in the meantime, you had a great time at the party, right?"

"I did." Pippa smiled. "It was the best night of my life."

"You'll be having happy dreams of this guy."

"Oh yes, I will." Pippa grinned. "My gladiator."

"You have a glow," Cheryl said.

"Maybe that's because I'm happy." Pippa smiled.

~

That happiness lasted until the morning sickness started. Starting each day with salty crackers and slow nibbles of an apple slice just to be able to get out of bed without being sick, Pippa knew this was more than a flu.

The at home pregnancy test confirmed it.

She called to make a doctor's appointment and thought, *what am I going to do?*

3

———————

This time her mystery man had given her a glow, but it was a glow of pregnancy.

There could be only one father.

A man, with the body of a gladiator; a voice, which reached deep inside of Pippa; and a face, she'd never fully seen.

A man whose name she didn't know.

"But we used a condom," she told her doctor in bewilderment. "How did this happen?"

"Condoms are not one hundred percent protection. There is a small margin of error. Around one percent," the doctor said.

"Great," Pippa said. "And I'm a one-percenter."

He cleared his throat. "Do you want this child?"

She blinked. Everything was happening so fast. She needed to think. But about this, she felt no hesitation.

Her hand moved to her belly, an automatic protective move.

Of course, I want this baby. No matter who his or her daddy is. I'm going to be a mother.

"Yes."

"All right," he said, nodding and pulling out his prescription pad from his pocket. "We need to get you on some good prenatal vitamins and schedule your next visit."

As she left his office, Pippa still couldn't believe it.

I'm going to be a mother. A single mom. This wasn't how I'd thought my life would turn out.

When she'd set out for the Halloween party, planning to have a memorable evening she'd look back on for the rest of her life, she hadn't planned this. Now, she was having trouble wrapping her mind around the consequence.

The next day at work, she told Cheryl and watched Cheryl's jaw drop.

"Oh honey, I'm sorry. I never thought this would happen." Cheryl said.

"I didn't either," Pippa said, giving her friend a tiny smile.

"Girl, you have the worst luck," Cheryl said.

"I'm trying not to think of it that way," Pippa said. "This baby, though not planned, will be loved just as much as any other baby."

Apparently for around one percent of the female population, contraception did not work. The doctor had explained this was true of using the pill, or a condom, or any other form of birth control.

Lucky me, to fall into that one percent.

She thought about looking for the handsome gladiator. But how would she ever find him?

I don't even know his name. And I can hardly walk onto the Naval base and say, hey, one of your SEAL's has knocked me up, can you help me find him. They'd think I was a real slut.

But I don't sleep around. He was the second man I ever slept with. Now, he'll be my last.

My life will be complicated enough with a baby without bringing a man or dating into it.

She bought a book of baby names and poured through the book. For a girl, she picked out the name Tania which meant 'fairy queen.' She only got as far as the B's when looking for a boy's name. Bryce seemed to jump out of the page for her. Bryce meant 'of Britain' which wasn't the reason she picked the name. She couldn't have explained to anyone why she'd picked that one, other than it just felt right.

The day Bryce was born, and she held him for the first time, looking down at his dark hair and his sweet little face, she felt that rush of mother love first time mothers feel and thought, *oh you look like your daddy. I wonder where he is now and what he would think of you if he could see you. I wish I could show you to him.*

A single tear spilled down her cheek amid her happiness and love for her child.

Every child deserved a mother and a father who loved them. She wished she could give that to her new son.

She closed her eyes and sent up a prayer.

Please bring Bryce's father home safely and please, if it is meant to be and best for our child, please bring him to us.

Maybe someday, if her prayer was answered, it would happen.

~

Two years had passed since Diesel had made love to the beautiful fairy princess with no name. He'd often dreamed of her, but the SEAL missions he was sent on kept him busy on deployments and not back in the states often.

One year had slid into two, until he'd thought of her less and less.

She was now a fond memory and a good dream when she showed up as he slept.

This week, he was back in town, and his father was visiting. It was great seeing his dad and showing him around, introducing him to the guys. His father wasn't getting any younger, and the pride in his eyes said everything to Diesel.

Bryce Taylor was enjoying the visit with his son, but it would soon be at an end.

Diesel had been called in for a meeting and would be shipping out again, soon. Since they couldn't have lunch together today, his dad decided to pick up lunch somewhere and take it to the park to enjoy the great weather. Too soon, he'd have to go back home where the weather wasn't as nice.

Sitting on a park bench, he watched as a little boy about two years of age played in the park.

Something about the boy drew his eye.

As the boy got closer, Bryce blinked twice to clear his eyes, and then rubbed them, but nothing changed, and the sense of *déjà vu* could not be blinked or rubbed away.

The boy playing in the park had dark wavy hair and dark brown eyes. The shape of his brows and the lively dark brown eyes full of mischief reminded him of Tanner, when he was two years old. This little boy was the spitting image of his son.

Bryce could have stepped back in time to be looking at his own son. The boy resembled Tanner so much it was uncanny.

As he spoke, the boy's voice took Bryce back twenty-six years. He even sounded like Tanner.

Good Lord, he could be Tanner's.

His gaze went immediately to the mother. She was young, with long brown hair, and green eyes. She wasn't wearing a ring.

Is she a single mom? Had she dated Tanner?

He had to find out. He didn't want to alarm the woman

or make her think he was some kind of creep, trying to get close to her for nefarious purposes.

How could he ask the questions pressing on him that he wanted to ask?

Bryce watched mother and child walk to the parking lot, holding hands, and then he stood, gathering his half-eaten sandwich. Following them, he dropped the rest of his sandwich into a trashcan he passed on the way, his appetite gone.

Mother and child moved toward an older model blue Chrysler with a red door. It had obviously been in an accident. He hoped neither of them had been hurt.

She opened the car door and put the boy into his car seat. Then she buckled him in and closed the door. Getting into the driver's seat, she closed the door and turned the car ignition over.

Her car wouldn't start.

He could see the frustration on her face.

A grin crossed his face. Someone was looking out for him and for her.

Good thing I'm a mechanic, he thought. *I can fix this and maybe learn more about her and the boy.*

He walked over to their car and said, "Having car trouble? Can I help?"

She scrunched her nose. "It won't start."

"Pop the hood, and I'll take a look at it."

She popped the hood.

He went around to the front of the car, lifted the hood, and looked inside. Then he came back around to the window and said, "I see your problem. Let me show you."

She got out and checked on her child in the back seat in his car seat before walking around to the front of the car with him. The boy was starting to doze off.

"It's getting close to his nap time," she said.

"He's a cute little tyke. What's the boy's name?" Bryce asked.

"His name is Bryce," She smiled.

Bryce froze when he heard the boy's name.

If Tanner was his dad, then the boy's mother had named the boy after his grandfather.

His emotions threatened to overtake him, and rare were the times in his life that this had happened. He blinked away a tear, focusing on the car again, redirecting his mind with a firm control. "Here's your problem," he said. "See all this corrosion on this battery terminal?"

"What's corrosion?" she asked.

"See this salty-looking white stuff?"

"Yes," she said, her tone saying she wished she didn't.

He grabbed the negative terminal, and the loose wire came right off. "It's loose. That's what's causing this." He pulled his Leatherman multi-tool out of his pocket.

"That looks like a big Swiss army knife."

He pulled out the blade and scraped as much of the corrosion off as he could. Then he put the wire back on the terminal and took a pair of pliers and tightened the nut. "Now try it," he said.

She got back in the car and tried the ignition again. It started right up.

He closed the hood with a bang. "You should be good to go now, but you might want to get this checked out by your mechanic. I don't have my other tools with me. It would be a good idea to have a competent mechanic go over this car. Cars this age need good maintenance to keep them running."

She appeared to wince. "Yes, I should probably do that. Thank you. Are you a mechanic? I don't have one."

"Yes, but I live in another state. My son is also a mechanic and a Navy SEAL. If you need some work done,

I'm sure he'd be willing to help you when he's not off on deployment. His name is Tanner. Tanner Taylor."

He watched her face, but not even one iota of change came over her, when she heard his son's name. So, he tried again. "But all his SEAL buddies call him Diesel."

Again, she showed no reaction.

Bryce wasn't sure what to think now. His gut was telling him that the little boy, who was now dozing in his car seat, had to be Tanner's. "I'm Bryce Taylor."

She held out her hand. "I'm Pippa. It's nice to meet you. Thank you again for fixing my car."

"You're welcome," he said. "Well, you'd best be getting the little fella home to sleep in his own bed."

Soon Pippa and little Bryce were on their way home, and Bryce Taylor had the information he'd wanted. She was a single mom. The boy was two. And his name was Bryce.

This irony was unbelievable to Bryce Taylor.

The boy had to be Tanner's. And it was time he had a talk with his son.

~

The next day Bryce took Tanner out for breakfast. On the way, his father had been quieter than usual, so it was a relief to Diesel when they ordered, and Bryce finally said, "Son, I asked you to breakfast because I have something serious to tell you, and I wanted to do it early, before you have to go to the base and have other things to focus on."

"Are you all right, dad?" Tanner grew serious. "Is it your health?"

"No, no." Bryce waved that away with his hand. "Nothing like that."

Tanner sat back in his chair, relieved. Whatever his dad had to say, everything would be fine.

Nothing to worry about.

If his dad's health was good, everything would be okay. His dad had no idea of the things Diesel had seen and had done under orders. Things a civilian might worry about were easy, compared to those life-or-death situations the SEALs lived in and around. He took a sip of his coffee, ready to listen.

"You've slept with a lot of women, according to your brother, Andy."

"A few." Diesel wondered where this was going. Was his dad going to ask him about sex? Or picking up women?

"Locally, too, I imagine."

"Yes, a few live here." Diesel hoped his dad didn't want to be fixed up with a local woman he knew. He hoped it wasn't that because he might not be okay with that.

Bryce cleared his throat. "Good." He took a swallow of his coffee and then continued, "I was in the park the other day and saw a young woman with a small child who was playing."

Diesel nodded, wishing his dad would get to the point and stop dragging his feet with whatever he had to say. *Out with it, dad* was what he wanted to say, but instead he just nodded, giving his dad the time and respect, he deserved.

"Her little boy is two years old, and he looks and sounds just like you. So much, he could be a clone of you at that age."

"Really?" Diesel frowned and tried to think back two years to remember if he'd been dating anyone local that year.

"Yes. And I want you to take this seriously."

Diesel nodded. He had slept with several local women, but not in that year. They all wanted to chase him into their beds, so they could brag that they'd slept with a SEAL. He'd enjoyed the excess at first, but hook-ups had gotten old quick. He'd stopped dating the locals because they wanted too much permanency and he never stayed around for long.

If he could just meet the perfect woman like that one he'd met at the costume party that time.

Her, he wouldn't have minded seeing more often. Once was not enough.

He sat, thinking. "That year I shipped out November first, and before that, I was dating Kira off and on. But she doesn't have any kids. And she doesn't want them."

"Did you go out with anyone else local that year? Even for one night?"

"No, I didn't..." His voice trailed away as his thoughts began to churn. "Though there was a Halloween party. And a beautiful girl who wouldn't give me her phone number. But that was just one brief evening event."

"So, you didn't sleep with her?"

"We, uh, got together dad. So, technically, yes."

"Then technically, I would say this Pippa is the same girl, and her little boy is your son and my grandson."

Diesel shook his head. "That's crazy."

"No. It's not. And you need to talk to this girl Pippa and meet the boy."

Their food came, and Diesel was suddenly starving. "Let's shelve this for now and dig in," he said. He didn't want the topic to ruin his meal. He'd deal with this later. He needed to eat, and then get back to the base and work.

～

Full of boundless energy and the smile and face of a Gerber baby, Pippa often looked at little Bryce, lifted him into the air, and looking into his eyes said, "You're a handsome boy, just like your daddy."

If only she knew who and where his daddy was. He was missing out on seeing this beautiful child grow up. This child, who was now her whole world.

There were only so many SEALs in the world. She just didn't know how to find hers, or if he'd even want to be found.

What if he she found him, and he didn't want anything to do with Bryce? That would break her heart.

~

Stan Nitty was finally out of prison.

He collected his personal belongings and walked out a free man, after serving half his sentence. He'd been on good behavior and convinced them he had changed and felt remorse for what he'd done. Privately he felt otherwise.

That guy had deserved what he'd gotten and then some. But that was in the past now. Time to move on.

Now, he was out, and things were going to change. He would find Joyce. It was time he got his wife back. He'd been inside the joint a long time without a woman, and he wanted to sink into her softness again and take what was his. Wherever she was, he would find her.

Traveling to the cache he'd hidden in the woods; he was pleased to find his weapons and ammo were still there. He collected them and then set off to the town where Joyce had last been seen. It was time to track down his woman.

The search only took Stan a week. Joyce hadn't been very careful, even though she'd changed her name.

Pippa. What a ridiculous name. Her parents were crazy to saddle their daughter with a middle name like Pippalousa. What the hell kind of name was that? Joyce Nitty was her proper name and it was time she took her proper name back.

His former cellmate knew a guy who could find anyone. Everyone left an electronic trail of some kind. It had taken the guy just two days to find Joyce, now calling herself Pippa. She lived in Virginia and was working at a grocery store there.

Maybe his wife thought he couldn't find her after he was sent to prison. Or maybe she thought he'd give up. But he would never give up on taking back what was his.

Now that he'd found her, he couldn't believe his eyes. She had fuller curves than she'd had before. Bigger breasts which was good. But she was there in the park with a toddler around two years of age. And that little boy had just called her mama.

A little boy with dark curly hair and brown eyes. The

boy that looked nothing like him. And anyone who could count would know that the child couldn't possibly be his.

So, the bitch had spread her legs for another man. And now, she had a baby. A boy. She'd let some other man fuck her, and then had a son that should've been his.

How dare she.

He'd picked her out especially to be his. She'd been young and beautiful and untouched. A virgin. She should've been popping out sons every couple of years to carry on the Nitty name. Little Stan juniors he could teach to hunt and fish. Now, she'd tainted herself.

He was so angry he couldn't see straight. When he got his hands on her, he'd make her pay. Before, he would've tried to woo her. He'd daydreamed of that and of keeping her naked in bed to please him. But all that was over now.

She wanted to behave like a slut, so now she'd be treated like one. And she'd just given him the best way possible to control her. Because he knew his wife remembered the feel of the back of his hand.

And she loved children.

She'll do anything to make sure nothing happens to that little boy.

~

Pippa pushed Bryce on the baby swings and laughed as he kicked his legs out and squealed. He loved going as high as she was willing to push him, and she had the feeling he would have taken off and flown if he could have.

Like his daddy. Probably.

It wasn't the first time she'd had that thought. She guessed that he took after his daddy in much more than looks.

If only she knew more about his daddy. In particular where he was and what he would think about having a son.

She dared not hope to run into him in this town full of SEALs and she'd given up praying for that. It felt like no one was listening. Or if listening, not inclined to answer her prayer with the answer she desired.

Sometimes she wasn't sure what she desired. She only wanted him found if it would be good for their son. If not, then she'd rather he be kept away.

Maybe this was for the best after all.

She and Bryce were both happy. In fact, Bryce was one of the happiest toddlers she'd ever seen. He never threw a tantrum or cried or reached for things he couldn't have.

Pippa tried to do the same.

She would not cry one more tear into her pillow over her situation. She'd been blessed with a healthy son who she loved with all her heart.

That would have to be enough.

Stan watched Joyce for two weeks to find her patterns, so he'd know the best place to make a grab and go.

He'd lined the van to soundproof it and darkened the windows. He'd bought toys and had a special juice he'd mixed himself, for the kid. All kids liked juice, and this one, mixed with that cherry children's cough syrup, would make the kid sleep. He didn't want to have to listen to or deal with the kid.

Surprised to see her leaving work early today, he chose to follow her.

She'd changed the pattern. But that could be good if no one was expecting her so early.

He parked down the street and watched her go into her

apartment, and then watched the sitter come out, get in her car, and drive away.

The timing was right. He felt it in every cell of his body as he moved the van to the graveled area behind the apartment building and parked. Exiting, he made his way to her door.

Didn't take much to break in, as flimsy as the locks were and no deadbolt on.

For someone who'd run away to Virginia and changed her name to hide, she wasn't very safety-conscious in her own apartment.

He moved into the apartment, quiet and slow, listening.

She was in her bedroom, humming a song for the kid, who was singing nonsense words to her tune.

Had it been his kid, he would've told her to cut that shit out. Boys didn't need to learn that stuff. He'd raise his boys the way his daddy had raised him, so they'd grow up tough and hard and not be mama's boys.

He had a feeling this kid was going to be a screamer. Kids screaming in restaurants and out in public drove him nuts. No way was he going to listen to that in the van.

He stepped into the room and moved quietly behind her.

She was putting the squirming kid into pajamas while the kid clearly didn't want to be still that long. She was too busy and focused on her kid to notice Stan.

Then he was right behind her.

His hands were on her, one over her mouth and the other around her neck.

He knew how to make her pass out, and once out, she'd be like a rag-doll, easy to tie and carry. Within minutes, he had her trussed up and slung over his shoulder.

The boy started crying and reaching up for his mama.

Stan ignored him.

All kids cried, and the neighbors would've heard it before.

In the living room, he laid her down on the couch, and then went back for the boy.

The boy was still crying out for his mama, tears running and a bubble forming under his nose.

Snotty nosed kid.

Stan pulled the water bottle out of his pocket and opened it; ready to pour the juice into one of those kiddie sippy cups he'd seen on the table by the bed. Taking the lid off, he saw it was empty. He poured in the juice.

The kid had quieted, watching him. He then toddled over and reached for the cup.

"Juice," he said.

So, the kid could talk some.

"Yeah. Juice." He handed the kid the cup.

The boy started to take a drink. Then he remembered his mother. "Mama," he said, and he toddled into the other room to look for her. "Mama."

Stan followed the kid into the living room carrying the cup. "Mama is sleeping. Taking a nap." He held out the cup. "Here's your juice."

The boy took the cup, and then carrying it, went over to his mother and laid his head down on her arm, still holding the cup, which now tipped, leaking juice out on the floor.

"Mamma, night, night," he said, his head still next to his mama as he patted her with his other hand.

"She's tired," Stan said. "Drink your juice."

The boy picked his head up, looked at Stan for a minute, and then took another drink.

How long was it going to take the kid to drink that juice? Too long already.

His patience was already shot.

Damn kid.

If he didn't need the kid to control his wife, he'd have taken care of the kid right now. One way or another. But for now, he was stuck with him.

"Drink your juice all gone and you can have a cookie," he said. He did have a cookie in his jacket pocket, but the kid would be asleep before he got a chance to eat it.

～

Pippa didn't hear him until his hands were on her mouth and her neck, cutting off her air and making everything go black. The last thing she remembered was her son's face, looking up at her as her ex-husband's voice said in her ear, "I've waited years for you. But you couldn't wait on your husband. I'm back, and the waiting is over."

Then she went out like a light.

She woke, looking for her son and not seeing anything but the darkness in the van.

Stan was driving.

Is he drunk? He used to drink and drive.

If Bryce was in the van, she hoped Stan wasn't drunk.

Where's Bryce?

She hoped he hadn't hurt her baby boy.

"You're awake and probably wondering where that little boy is right now," Stan said. "I'm taking good care of him. And I'll continue to take good care of him — if you don't give me any trouble."

He'd gagged her, and she couldn't speak, so she had no way to answer him.

Turning up the radio, he started singing to "Patience" by Guns N' Roses. She didn't know if that was supposed to be for her benefit or his.

She glared at him because she couldn't speak and thought, *Let the mind games begin. Only this time you won't win because I'm stronger than I used to be. And now I have a son to be strong for.*

She tried to focus on where he might be taking them. Tried to listen for sounds. To feel the direction of the vehicle. But it was no use. And she'd been knocked out for she didn't know how long.

What if no one knows we are gone? What if they don't even know to look for us?

Diesel and his father were able to track down the mystery woman by using her license plate number, which his father had written down after she'd driven away from the park with her son.

Possibly his son.

Unsure of how to approach her, he'd decided on the direct approach. Too much time had passed since they'd met—if this was truly the mystery woman he'd dreamed about so many nights away in other countries, doing his job. If she was his fairy princess and her son was his baby, dancing around it would just waste more time.

If the boy was his son, he didn't want to waste another minute.

Now he stood outside Pippa's apartment, ringing the bell, but no one answered the door.

Then he loudly knocked three times.

She wasn't home.

He'd have to adapt and adjust his plan. He went back down the stairs, got in his truck, and headed for the grocery where she worked.

Intel he and his father had gathered said she worked six

days a week at the grocery store checking groceries, and then took a night class from seven to eight-thirty on Monday, Wednesday, and Friday nights. It being Wednesday, and nearly seven, she should've been home from the grocery by now to leave her son with the sitter.

Her pattern was broken.

Diesel scowled at the clock and wondered what had caused her to change her pattern.

Starting the truck, he backed out of the parking lot and headed for the grocery. He'd have to see if she was still at work, and if she wasn't, he'd ask if she'd been at work today and when she'd left.

She wouldn't have gone to class with her son. The course she was taking was court transcription, and there'd be no way she could do that with a child in her arms.

Maybe the boy was sick, and she'd taken him to urgent care.

He hoped nothing bad had happened to either of them. But he was getting that feeling in the pit of his stomach when something went wrong. And that feeling, which was battle-tested, had never been wrong. Not even once. He'd learned long ago to trust his gut. The more the minutes ticked on, the more his gut was sending out those warning signals.

Driving to the grocery store, the feelings only increased.

He parked, walked inside, and looked for the manager.

The man was in his office on the phone.

Diesel waited for him to hang up. When he did, Diesel said, "I'm concerned about my friend, Pippa. She works here as a checker."

The manager frowned and said, "Concerned? Why?"

"She didn't arrive home tonight."

"Who are you?"

"A friend of Pippa's. She usually comes home, and then

goes to that class she's taking after the sitter arrives, but she never came home tonight."

Concern for Pippa changed the manager's facial expression and body language. It also redirected his attention to finding her. "Did you try her cellphone?" He had his phone in his hand and started to dial. "I sent her home an hour early because we were slow, and I had too many checkers standing around. She should've been home a long time ago."

The phone went immediately to voice mail, and the man's frown deepened. "She's not answering. She must not have her phone turned on." He shook his head. "That's not something she does because of Bryce; in case the sitter has to call her. She never turns off her phone."

Diesel froze.

Bryce? That was his father's name. *When were you going to give me that bit of Intel, dad?*

The manager was looking at him strangely. "Who did you say you were again?" he asked.

"I didn't." He pulled out his I.D. showing his name and his military credentials, what he was able to divulge about himself.

"And you know Pippa how?"

"I believe I may be the boy's father, and I believe something has happened to Pippa."

The manager started dialing the phone again. "I'm calling the police."

"Good. You do that." Diesel then went silent. He'd be gone before they ever got there. Disappearing was something he excelled at. Infiltration was a specialty of his. But searching for, hunting for anyone or anything, for that he'd call on his SEAL brother, Osprey, who was the best hunter he knew.

He was out the door and on his phone to Osprey before

the manager even finished the call to the police. And within just a couple minutes, he was gone, as if he'd never been there.

Retracing her probable and usual route from her work to home, he talked to Osprey, explaining the situation.

"Give me every bit of info you have, down to the smallest detail, even if it appears unimportant," Osprey said. "You going to her apartment to search?"

"Headed there now." If there was anything in her apartment that could clue them in on where she might've gone, he would find it.

At her apartment again, he ran up the apartment steps all the way to the top floor without being out of breath and stopped at her door. He tried the door, believing it would be locked, thinking he might have to break it down to get in, but it swung open with an easy push.

Damn. If he'd done that when he was here before, he wouldn't have wasted time at the grocery store.

The door squeaked, and he scanned the first room and then stepped inside.

There'd been a struggle.

A table lamp lay broken on the floor, a bowl of cereal O's had spilled and scattered all over the floor. A child's juice cup, which must've been Cranapple, or berry had spilled onto the beige carpet, leaving a stain which reminded him too much of fresh blood.

Though it wasn't blood. He'd seen plenty of spilled blood and knew exactly what the color of blood looked like, and whether it was freshly spilled or blood that had been there a while. He bent down.

This spill was recent enough to have been early evening.

She'd come home and shortly afterward; someone had taken them both.

He moved to the kitchen just off the first room. Clean,

nothing spilled or broken there. Remarkably clean for having a baby in the house.

Her purse sat on a kitchen chair. He went over to it and looked inside. If her cell phone was inside and turned off, he'd have his answer to why a call wouldn't go through.

No cellphone.

He moved into the bedroom, and then the bathroom. Nothing looked out of place in either.

In her bedroom, a crib was set up in the corner, and her bed took up the middle of the room. A changing table stood next to the crib. No longer in use, she now used it as storage, and piles of neatly folded baby clothes sat on top of it.

Back in the front room again, he noted there was no television, no radio, just books and a basket with yarn and crochet hooks, and toys for toddlers.

Her life centered around her child. Everything about the place said a mother and her baby lived here.

He felt very much out of place here. Like an intruder. Which he was.

He'd entered many homes before, some with women and children. But he'd never felt so much like an intruder until now. This woman was trying to create a good home for her son.

His son if he was to believe his father.

Before his dad had flown back home, he'd suddenly turned detective and decided to find out about the woman and the baby.

According to the friend Pippa worked with, Pippa didn't know who the father was.

If Pippa was the woman he thought she was, then there was a very good reason she might say she didn't know who the father was. She didn't know his name. And he hadn't known hers.

Until recently.

He could've been angry with her about having the baby and not telling him, except for those facts.

But if she was hiding because she didn't want to tell him, that was something else. And if that were the reason, then he'd have more than a few words to say to her about that.

Fathers had rights, too, and his son was not going to grow up without his father in his life. No way in hell.

Between his connections and his SEAL training she hadn't stood much chance of hiding from him, if hiding was what she was trying to do. Even though, technically speaking, SEALs weren't supposed to be digging around on their own time and using government resources and manpower to achieve their own goals.

Pippa's friend Cheryl had told his dad that Pippa had been trying to hide from an ex who might hurt her if he found her. An ex who was not only an ex-husband but was an inmate in prison.

Matt, who was a computer genius and had an uncanny ability of being able to find almost anyone, had turned up the fact that Stan Nitty had just been released from prison a few weeks ago.

Even if Pippa wasn't the woman his dad now insisted she was, and the boy wasn't his son, she still needed to know her ex was free again, so she'd be aware. For her own safety and precautions.

No court-ordered document would protect her if a violent man like her ex came after her.

Diesel had seen the pictures of Pippa, which were part of the divorce proceedings. The marks upon Pippa's neck made him want to do bad things to Stan Nitty.

No man should ever beat or injure his wife. That kind of thing made Diesel's blood boil.

Nitty was a dangerous man and if he decided to come after Pippa, she'd be in danger.

Diesel wasn't about to let anything happen to Pippa, whether the boy was his or not. It would give him immense pleasure to wipe scum like her ex off the face of the earth.

No woman deserved to be treated they way Pippa had been.

Court documents had been easy to find and read. It was all there. The pictures of her neck where the man had squeezed showed bruises shaped like finger marks.

He couldn't keep those images out of his head.

Diesel would take pleasure in breaking every one of the man's fingers and showing him just what that squeezing would've felt like to his wife. And Diesel knew how to exact pain without killing. Though he was a trained killer, courtesy of the United States government, killing would be too fast for scum like Pippa's ex. The man had served time for felonious assault and was now out of prison.

No one seemed to know where he currently was, but he'd been sighted outside of Ohio, so he wasn't staying put and checking in with his probation office.

The man was on the move.

And Pippa and her son were missing.

Had her ex tried to contact Pippa? Had he found her?

If the scumbag had found her, he'd find the boy, too. Which meant the boy might be in danger.

Diesel needed to find Pippa, and *now.*

6

———

After driving the route, Pippa would have taken, more than once, and going over her apartment, Diesel was at a dead end. He drove onto the base, and ran over everything again in his head.

It was time to call Rich, and to see if any of his brothers were free to help him find the mysterious woman of his dreams, who seemed to keep slipping through his fingers.

He made the call, and the answer didn't surprise him.

SEALs were brothers and looked after their own. And that included their family members.

Rich was the first to step up, before Diesel even had to ask. "Hell, yeah, we're with you on this. And we'll find her, brother. You know as a team we're unbeatable." Rich added, "Come over to Chicks. Many of us are already here."

Turning around, Diesel drove off the base again, and headed to Chick's Bar. He made record time and managed to avoid a traffic ticket.

Inside, several of the men were seated at the table. Rich, Osprey, and Kik sat, having a beer.

"We have a potential team of six," Rich said. He gestured to the men. "You have us. R.T. and Cutter want in, but we don't really need six. Three is enough. So Matt is going to stay on base, but stay in contact. Cutter will jump in, and do perimeter patrol, if needed. We three are the extraction team."

"Four," Diesel said crossing his arms.

The men noted his body language, and knew not to argue with him. This was likely his son they were rescuing, along with the boy's mother. Of course, Diesel would insist on being in.

Matt, R.T. and Cutter joined them at the bar.

"We'll find her quicker than anyone else could," Rich said.

Matt nodded in agreement. An expert in computer skills, Matt could hack into any computer, and find out anything.

And Osprey? He lived for the hunt. Game, people, anything he set his sights on as his intended target, he found, took down, and he delivered what he targeted. "We'll find them."

Diesel didn't know of any other men more qualified to help him right now, than these six SEAL brothers. He couldn't have done better if he'd picked them himself.

Popping another antacid, he went quiet. He grabbed another, eating them like candy.

"You all right, brother?" R.T. clapped a hand on his shoulder. "Never seen you need those before." He gave a friendly squeeze saying, "You know you could sit this one out, and let us handle it. You're too close to it."

Diesel shook his head. "No way."

"All right, then. Let's go for a thirty-minute run. You've got to do something, while you wait. Matt will let us know, as soon as he has something," R.T. said.

"You know it," Matt said, picking up his to go order. "I'm heading back to the base now, and will be on my computer shortly."

If there was a way to track someone online, Matt had the skills to do it. Matt had tracked down Pippa's ex using his well-honed computer skills, and now he'd narrowed her possible location down to a house on the outskirts of town, which appeared, at first, to be abandoned.

Stan Nitty had saved whatever money he'd gotten from the sale of the house he'd shared with Pippa, and had taken a portion of it to buy a run-down house on the edge of Virginia.

~

Diesel and the team surrounded the house, and watched for less than an hour, though it seemed much longer to him.

Minutes had never crawled so slow in his life.

They waited for the sun to go down, so they could use their night vision goggles to see who might be inside and where.

At first glance, the house appeared abandoned. But SEALs knew appearances could be deceiving.

At last, the sun went down, and they donned their night vision to do a visual search, from a distance that wouldn't give away their positions.

No lights shined in the windows, and no sounds could be heard.

Until the child started crying.

Diesel froze.

The sound tore at his heart in a way nothing ever had before.

That was his son. Dammit, he just knew it.

The first sound he'd ever heard from his son, and it was a sound of distress.

It almost made him frantic. He had to reach the boy. To

save him from whatever was happening to him right now, or what might happen to him.

But he also had to stay calm, focused, stay on the goal, and the mission. Keep his head clear from emotion to do his job. This might be the hardest mission he'd ever been on.

Most of the time SEALs lived for the next mission, but this was one mission he wished had never happened.

His little boy should've been safe at home, playing with his toys, being doted on by his loving family. Not trapped in a damn shack by some lunatic who wouldn't let his ex-wife go.

His child, who he'd never once held in his arms, needed him.

The urge to charge in immediately, to destroy the man who'd abducted the child, and the child's mother, was so strong it made him want to do *something*.

He tamped that down, controlled it. Forced it to bend to his will. He had to do what was best for the boy, for the safety of the boy, for the complete success of this mission.

There could be no mistakes. Failure was unacceptable.

"You're too close to this," Rich said softly.

"Don't even think of telling me to sit this one out," Diesel said. "That's not an option."

"We won't fail," Rich said. "He's one man against six SEALs."

Lights in the house turned on, in the kitchen, now that it was dark. Up to this point the woman and child were in the kitchen, and the man had been moving in and out of it.

After the boy started crying, the lights in the kitchen were turned on.

Patiently the team waited for Nitty to move away from the woman, and child, into another room. They wouldn't chance the boy, or the woman, getting hurt but would wait for the right moment.

Trained SEALs were used to waiting and spent far more time waiting during an op than most people would have guessed.

Real life opps were not like Hollywood movies.

Finally Nitty moved down the hall, into a back bedroom, and Rich signaled to the team to move closer to the house.

Diesel and his team moved closer, watching as they moved.

Cutter would stay outside, on perimeter watch, and would communicate any movements, as he didn't have to remove his night vision goggles.

Nitty was in one of the bedrooms cleaning his gun.

Pippa was in the kitchen, seated on a chair, and tied to it.

Little Bryce was playing with a toy car, rolling it back and forth, along the floor.

Diesel took all this in.

God, he could kill for what was happening to Pippa.

What I wouldn't give to be sitting on a kitchen floor playing cars and trucks with my son.

He took a breath and gritted his teeth.

Focus. On. The. Mission.

Then it was on.

The team moved without speaking, using hand signals. One, then two, then three, and then they were go - into the house, and moving to reach the one man they wanted to take out.

Rich moved in through the front door, gun ready.

The first room was dark and empty. He removed his night vision, and pulled a black ski mask over his face, so no one would recognize him.

Kik followed him and repeated his movements.

Diesel was third, and seeing everything through his night vision as they all were, until they pulled the goggles up, and the ski masks down, the only sound in their earpieces was their breathing.

Without their night vision, they'd have to rely on Cutter and Osprey's eyes, as they patrolled outside the house.

"Nitty, back bedroom. Just laid his gun down reaching for something on closet self. Go, go, go!

Nitty reached for a box on the closet shelf. He'd laid his gun on the bed.

R.T. brought up the rear, and Diesel could hear him breathing heavier than usual. He'd mentioned allergies earlier, and said he needed to take his meds when they were in route.

It sounded much too loud to Diesel, but then his nerves were on edge, worried about his son. Staying cool was taking lots more effort than any op had ever required.

Rich moved silent and quick, toward the back bedroom Stan Nitty was in.

The man had put down his gun to reach for a box, so his hands were up.

There was no better moment to go. This should be a quick in, and out, as the man had no idea they were there.

Then R.T. sneezed.

Nitty turned toward the door, dropping the box, and grabbed for his rifle.

He fired and one shot hit the door trim, beside Kik's head, splintering the wood.

Rich, calm and cool, shot Nitty in the shoulder of his shooting arm, knocking him backward against the closet door.

Nitty looked down, shock flooding his face, on seeing that he'd been shot, and blood was now staining his shirt. "Who the hell are you?" he asked.

Not one of them answered. He'd get no Intel from them.

Nitty had a stockpile of weapons and ammunition, but

he was just one man, and one man with a loaded gun, or even with multiple guns was no match for a team of trained SEAL's.

The entire operation was over in less than ten minutes.

Kik wrapped an arm around Nitty's neck, and then applied pressure, and Nitty soon slumped.

Stan Nitty now lay on the ground, passed out.

Diesel hurried into the kitchen, took one look at Pippa, and said, "Are you hurt?"

Then he bent down on one knee, to untie Pippa from the chair she was tied to.

Pippa heard the voice behind her, and chills ran down her back. She knew that voice, behind her ear.

I know that voice. From one night. One wonderful night I could never forget.

The man dressed all in black military clothing and gear, like a commando out of some movie, knelt in front of her, and started untying her hands.

A long white scar peaked out from his right sleeve. She'd seen that scar before.

Could it really be him? She knew that scar.

He was working the knots loose, with quick and sure hands, and a calm, strong presence.

She knew that voice.

My gladiator. He's here. Am I dreaming?

She realized she hadn't answered him yet.

"No," she said in a soft whisper. "He hasn't hurt us yet. But he was going to."

"No," he said. "He wouldn't. I wouldn't have let him."

She drew a shuddering breath. "How did you find me?"

It all seemed like something out of a fairy tale, the way he'd suddenly appeared. The hero of her dreams was flesh and blood, and right in front of her.

She couldn't help staring.

He'd untied her, and now he pulled his goggles up, so as not to scare the boy, as he moved around in front of the chair where the boy played. Then he bent down on one knee again, and looked at the boy.

Bryce looked up at him, smiled the sweet smile only a two-year-old can give, and then said, "Play trucks."

It was a command. Not so unlike his father's.

Tears filled Pippa's eyes. "I have something to tell you."

Diesel turned his brown eyes to took into hers, and her son turned to watch her, too. He knew what she was going to say, but he needed her to say it.

He needed her to tell him what she should have told him a long time ago.

"We made a beautiful boy one night. I'm glad you'll be able to meet him now. I'm glad you found us. Thank you for saving our lives." Tears started rolling down her cheeks, and that was all she could get out.

Diesel had tears in his eyes now, too.

How could he be angry with her, when he'd looked into her eyes, and seen the feelings and emotions there? The way she loved and cared for their son?

Our son.

It really was true. Not some fairytale, or imagined thing from his father.

The old man knew. From the moment he saw little Bryce, he knew.

A little hand patted Diesel's rock-hard thigh, and he turned his head to look at his son again.

"Play trucks now," he demanded.

He and Pippa both laughed, as they looked at their son.

"How about we go home, and play trucks there," Diesel said.

But Bryce was already playing trucks by driving the truck up Diesels black boot.

Diesel had a grin from ear to ear, so big that his face was hurting. He looked at the other team members, who'd gathered in the room.

"I have a son," he said.

"Looks just like you," Kik said.

"Stubborn like you, too," Rich said.

"Bring that boy on out here, where I can see him," Cutter said. He was outside, guarding their prisoner, Stan.

"Let's go meet Cutter," Diesel said.

He held out a hand to help Pippa up, and she stood, moving her arms and legs, getting the circulation moving again.

She went to pick up Bryce, but Diesel said, "Let me."

He reached his arms toward the boy, waiting to see if Bryce would come to him, and grinned even wider when he did. Lifting him up, into his arms, he held him, and blinked a few times to clear the sudden moisture which affected his vision.

They walked out of the house into the yard where Cutter was watching Stan.

Still out, he looked less dangerous to Pippa, especially with SEALs on her side, and in control.

Stan couldn't hurt her now.

"We've talked about the way this needs to go down from here," Rich said. "Since this was an unauthorized op. We're going to fade into the background. What we need for you to do, is call the police from here, using this phone."

He handed her Stan's cellphone. "Tell them he abducted you, tell them exactly what happened, up until we arrived. Leave out the part where he had you tied up. We can't be here when they arrive, and you can't mention us. It's got to be as if we were never here."

"Okay." She nodded. "I can do that."

"When you call the police, tell them he's been shot, and

may need an ambulance. You didn't stay, because you were in fear of your life, if he came to again."

"Now, here's the story you need to tell. He had you in this house, and was threatening to kill you. You saw a chance to take his gun, and shoot him, and you took it. Then you grabbed your baby, and ran like hell. Used his van to drive yourself away from him, and back home."

"But I don't know how to shoot a gun, especially one of those big things."

"Give her a quick lesson, Diesel." Kik said. "Just enough that she'd know how to pick it up, and pull the trigger."

He held out the gun used to shoot Nitty toward Pippa. "The gun is clean and empty at the moment, so it's safe, but now we want your prints on it, so go ahead and take it."

"Hold it like this," Diesel showed her, using his own gun. "When you shoot, you'd pull this trigger."

When she hesitated, he said, "It's not going to hurt you. We're having you dry fire first, that means no ammo. It's just to get your prints on it."

She copied everything he did.

Then he loaded it, and had her place the gun against her shoulder, and fire into the woods.

The recoil hurt her shoulder, and she was sure she'd bruise.

This was the first time she'd ever shot a gun.

Being married to Stan had made her nervous around guns, and she'd never wanted to learn.

He'd been happy to keep her ignorant of her own self-defense, and dependent upon him. In fact, he encouraged her fear of guns.

It was just one more way to control her.

Done with the quick shooting lesson, she handed the gun back to Kik, who still had his gloves on.

Kik took the gun, and went to prepare the scene.

"I'm scared," she said. "What do I tell the police again? Won't they arrest me, and take the baby?"

"That's not going to happen. When you call in, tell them you want to charge him with kidnapping you and your son, and that you were terrified for your life. He tried to choke you to death once. And that's on record. This time you shot in self-defense, and got away. With his record, they'll send him back to prison, and he won't get to you again."

"But what if he gets out again?"

"I'll be there," Diesel said. "He's not ever going to get to you, or Bryce again, but even if on some wild chance he does, I'll be there."

He'd be there? What exactly did he mean?

Her heart thumped hard inside her chest.

"Thank you," she said. "Thank you, all of you. I don't know what I'd have done if he'd hurt Bryce."

"It's over now," Diesel said.

"Time to go." Rich tapped his watch.

R.T. carried Stan's limp body inside, to arrange it, and came back out carrying the ropes used to tie Pippa to the chair.

"Why aren't you leaving them?" Pippa asked.

"Doesn't fit the story," R.T. said, and then winked. He tossed the ropes into an SUV, and climbed in.

"Make that call," Rich said.

She took the phone, and called the police, following their instructions.

"Here are the van keys," Cutter said, tossing them to her.

"I've got Bryce," Diesel said. "There's no car seats, so I'll buckle him into the passenger seat."

Pippa wished there was a back seat, but Stan had stripped it out, so he could toss them into the back of the van, close to the driver's seat where he could watch them.

She watched Diesel strapping their son in, as careful as any other dad.

This all still seemed unreal, like a dream she hadn't woke up from yet.

"R.T. and I are going to tail you back to your apartment, and wait out of sight, until the police leave. Then we'll go get my truck, and talk."

She nodded, her gaze clinging to his face.

Lord, he was more handsome than she'd known.

"I guess we have a lot to talk about."

"We do. For now, let's stay on track here. You get this van to the apartment, with all the evidence inside, and they'll come here, and go over this place with a fine-tooth comb. All you'll have to do is sit tight at home, and take care of Bryce."

"Sounds good."

Going around to the driver's side, she climbed in. When she started the van and pulled out, a dark SUV slowly pulled out behind her.

R.T. and Diesel would be behind her, though soon they were out of sight. Still, she felt safer knowing they were there.

7

———

The police had come and gone for two days, taking statements, and collecting evidence. Pippa had to tell her story repeatedly and wished that it would all be over soon.

Everyone agreed it was likely Stan would be sent back to prison with a much longer sentence this time.

Her boss had given her time off, and she'd also taken a week off from her classes. Since she hadn't missed any days, losing one week wouldn't be enough to affect her grades.

Everyone was being nice to her and to Bryce, showing their concern, but she was tired of going over the story again, and again. She just wanted it to be over.

It had been over a week now, and though they knew the police would still be keeping an eye on the case, and any odd behavior she might do; it was finally okay for Diesel to start coming around.

He'd begun by showing up, when there were witnesses, introducing himself to her, as if they hadn't just met at the crime scene where he and the other SEALs had saved her life. He hadn't told her he was coming, so her surprise was more genuine.

Everyone seemed to take it as believable, that seeing

them on the news had made him realize the boy might be his.

Even a few of the police officers were encouraging the romance.

A winsome two-year-old, a woman who needed rescuing, and a military hero, well that kind of love story, who could argue against that.

At last, Diesel and Pippa were alone. Or as alone as a single mother with a two-year-old could be. Bryce was napping, and they had a chance to really talk now.

They'd been talking for the better part of an hour.

"Are you sure you want to be a part of our lives? I mean, you hardly know us," her voice was serious, but uncertain.

"I know I dreamed about you, many nights, when I was deployed over the last two years." He reached out a hand for hers, grasped it, and pulled her nearer.

"I dreamed of you too," she smiled. "My gladiator."

He smiled, and continued. "I dreamed of you, and of finding you. Dreamed of making love to you, again. Of touching your skin, kissing your lips. Of sliding my arms around your waist, just like this." His arms slid around her waist.

"Of tasting you again, and again." He kissed her lips softly, and then released her, to finish what he'd waited so long to say. "Of making love to you, all night, and waking up with you still in my bed, in my arms. For two years, I've thought of finding you. Now, you're here."

His arms pulled her closer, until their hips met, and he felt the softness of her fuller, more rounded belly since having the baby, as he looked down into her eyes. "And I don't want to let you go."

Her gaze searched his, looking for what lay deep within, below the surfaces. "Is it only sex?" she asked, "I desire you, I dream of you too, but is it only sex?"

"If it were, any woman would do. No, it isn't only sex. I want you." His eyes searched hers now, seeking his answers. "And I'm hoping you want me, too."

"I do," she breathed the words out. "I want to know you. More and more, to know you. But I'm afraid."

"What are you afraid of?"

Her lips trembled. "That you'll change. And then, you'll hurt me."

"Because of him," he said softly.

"Yes."

He sighed. "Do you know how to conquer a fear?"

She shook her head, unable to speak. Her wide green eyes watched him.

"You conquer a fear by working through it. By facing the fear, and then moving through it. The way out of fear is *through*. It's how you get to the other side."

She nodded, listening.

"We can take this slow. We *should* take this slow. It would be best for you, and for Bryce, too," Diesel said.

"Yes," she said quickly.

Relief showed on her face.

"I'm not going to push you to chose me. I want you to choose me for me, and I want to choose you for you, neither of us owning the other. Bryce has been fatherless for two years already, and I'll be in his life now, no matter what you decide, but neither of you know me that well, not yet. This will take time."

She gave him a little smile. "Bryce is the easy one, I think. Children just love right away, like puppies. It's so innocent and pure. First loves are like that, too. We go into them wide-eyed and thinking no one will hurt us, no one will leave us. And then, they do." Pippa stared off, away from him.

"Pippa," he said softly. "I would injure *myself* before I

would ever hurt you or Bryce. I'm not the kind of man who hurts women, or children. I'm a protecting kind of man, the kind who saves them."

"Yes, you are," she smiled a soft smile. "You certainly saved me. And Bryce, too."

"How about we start with this? I want to protect you and Bryce, for the rest of my life. To make sure no harm comes to you. But I want more."

"More?" she whispered the word.

"Yes. More. I want to be the protector of your heart."

She breathed in sharply, and held her breath.

"Will you allow me to do that for you? To guard and protect your heart?"

This was beyond anything she'd ever dreamed of. It hardly seemed real.

She placed her hand on his warm, strong forearm. Feeling his strength in body, and the strength of his love, and this gift he was giving her now.

"Yes," she breathed out. "Yes."

~

Though they would marry nine months later, with a daughter on the way, both considered the day of that first vow to be their first wedding day, when Diesel became her protector, and the guardian and keeper of her heart.

THE END

ACKNOWLEDGMENTS

My infinite love and gratitude to all who played a part in the origins of this story, all the way to this new launch of the revised story, and my new Green Brotherhood: SEAL Team XII series.

From the beginnings of the original short novella I was invited to write by Susan Stoker, and for recent encouragement to publish this story with my own press, my eternal thanks to Susan Stoker; Special thanks to Elle James who introduced me to Susan, and suggested I write in her world. Kindle Worlds was a good run while it lasted, and I appreciate you both inviting me into your worlds.

Thank you to my gun instructor and gunfight scene advisor for many years, Army veteran Bobby Buls; thank you to Marine veteran and advisor Charles Welshans; thank you to Delilah Devlin for editing several of my books in the series; thank you to my cover artist Sheri L. McGathy; and to my sister Kim who read all my books and worked as my PA; thank you to my best friend author Susan Boles; and to all my readers who loved that first short story and wanted more.

From that first small novella, grew this new series I'm excited to launch with this first book, and I'm thrilled to be able to thank my new SEAL advisor, Navy SEAL veteran and author Bill Hellman who is helping me make my SEAL stories even better and worked with me to create this new SEAL Team; thank you to my cover artist and logo designer for SEAL Team XII Sheri L. McGathy; thank you to my family, and especially my husband Mike, bus driver, maintenance man, and sometimes "arm candy."

I love you all.

REAL MOVIE HERO

1

LITTLE CREEK, VIRGINA

Reed "Railroad" Tindal aka "R.T." sat outside on the deck of Chicks bar, at the marina, enjoying his beer, as he and two of his SEAL brothers watched a boat pulling into one of the slips.

It was a perfect evening for sailing. Just enough of a breeze and the sun starting to set.

"That's the life," "Cutter" Antonius (Tony) said. "What I'm going to do after I retire. Nothing but sails, suds, and sweethearts."

"A girl for you in every port," Tanner "Diesel" Taylor said. "Not much different from what you have now."

Diesel liked to have a beer in every port, but Cutter, he was all about the women.

Around SEALs there were always women. Drawn to them like moths to flames.

A seagull landed on one of the posts near them and looked at them for food.

Sheri, their favorite cheerful dimpled waitress, showed up again to see if the men wanted another beer. "Fred has joined your party," she said. "Do you want some pretzels for him? And another beer?"

Reed shook his head. "Sorry, guys, I'd hang for another beer and to stay and chat," Reed said, "but I'm headed out to see a movie premiere."

"Oh, lucky you," Sheri said.

"Which one?" Diesel asked.

"*Turn and Deliver*, with Cole Kennick," Reed said.

"He's very handsome," Sheri said. "I like his movies."

"There should be plenty of good action scenes in that one," Cutter said. He raised his nearly empty glass. "And I'll take another beer, hun."

She smiled her dimpled grin at him. "You've got it."

"Cole Kennick does a better job keeping it real than most," Reed said.

"How'd you get passes?" Diesel asked.

"Won them from the local radio station," Reed said. "I've got one unclaimed pass." He turned to their waitress. "If you'd like to go, Sheri."

"You know I can't," Sheri shook her head. "My boyfriend wouldn't like that."

"It's just a movie," Reed said. "Not a kiss."

She put one hand on her hip. "Now you know that movies lead to kisses, and that is how people get into trouble."

"Are you saying you couldn't keep yourself from kissing me?" Reed teased.

Throwing one hand in the air she said, "Now you know that's not what I meant." Shaking her head, she turned and walked away.

"Well, guys, looks like I have one pass up for grabs if one of you wants it," Reed said.

"Can't tonight," Cutter said. "I'm meeting a chick here."

"That does not surprise me," Reed said.

"Another hot dancer with long legs?" Diesel asked.

Cutter grinned. "You know it."

The man was predictable as hell when it came to women, and he always seemed to be dating a dancer.

Reed turned to Diesel. "Do you want it?"

"Dad is flying in tonight, and I'm picking him up at the airport," Tanner "Diesel" Taylor said. "So, this is my limit tonight." He raised his beer. "And I've got to go." He drained his beer, and then pushed his chair back to stand.

Reed stood and said good night to both before heading toward the door.

Too bad the extra ticket would go to waste.

He'd just picked the tickets up from the station before heading to Chicks so there hadn't been time to ask around. Plus, he hadn't figured on both his brothers being busy tonight.

It was a weeknight, not a Saturday, and generally they all hung out at Chicks enjoying the views and brews. Tonight, it had just been the three of them.

It looked like he was headed to the premiere alone. But that didn't bother him. He would enjoy the movie either way.

"I can't go tonight," Tanya told Christie over the phone, her voice hard to hear, while Tanya's dog, Brutus, whined in the background, and her cat, Miss Priss, meowed mournfully. "There's no way I'll make the movie premiere. I hate to let you down, but it's crazy here."

"Oh, no," Christie said, her stomach dropping to her toes. "What's going on?"

Tanya is bailing.

Dismayed, Christie glanced at her watch. *We're supposed to meet in front of the theater in twenty minutes.*

The movie premiere passes Christie had won last week

from the local radio station were only good for tonight's premiere.

It's too late to call someone else.

Christie looked down at her red and white dress which showed off her curves.

And I'm dressed forties style. There's no time to change clothes.

The whole idea was she and Tanya were going to have a "girls' night out," dressed in 1940's attire. First, they'd see the movie, and then they'd go for drinks afterward. Both women enjoyed dressing in vintage fashions, and they'd each bought new dresses to show off.

Christie couldn't help but be disappointed.

Tanya interrupted Christie's thoughts. "Cole Kennick must be the hottest man in Hollywood, and you know how much I wanted to go to the premiere with you. But Miss Priss just yakked all over my bedspread, right after I finished cleaning up after Brutus. They're both sick. I'm thinking I might need to call the vet."

"I'm so sorry. Are they going to be all right?" Christie's concern for the animals pushed aside her disappointment at her best friend bailing on her. "Do you want me to come over?"

"No, I can handle this," Tanya said. "You go on to the movie. I don't want to be the reason you miss the premiere."

"What do you think it is?" Christie asked. "Did they both get into something? Maybe eat something bad?"

"They've eaten something I didn't give them, that much I do know," Tanya said. "What it is though, I can't tell."

"Oh my god." Christie didn't say her next thought.

Poison. The nasty neighbor might've poisoned them.

Tanya's neighbor was always complaining about Brutus and his barking. Brutus was a German Shepard and very protective of Tanya. Tanya's crazy neighbor jumped at any excuse to call the police. On the other hand, Miss Priss was a beautiful white Persian cat who never bothered anyone, although she did shed white hair everywhere.

"You'd better take a sample of the puke to the vet, in case he needs to test what they got into," Christie said.

"Already thought of that. Go enjoy the movie," Tanya said, her tone reassuring. "Don't worry. I don't want to ruin your fun evening."

"You're not going to ruin my evening," Christie said. "But I will miss you."

"Well, you'd better hurry or you'll be late," Tanya said. "And I don't think they let you in late to premieres."

Christie sighed. "All right, but I'm calling you just as soon as the movie is over."

"Thanks, Christie. And again, I'm so sorry about this."

"It's okay," Christie said. "You just take care of those sweet fur babies."

"Thanks for understanding," Tanya said.

"Hey, that's what best friends do," Christie said.

"Thanks bestie," Tanya said. "Chat soon. Don't be late!"

"I won't, "Christie said. "Bye."

"Bye."

Worrying about Tanya's fur babies, Christie grabbed the movie passes and hurried out the door to her car.

Fortunately, she made every streetlight by driving two miles under the speed limit and arrived just in time.

The line inside the Cinema One complex was long and filled the lobby. Christie stood at the end of line waiting.

At least I only need one seat.

Two ticket takers stood at the entrance. A man and a woman. The woman held a basket to collect their cell phones. She was explaining that everyone would get their phones back when they came out of the movie and she'd always be with the phones. Taking the phones was to prevent anyone from sneaking to take a video of the movie. The woman reminded everyone that pirating was against federal law.

Christie handed the man her pass and placed her phone into the basket the woman held. As she moved away, her gaze lingered on her phone reluctantly.

I hope Tanya won't need to reach me soon and that the vet tells Tanya her fur babies will be okay. She's got to do something about that mean neighbor. That woman has gone too far if she has poisoned them, and I'll bet she has. Poor Miss Priss and Brutus.

Inside, the theater was semi-dark and nearly full.

Christie stood at the bottom of the theater's stadium seating, letting her eyes adjust to the darkness and looking for one good seat.

Oh, there's one next to that fit, handsome man with the brown hair wearing the brown leather jacket.

Her gaze stopped and held as he captured her attention. His build was solid. Strong. Something about him drew her attention—and then she noticed, he was looking right back at her with his intense hazel eyes. But then, his gaze swept past her to the other side of the theater, as he sat quietly scanning the room.

Is he waiting for someone? Saving that seat? I hope not. It's a good location, and I'm running out of options.

She headed for the seat, hoping it would be free.

Reaching his isle, she leaned forward, drawing his full attention, and asked, "Is this seat taken?"

"No." He shook his head, his eyes watching her.

She smiled, and the teenager seated on the end of the aisle moved his feet, so she could slip between the rows.

"Excuse me," she said, and began the "theater row shuffle", being careful, as she was wearing her highest heels.

The new red ones, with the little bows on the front, and tall, narrow heels.

She'd had so much fun planning to glam it up on their girls' night out, and both she and Tanya had pretty dresses any pin-up girl would be proud of. Now, Tanya wouldn't see her in her new red and white checkered dress. The cool summer dress was form-fitting, and showed her curves, making her feel attractive, and glamorous, in a Marilyn Monroe kind of way.

All dolled up for a night on the town, and no one to spend it with.

There was no one here, that she knew, to see the dress and to appreciate it along with the time and effort she'd spent on her blonde hairdo, and makeup to complete the look. Plenty of men had ogled her since she'd stepped out of her car, in the theater parking lot, but that wasn't the kind of attention she wanted.

Tanya would've appreciated the dress, and the time it took to find the perfect dress, and to do her hair and makeup just so. Still, the entire row of men she passed, and men in the rows behind them, watched her every move.

Stepping daintily to the left of the handsome man in the brown leather jacket, and in front of the empty seat, she turned and sat while trying to play it cool, like she just needed a seat and not like she'd hoped to sit with him. Wondering where to put her purse and keeping in mind how a movie theater floor could be sticky, she bent and placed her new, shiny red purse on top of her feet, balancing it on her toes.

The air-conditioning sent a cool draft across her bare shoulders, bringing goose bumps, and making her want to shiver. She'd forgotten how cool the air could be in a theater when she'd ordered this dress. Wishing she'd worn a shawl; Christie hoped all the people in the theater would create enough body heat to warm the room up. At least when she leaned back against the seat, the vent blew in front of her, not on her back. Though her neck and collarbone were receiving the draft, chilling her front side.

Now that she was seated, she realized how much taller than her the handsome man was. Sitting next to him made her feel downright delicate. His chest, shoulders, and arms were muscular, and he exuded strength.

Oh my, but he's handsome, and he smells good.

She glanced down at his hand.

No wedding ring. I wonder why he's here without a date, or a friend? Women probably fall all over him. I wonder what his name is.

On her other side, a large man in an orange T-shirt and jeans sat holding a huge tub of popcorn. "Here by yourself?" he said. "That's terrible."

Taken aback by his sly tone, she leaned away from the nosy man and closer to the handsome man, aware of him now watching her and the nosy man.

"Why would you ask?" she said, frowning and then catching herself, as she decided she shouldn't be speaking to this stranger about whether she was out alone. "That's none of your business," she said, feeling herself bristle.

Maybe this seat wasn't such a good one after all.

Though the view of the screen was excellent, and she was near enough to the aisle to get out without having to climb over half a row of people, now she hoped the nosy man wouldn't continue to bother her.

Mr. Nosy leaned forward, as if to say something else, and his hand reached toward her, but then he stopped, looking past her to handsome man.

She turned to glance at handsome man, wondering what he'd done to stop Mr. Nosy.

Handsome Man's hair was damp, likely from having

taken a recent shower. Hot as it was outside, his hair would've dried otherwise. She became aware once again of his aftershave or cologne, a manly enticing scent.

"Most people are here because they received a pass to the premiere," the handsome man said dryly.

Mr. Nosy shut up and went back to eating his popcorn, taking a huge handful.

Christie exhaled stress she didn't know she'd been holding.

Better Mr. Nosy keeps his attention on his popcorn, and not on me.

"Thank you," Christie whispered under her breath, just low enough the handsome man could hear.

"No problem," came his low answer.

He smells good.

And that low voice was doing things to her insides as his scent assaulted her senses on another level. Pheromones flooded her body, making her aware of her breath, her heartbeat, the way her palms were starting to warm. The slight flush in her pale cheeks and chest, which always happened, would begin now.

Her pheromones could get her into trouble sometimes when they kicked in before she figured out if a guy was a good man to be with or not.

As the lights began to dim, she thought, *Good thing we'll be in a dark theater. Handsome Man will never know how I'm reacting to him.*

∽

R eed Tindal sat scanning the crowd.

Attentiveness was by now an ingrained habit, though he was casual about it, unless he needed not to be.

A trained SEAL, when he was awake, he was always aware of his surroundings.

The pretty blonde with the creamy skin and stunning green eyes had caught his attention before she'd noticed him. Then their gazes had connected, and he'd felt that flicker, the one that always happened when attraction kicked in. This attraction was strong. Strong enough to take him by surprise, as she usually wouldn't have been his type.

She was wearing a delicate red and white checked dress with little straps and high heels.

With soft blonde shoulder length curls tied with a red ribbon, smokey eyeliner, and cherry red lipstick, she was girly from her head to her red painted toenails, which peeked out of her shoes. Those red high heeled shoes with red bows on the front were the kind that always made him wonder how a woman would run if she had to, without turning an ankle. He hoped this beauty never found out. She turned heads dressed like that, and some heads were best avoided.

He wondered what her story was, and why she was all dressed up to watch a movie by herself. There was a story there. He couldn't imagine any hot-blooded male standing up a woman who looked as good as she did.

Reed was used to dating women who were more practical. Sensible about things like shoes, wore jeans instead of dresses, and carried guns. There was nowhere on that pretty dress where this woman could carry a gun or anything else. In fact, he'd bet she didn't even know how to shoot a gun.

She looked like the "take care of me" type, not the "I'll take care of things myself" type.

Everyone was seated. A man in a black suit stepped onto the stage and welcomed them to the premiere, then the lights were dimmed, and everyone settled in to watch the show.

The blonde, caught up in the story, would catch her breath, only to release it when Cole escaped the bad guy's malevolence, and avoided getting so much as a mark on him.

Her breathy sighs and little gasps caught Reed's attention each time, though he was also focusing on the movie. He was good at doing two things at once.

The movie held her complete attention, and she seemed unaware of anything else, though Reed had noted her initial reaction to him.

Reed could have been caught up in the movie as well if he'd let himself. Cole was one of the few actors who did their own stunts, and he kept his movies more real than most. Which meant Reed didn't disengage and start critiquing action shots five minutes into the movie.

Had he been at home, he might have been as caught up as the woman was. But out in public, nothing would ever take up his total attention. However, that was not to say he wasn't enjoying the movie. In fact, he was enjoying the movie as well as her reactions to it.

Total opposites, he thought as he noted her reactions to the movie. She was so caught up in the movie, she didn't notice anything else.

Reed had grown up in a neighborhood where boys had to fight, or be picked on, so he'd learned early on to fight, and to pay attention to who was where, always. He viewed her as he would a child, or any other innocent civilian, who hadn't learned to be wary. He was glad to see her relaxing and enjoying the movie.

This was why men like him fought. To protect the innocent, and preserve a peaceful way of life, and freedom. These were some of the reasons he fought.

Actor Cole Kennick played roles in which he did the

same, which was one reason Reed enjoyed watching his movies.

Some feeling he couldn't have named, other than to call it a sixth sense, made him turn his focus to a man at the front of the theater, dressed all in black.

Not one of the staff.

Another patron, perhaps.

He stood at the far-right corner of the theater. Something about him was very off.

The man turned to face the crowd, and began to move his arm upward —

Damn.

Reed went calm and cool, even as he thought the word, his training kicking in, knowing the man was going to shoot.

Everything around Reed slowed.

"Everyone down!" he yelled, as his hand landed on the pretty blonde's shoulder, forcing her to the ground behind the seats.

The shooter raised his gun to fire.

2

———————

Christie didn't understand what was happening, as the handsome man next to her shouted, and the sharp reports of gunfire — not coming from the screen, but somewhere in the theater - erupted. At the same time, the man's strong, warm hand closed over her bare shoulder, hard, pulling her away from her seat, pushing her forward and down onto her knees on the sticky theater floor.

"Stay down," he said, his tone brisk and harsh.

His right hand reached for the gun he carried in a belt holster behind his back. "Stay here."

She followed his directions, crouching low, with her hands over her head, so scared she was shaking, but she couldn't resist looking at the shooter through the small space between the seats.

Dressed in a black hoodie, she saw only his tall, lean figure and a long gun pointing toward them.

Oh my God. We're all going to die. Her thoughts raced as the shots continued. *I'm not ready, Lord. Please don't let me die now.*

The handsome man leapt over the seats in front of them,

firing, up and over the crowd, his aim deadly, his body moving in a straight line, charging the shooter.

The man in black went down.

The confrontation was over in seconds, which dragged like minutes. Less time than any of them would have guessed, other than Reed, who'd been well trained to eliminate this kind of threat. He knew what could happen in just a few seconds, and exactly how fast he needed to be.

Reed hoped like hell that nobody had been killed. The shooter had gotten off a few shots before he went down.

Women's screams still filled the air along with crying.

A man called out, "I've been shot."

The screaming stopped.

There was a moment of silence, following the gunshots, which gave Reed a chance to take a deep breath and added to his sense of calm.

A few people raised their heads to look at the shooter.

Sounds of women crying replaced the silence.

A man moaned.

Reed reached into his left pocket, as his right thumb pressed a button on his gun.

The empty magazine fell to the ground, as he slapped in a new one, and kept moving forward, down to where the gunman lay on the floor.

He'd make sure the man didn't get up and start shooting again. He had to make sure he'd delivered the kill shot he thought he had. He'd take no chances.

First thing he did, was kick away, and remove all weapons, out of the man's reach. Then he bent to check the man's pulse.

Nothing. The man was dead.

Reed pulled out his cell phone, and dialed 911, thankful he'd ignored instructions to hand his phone in along with all the others.

Likely, he was the only one in the theater able to call. Something the shooter had probably counted on. Like counting on all the patrons to be unarmed.

"Springfield dispatch," a female voice answered.

"I need to report the live shooter at Springfield Cinema One, is now down," he said.

"A live shooter at Springfield Cinema One," the voice repeated. "Did you say down?"

"Yes," he said. "One live shooter down. No others in sight."

"Who am I speaking to?"

"Reed Tindal. I'm a Navy SEAL."

"Are you armed, Mr. Tindal?"

"Yes. One patron has been shot. I'll assess and report back. We're going to need at least two ambulances."

"Please stay on the line, Mr. Tindal. Police and ambulances are on their way."

"Roger that."

He moved back to where the pretty blonde was still crouching on the ground.

She looked up at him, her eyes wide.

"You can get up now," he said. "It's safe."

She rose, slowly and shakily. "Safe," she repeated, as if to reassure herself.

"Yes," he answered. "You're safe. What's your name?"

"Christie Anderson."

"Okay Christie." He handed her his phone. "Take this. Stay on the line with dispatch. I'm going to check on the wounded."

The blonde blinked, as if waking from a fog, but then took the phone. "Of course."

"Good," he said.

She put his phone to her ear, and said, "Hello?"

"Where is Mr. Tindal, and who am I speaking to?" the dispatcher asked.

Mr. Tindal, that was his name.

She filed his name away in her memory as the man who'd saved her life. "He's checking for wounded, but I'll stay on the line," Christie said. "I'm Christie Anderson."

"All right, Christie. Stay with me, until the police arrive and let me know what's happening."

"Yes, ma'am."

Christie watched Mr. Tindal moving quickly, his glance going up and down aisles, while he reassured theater patrons that everything was over, and would be okay now. His expression hardened when he found the man who'd called out he'd been shot.

The dispatcher asked, "Ask Mr. Tindal how many are injured?"

"Okay," Christie said. "Hang on. I have to move down to where he is, right now. He's with a man who got shot."

"Keep talking to me. Tell me what's happening."

"Well, I won't really know, 'til I get down there," Christie said.

"Okay, just stay on the line."

"I will." Christie started moving down toward where Mr. Tidal was.

The wounded man who'd shouted out, was in a theater seat, and Mr. Tindal was getting the nearby patrons to move out of the way, so he could get to him.

As Christie got nearer, she saw the man had been shot in the arm. Blood was everywhere, and the man's skin was pale, as if he'd already lost too much blood. The man in the row behind him, was also shot, bleeding from his arm.

She breathed in sharp, the images nearly stopping her.

The dispatcher, who'd been listening said, "What is it? Christie, are you all right?"

Nausea hit her stomach, and she pressed her free hand to her belly, to try to calm it back down. She couldn't get sick at the sight of blood, she had to pull herself together. "Yes." She swallowed hard. "There's just a lot of blood. Two men have been shot. I'm down here with Mr. Tindal now."

Mr. Tindal pulled something out of his pocket, and then started to unwind a strap of some kind. He opened the thing into what looked like a circle.

"He's got something he's making into a circle," Christie said.

"That's probably a tourniquet."

"I feel like I should be helping him," Christie said.

"Do you have any medical training?"

"No," she said.

"If he's a SEAL, he may have been trained as a medic. He'll know what to do, until the ambulance arrives. You just stay on the line."

Christie could hear sirens in the distance. "I hear sirens now."

"They're almost there. You just hang on."

Christie reached Mr. Tindal. He glanced up and gave her a nod. "Put the call on speaker, then put it down and help me."

"Okay." She tapped the speaker setting and said, "You're on speaker phone now, so you can hear us both. I need to help him."

"Tell me what's happening," the dispatcher said.

Mr. Tindal responded, "We've got two men shot, both in the arm. Need tourniquets. I've got two with me." He reached into his pocket, pulled out a second tourniquet, and handed it to Christie. "You're going to put this one on that guy, while I put one on this guy."

Christie stared at him. "I don't know anything about tourniquets."

"It's not hard," Mr. Tindal said. "Open it up. And hurry."

Looking at it, Christie found the ends, and let the rest of the band fall, opening easily into a circle. She hurried into the isle behind the first wounded man and saw blood all over the second man and on the empty seat that had been cleared, so Mr. Tindal could get to him.

But Mr. Tindal was only one man and he'd said to hurry.

"Now, put it on his arm," Mr. Tindal said. "Get as high up as you can get, without going up onto his shoulder."

The wounded man whimpered, as Christie awkwardly complied, squatting on her high heels, trying not to cause more pain.

"Now what?" he said.

"You need to cinch it down tight," Mr. Tindal said. "Watch me."

Christie paid close attention as Mr. Tindal tightened the strap, doubled it back, and then began twisting a metal rod like a windlass, before looping it into a strap of Velcro.

Mr. Tindal looked her in the eyes. "It needs to be as tight as possible. Better to hurt him now than to let him bleed to death."

Christie felt the blood drain from her face.

The only way to get enough leverage to turn that tourniquet properly, the way Mr. Tindal was doing, was to kneel on the bloody seat next to the man who'd been shot and put her weight into it.

Her new dress would be ruined. But she had to do it anyway.

She turned back to the man she was working on, her hands fumbling on their own. This near to the man, the stench of blood made her stomach roil, but she pressed on.

Christie tightened the strap, then started twisting the windlass.

With each turn, the man's face screwed up tighter in

pain, but she didn't stop until it was too tight for her to turn. Then she strapped it down.

Mr. Tindal watched her appraisingly and nodded his approval.

Good. She exhaled. *I must have done it right. I hope this man makes it.*

"Both tourniquets are on," Mr. Tindal said into the phone. "ETA on those ambulances?"

"Three minutes," the dispatcher said.

When he set the phone down, Christie said, "It's a good thing you had two of those."

"I always carry two tourniquets," he said. "Because we have two femoral arteries."

"Oh," Christie said.

She knew little about anatomy, and wasn't sure where femoral arteries were, but was glad he knew, and that he knew what to do.

"By the way, you did a great job," he said.

Blushing, she glanced down. "Thank you," she said, embarrassed by his praise.

Police officers streamed into the theater, alert, armed and ready for trouble.

Mr. Tindal sat back on his heels, having finished with the civilian he'd been treating.

The first officer approached him and said, "Reed Tindal?"

"That's me." He nodded at the man he'd treated. "This one is wounded, and there's another." He pointed to the other man.

The officer nodded. "Are you armed?"

"Yes," Mr. Tindal stood slowly. "Behind my right hip."

"Ok. I'm going to ask you step out of the isle, and down the stairs."

Christie noted that the police officers had arrived with

guns drawn. They'd eased off but not holstered their weapons.

Mr. Tindal obeyed, moving out of the isle, and down the stairs followed by the first officer.

Was all this necessary? Couldn't they see he wasn't the bad guy? He was the man who'd stopped the bad guy. Everyone in the theater owed their lives to Mr. Tindal.

"Turn and face the wall, please," the officer said.

Mr. Tindal automatically pressed his palms against the wall and didn't seem upset.

"This the gun you used tonight?"

"Yes sir," Mr. Tindal said. "It's reloaded. Habit."

"Right," the officer said.

Mr. Tindal waited in silence, as the officer disarmed him, and looked at the gun.

Reed faced the wall and waited for the officer to follow procedure. Now that the police were here, he could stand down. He waited as the officer disarmed him and thoughts of Christie ran through his head.

As Reed had watched Christie appraisingly, he'd reassessed his first impression of her.

It was always a make-or-break moment, especially for civilians who'd never seen this kind of thing before. Most people were much more capable than they thought, and it always cheered him to see them realize it.

This petite, throwback blonde had done better than many soldiers he'd seen reacting to carnage their first time. She listened well, didn't question what had to be done, and did it to the best of her ability.

Maybe she isn't as much of a "take care of me" type female as she appears to be. She hadn't fallen apart. She'd followed directions without getting emotional. Though not the "Step up, I'll take care of things myself" type of female, perhaps there's more to her than just her looks and femininity. She's willing and capable of taking care of others.

Now she intrigued him. He wanted to get to know her better, find out more about her. However, this wasn't the time.

He waited for the officer to finish.

His Sig Sauer P229 had been properly de-cocked, and the hammer was down. The officer had only to unload it.

"I've also got a knife on my ankle," he said, knowing a pat down was the procedure, and it was best to tell where any weapons were, so he could be disarmed.

"Thank you," the officer said, after patting him down and removing the knife. "You can turn around now."

"Thanks," Reed said. He'd expected all this and wasn't concerned by it. Now they'd have to wait for detectives and crime scene investigators to arrive, and then he'd have to answer a lot of questions.

He didn't look forward to that part, and what would turn into a long night.

Reed glanced over to where Christie was, to see how she was doing.

She was sitting quietly, while a female officer spoke to her. The bottom of her dress, and her hose where her knees had met the bloody seat cushion, were stained with blood.

Too bad her dress had been ruined. She looked hot in that dress.

The EMP's were here now, bringing in stretchers for the wounded men.

Everyone made way for them. There wasn't much room in a theater for two stretchers, and the wounded men were in theater seats, but they made it work, and soon the two men were out of the theater and on their way to the emergency room.

Now the detectives would really get to work, and the questioning would begin.

Christie didn't remember much more than a blur of color and sound after it was all over.

There were uniformed police, white-shirted EMT's and paramedics, and detectives in business casual suits—all of them asking questions.

Are you all right? Where were you sitting? What happened next? What did you hear? Did he say anything? How many shots...

She mumbled out what she could remember.

There was a big gap where she'd been too petrified with fear to move, or to think.

Then after, she remembered Mr. Tindal asking for her help, handing her his phone, and the tourniquets. Following what he told her and copying what he was doing to save a life.

She'd done that. She too had saved a life.

It all seemed surreal now. Hard to believe it had happened, though it had.

When there was nothing left to tell, and she'd been wrung completely dry, a detective finally gave her a business card and said, "Go home and get some rest. We'll be in touch."

Christie numbly took the card, said, "Yes, sir," and turned to leave.

Someone holding the basket with all the patrons remaining cell phones held the basket out to her and invited her to find her phone.

It was the only phone still in the basket with a pink cover.

She picked the phone up. "That's mine," she said before dropping the phone in her purse, without looking at it. She moved toward the door as if through a foggy night.

As she passed Mr. Tindal, who was still being questioned, she heard the detective thank him for helping.

"It could a been a lot worse. You saved a lot of people here tonight," he said.

"Just doing my job." Mr. Tindal shrugged, as if this was the kind of thing he did every day.

But then, for a Navy SEAL, maybe it was.

~

Christie got behind the wheel of her car and sat still for several minutes before moving.

Inside the pale blue Chevy, it was quiet. No one was talking; no one was moving about. There were no people who'd been shot and needed tourniquets. There were no women screaming, and no gunshots being fired. There were no more men shot, and nearly dying. There was no bad guy on the floor who might get up again to hurt more people.

The quiet in the car calmed everything, in a way the quiet in the theater never had, but she only briefly registered what it was doing.

She simply sat, while the police lights flashed silently.

And then, after a while, she started the car, without really thinking, and began the drive toward home.

The red light on her dash, which reminded her to get gas, was still on.

Gas. That's right. I need gas. Now. Won't make it home.

She drove until she saw the first gas station on her route, one she'd never been to before, and pulled in.

Pulling up to the pump, she parked and turned off her car. Her purse had fallen off the seat onto the floor, and she unbuckled her seatbelt, and leaned down to get it. Taking her purse, she reached in for her wallet, found her credit card and then got out of the car.

She moved to the back of the car and opened the fuel door, then unscrewed the fuel cap, and let it hang by its cord. She turned toward the pump and stopped in front of it to insert her credit card, but with her hand shaking, she missed, and dropped the card on the ground.

As Reed drove down the street, he saw Christie's red and white dress, as she stood on those high red heels at the gas pump, getting ready to put gas into her car. A pale blue Chevy.

She bent down to pick up something on the ground.

What is she thinking? This is a bad area of town for a woman alone to pump gas, especially wearing an outfit like that. Every man in the gas station parking lot is watching her bend over in that dress. Damn. Didn't she see the graffiti on the fence, beside the gas station? This is the wrong station for her to be stopping at to get gas at any time of day, but especially at this time of night.

He pulled into the gas station behind her and turned off his car to get out.

She'd attracted the attention of a group of men, who hovered at the edge of the building, near a parked black mustang with dark windows, and a beat-up old white van.

One man with tattoos on his neck and face gave a whistle as she bent down.

Another, a tall, thin, bald man with tattoos on his neck, who wore a tattered jean jacket, moved toward her.

She seemed focused on the credit card, trying to insert it into the machine and failing. She didn't seem to notice the men watching her, while nudging each other, laughing as their man moved toward her.

3

———

Reed got out and closed his door. He stepped purposefully toward her.

"Hey, Christie," he said, as he moved closer. "Let me give you a hand with that."

He noted the bald man stopped, realizing Reed was with her, and then turned to walk back to his group.

Christie stood, looking way too fragile and feminine, as her hand holding the card shook.

Her wide green eyes looked up at him in surprise when he called out to her, but she seemed not to recognize him at first. Then her eyes widened. "Oh. Yes. Hello, Mr. Tindal"

"Reed," he said. "Reed Tindal." His hand closed over hers, and he held it for a moment, to still the shaking. He noted that her hand was cold inside his, and he gave her a warm smile. Then glancing at the card, he said, "It's backward."

"Oh. Yes, it is. Thank you," she said.

"You're welcome," he said.

She pulled her hand away, turned the card around, and tried to insert it again, but her hand still had the shakes.

"Let me do that," he said.

She handed him the card.

He put it into the machine, and then it asked for her code. "Your turn," he said.

She paused, as if thinking, as a frown came over her face. Maybe she didn't trust him.

He turned his head toward the men, giving her a chance to put the code in privately, without him seeing the numbers. Lowering his voice, he asked, "Did those guys scare you?"

"Guys? What guys?"

He turned back to look more closely at her.

Christie is in bad shape if she hasn't noticed the guys clearly watching her every move. Had she even heard that whistle? Seen the man approaching her less than ten feet away?

As Reed watched her, he noted she had no awareness of her surroundings; her only focus was on getting gas.

He had to remind himself she was a civilian with likely no understanding of situational awareness.

And the men were still watching her, and now, him.

"No problem," he said. "Why don't you go on and get in your car while I finish this."

"Okay," she said.

The men's interest in her hadn't waned, though they were quietly watching, and talking among themselves, and hadn't made another step near her.

He doubted they would, now.

Reed had found that after SEAL training, few men messed with him. Only the rare asshole, looking for a fight, would pursue one.

Usually, Reed could de-escalate things with his calm response. He didn't want to fight unless he had to, but when he did fight, he fought to end things fast. His goal was to put the other man down fast, so peace could resume.

The calm confidence he always displayed could easily be read by any man with street smarts.

You never took your eyes off the calm man in the back, because that calm man was likely the one who would take you down fast and hard.

The group of men, though they watched, made no other move toward her or him. Likely, they'd also noted the stickers on his car, one which let him drive his car on base, and the other a SEAL bone frog sticker.

Reed watched her get into her car.

She was safe once again.

He put the nozzle into the gas tank and started filling it.

Christie rolled down her window.

He wondered why her hand had been shaking if she wasn't afraid of the men.

Is she still shaken up after the shooting? She shouldn't be out here alone like this, on any night, let alone this one.

Now that her window was down, they could talk again.

"So, how are you doing?" He watched her, looking for signs of shock.

The EMTs had been busy tonight, with a theater full of people to check out, and maybe they'd missed seeing her.

He'd been busy and hadn't paid attention to what was going on with Christie.

She hadn't been shot and had seemed fine. She'd been right there by his side, helping him with triage, intently listening, and following his orders, so he'd assumed she was fine. And maybe she had been then, but she clearly wasn't now.

"I-I'm okay. Just...cold." She shrugged and rubbed her hands up and down her arms.

The thing was, it wasn't that cold out tonight.

Humidity made his leather jacket too warm, and there wasn't even a breeze.

He would've frowned, but held that back, and kept a casual, pleasant expression on his face. "You were headed home?"

He hoped that was the case.

"Yes. I-I was running late to the premiere and had meant to stop for gas on the way," Christie said. "But I was going to be too late, if I got gas then, so I didn't stop. I didn't have enough to get home without stopping."

"If you'd said something, I'd have followed you, to make sure you were safe," he said. "I'll finish here, and then follow you home. Make sure you get inside safe."

"Oh, thank you. That's nice of you." She placed her hand on his arm and turned her green eyes up to him. "Thank you again for saving my life."

Her slim delicate fingers were cool upon his arm.

Shock was his assessment.

"Any time," he said, and then, redirecting her, added, "You okay to drive home? You still look a little shaken up."

"I'm okay now," she said. "I can drive."

He wasn't so sure. "How far is it?"

"About twenty minutes."

He'd have preferred knowing miles, as that's what he'd asked her, but wasn't going to press her on it.

If she were like his cousin, Katelyn, she wouldn't have any idea how many miles.

Christie didn't seem like a practical sort of woman. Girly from head to toe, she was the kind who needed looking after. An innocent. The kind bad men would pounce on if someone weren't protecting her.

The someone tonight being him, which he didn't mind in the least. It was in his nature to protect.

Though she wasn't the sort he usually went out with, and this wasn't a date now, he felt a strong need to protect her, as if she were his, under his protection. It seemed she brought that out in him.

Perhaps the live shooting event they'd been through together had created a bond, as intense situations tended to do; a friendship, if nothing more, though he liked her.

He liked her enough to want to ask her out and get to know her better.

She was rubbing her arms, and the movement moved the low-cut neckline of her dress.

He admired the view, but he wasn't the only one in this parking lot watching her, and he wanted her out of here and home safe again.

She smiled at him. "This is nice of you. To stop and help me get gas, and to follow me home."

Finishing, he closed and twisted the lid on the gas tank, pushed the cover over top of it, and then walked back around to her open window.

She sat inside, her hands resting on the bottom of the steering wheel.

From his vantage point, he could see down into her cleavage. His gaze went there, though he hadn't intended it to.

Her soft curves looked touchable and enticing. The view teased.

He'd have loved to see more of her breasts. Just as any other red-blooded male would have.

Looking up at him with those green eyes, she said, "Thank you. I appreciate you helping me with the gas."

"You're welcome," he said. "You ready to drive?"

"Yes," she nodded. "I'm ready."

"Then start her up. I'm right behind you."

"Okay," she said.

He walked back to his car, and she started hers.

Soon, they were driving the roads which led to her house.

She drove slowly, five miles under the speed limit, like someone who hadn't had enough sleep, or was driving home from a party after a few too many.

His concern for her made his brow furrow, as he wondered at her state of mind.

It was a good thing he'd seen her on his way home and had stopped.

Her house was on a street where older cottage-style houses lined both sides, and well-groomed trees stood in the grassy areas of the median.

She drove into her driveway and parked.

Her house was painted white, had soft blue shutters, and a black roof. Blue and purple flowers out front had taken over.

He pulled in behind her, as she opened her car door. He got out of his car and walked up beside her. "Nice house," he said.

"I've lived here for three years," she said. "I love it."

"I can tell," he said and smiled. "I take it you enjoy gardening, and flowers."

"Flowers? Oh, I'm all about flowers." She giggled.

Is she nervous, or is there something funny I missed?

"Oh, I didn't tell you." She stopped, putting her hand to her mouth. "I'm a florist. Flowers surround me all day. At work, here at home . . ."

He laughed. "So, you do enjoy flowers."

"That's a big understatement." She laughed. "I love flowers. And I love arranging them."

"That's great." He grinned.

Her excitement was good to see, and her happiness contagious. He'd also managed to take her mind off tonight's live shooting event, and onto a happier topic. "I'll have to stop into your shop some time."

"Oh yes, you should." She nodded. "I work at Floral Blessings, the new shop by the library. I used to work for a wedding planner, doing the big jobs, but now I'm in with Mrs. Brown, who really ought to be named Mrs. White, because she's so pale. She's a short, white haired, sixty-eight-year-old widow. After her husband died, she decided to start a new career selling flowers. She smiles all the time. You'd never know she was widowed less than two years ago."

They'd reached Christie's front door, as they walked and talked, and she automatically reached into her purse for her keys.

After about a minute of rifling through her purse, she pulled them out. The keys hung from a red and white polka dotted key chain.

He held the screen door for her, while she fumbled with the key in the lock. All the while he watched her, he noted she showed symptoms of shock.

"Come in for coffee?" she asked. "It's the least I can do, after all you've done for me."

It was late and they both needed sleep, not coffee, but he suspected she wasn't ready to be alone, or ready to go to sleep.

He certainly wasn't.

Maybe she'd quit thanking him if he allowed her to thank him with coffee. It would also give them a chance to get to know each other better. "Sounds good," he said.

"I have some Jamaican blue," she said. "Got it on a cruise, and I save it for special occasions."

"Sounds wonderful," he said. "Where did you cruise to?"

"Jamaica, of course," she said. "Grand Cayman, and Saint Thomas. Have you ever been?"

"Nope." He shook his head. "Been lots of places around

the world, but nothing in the Caribbean yet. No pleasure cruising."

"The islands are wonderful," she said. "Very relaxing."

"That sounds good, right about now," he said.

"I agree." She smiled and nodded.

As she busied herself making coffee, he took in the room.

White lace curtains hung above the window over the sink, and the window in the back door, a white lace table-cloth covered a small round table, and padded cushions with a pale pink and white polka dotted print sat atop the two chairs.

The pale pink was picked up in accessories throughout the kitchen; accessories that could've stepped out of an old movie, where the woman of the house wore an apron and a dress.

She noticed him looking and said, "I love anything retro, from the forties and fifties."

Ah. So that's why she's dressed like that, and why her house is decorated this way.

"It suits you," he said.

Those boys overseas would've had many a good dream about her, if a poster of her were pinned in their locker.

"Thank you." She rubbed her hands down her hips, in a self-conscious gesture; unaware she outlined her hips, drawing his gaze to those curves.

"I, well, this is why I'm dressed like this," she said. "Tanya and I were having a girl's night out, retro style. I'd step back in time if I could and visit those days."

"You look great."

"Thank you." Pink flooded her cheeks.

Is she embarrassed? Not used to compliments.

"Who is Tanya?" he asked.

"She's my best friend," Christie said.

He frowned. "You were alone tonight. What happened to Tanya?"

"She had an emergency with her animals. Had to take them to the vet. I think her neighbor poisoned them." She gasped. "Oh, no. I was supposed to call her after the show. I didn't think to check my phone. Oh, I hope they're all right."

She hurried to her purse, and pulled her phone out, turning it back on, and watching for it to turn on again.

Ding. Ding. Ding.

Her phone was blowing up with missed calls or texts, likely from people who cared about her and had heard about the shooting at the theater.

Christie sat on a kitchen chair, her shoulders dropping. She read through text after text.

Reed tried not to appear nosy or to look, but it was clear she was upset again. "Lots of messages. Everything okay?"

"Miss Priss and Brutus are going to be okay. They both ate something bad that I've never heard of. I hope it's not a poison. And Tanya is worried about me. She heard on the news about the shooting."

"Maybe you should call her," he said.

"After coffee. I promised you coffee. And she's probably asleep now." Christie put her phone down and got back up to get two coffee mugs out. She glanced back over her shoulder. "Sugar? Cream?"

"Black."

"Okay." She placed the coffee mugs on the table, and then got dream and sugar out for herself. "It's almost ready."

Pouring the coffee, her hands trembled again, making the coffee slosh over the side of the cup.

"Hey," he closed his hand over hers "You're still shaking. Let me."

4

―――――

Christie nodded as the warmth of Reed's hand grounded her and eased the shaking in her hand.

His warm hazel gaze met hers.

Letting him take the coffee pot from her to pour, she then sat, some of the stress easing.

"That shooting shook me too," he said as he poured the coffee into the other cup.

"I never would've guessed," she said. "You seemed so calm and knew just what to do."

"I wasn't expecting it," he said, "But I've been trained in how to react."

"You knew what to do," she said. "I'm so glad you did."

"Me too," he said, giving her a smile, his warm gaze making her feel safe and secure.

Everything about him seemed warm, safe, caring. She needed that warmth.

She stirred the sugar and cream into her coffee, and then sat for a while taking in his warmth without speaking, as they each sipped from their coffee cups.

His silent companionship was nice.

She really did not want to be alone right now.

Just sitting near him reassured her.

Finally, he spoke. "Want to talk about it?"

She nodded, and then tried to find the words. "It was…" she paused, unable to articulate what she wanted to say. "I don't have the word for it."

"You're not used to gunfire," he said. "I am. Very used to it. But it shook me, too."

She shook her head. "You didn't seem shaken. You took charge. Your military training. You took care of everyone."

"Yes. With your help." He spoke quiet, watching her. "My training has given me a faster reaction time. But it still takes time for the brain to process what is happening, and to act, even for a trained soldier."

"You seemed pretty fast to me," she said. "You saved my life, pushed me down, before you even started shooting. I owe you my life."

"No." He shook his head. "You owe me nothing. There's no debt owed."

"Then you have my undying gratitude, and thanks," she said.

"Christie, this is what I do," he said. "What I'm trained to do. For a Navy SEAL, taking bad guys out is just part of the job."

"You're a Navy SEAL?" Her jaw dropped as her estimation of him rose way, way, up, beyond where it was already.

He was like a hero stepped out of a movie screen, a real movie hero, not an actor, and this did more than confirm it. It set this fact in concrete.

He was a true hero, trained to be one of those guys who the military sent in to handle the toughest, most dangerous jobs.

"Yes," he said.

"Wow. I'm impressed," she said, her eyes wide. "I'm so glad you were there. I'm glad you're trained to do what you do and that you do it so well. And I'm just happy to be alive."

"Hey, I'm with you on that one," he said. "Happy to be alive." He winked at her. "Now, how about we enjoy our coffee and get to know each other a little better."

"Okay," she smiled. "That sounds good."

"Where are you from?" he asked.

"I'm from a little town in Pennsylvania that no one has ever heard of," she said.

"Try me."

"Gouldsboro, PA. In the Pocono Mountains. There's not even a flashing red light, and it's thirty minutes to the nearest grocery store."

He laughed. "No wonder no one's heard about it. How did you end up here?"

"I couldn't wait to get off that mountain, and wanted to see more of the world, so I picked a college farther away, and moved. I made it through three years, before I ran out of money, and started working for a wedding planner. Found out I loved working with flowers more than going to classes for a degree, so I finished the semester, and then never went back."

Wow, I'm just rambling, giving him way more information than he asked for. He's so easy to talk to, and I'm nervous and talking too much.

I need to ask him things, and not just talk about myself. "What about you? Where are you from?"

"Texas, my first nine years," he said. "And then Florida until my senior year of high school. I joined the U.S. Navy after graduation with the goal of becoming a SEAL."

"Why are you here now and not off on a mission?"

"I'm stateside," he said. "Because my grandfather passed. I had leave built up, so I'm here for a while to help my mom out."

"I'm so glad you were here tonight."

"I'm glad too," he said.

Their gazes met, searching and connecting, as the chemistry between them sizzled again, his male strength, and her inviting softness.

"I'm glad you're here with me now. You make me feel safe." Her voice came out soft, and she blushed.

His voice did things to her. And she was glad he was here. She wished he would stay. Wished he didn't have to go. But she would never ask him to stay. She'd just met him.

They finished their coffee, and when he stood, she followed, looking up at him.

"I'd better tell you good night," he said. "It's been nice getting to know you, Christie. Thanks for the coffee."

"It was the least I could do when you—"

He placed a finger on her lips, to silence her from thanking him again, as she was going to do.

She smiled beneath it.

His finger, warm and gentle on her lips, made her mind move from what she was about to say, to the new sensations he was creating.

He let his finger drop. "I'm glad we met, and I'm glad you're safe at home. You get some rest and be sure to lock the door behind me."

"Yes," she said.

She was tempted to say, "Yes, sir," as his last words had a ring of command to them, in a concerned, "I'm just looking out for you" kind of way. Like her grandfather used to do. Maybe it was because both men had served in the military and had learned the art of command.

Whatever it was, it made her feel very cared for. She didn't mind complying with that kind of command.

Reed walked with her to the door, noting the way she

moved. When he reached it, he said, "When do you have to go back to work?"

"Monday," she said.

"You don't have to go anywhere today?" This being Sunday, he hoped that was the case.

She shook her head, "No."

"Good," he said. "Get some rest now."

"I will. Good night. Or good morning," she said.

She looked confused. The sun was up, and it was morning.

"Or good day," she said.

"Good everything," he said with a grin. "See you later, Christie Anderson."

She grinned back. "See you later, Reed Tindal."

Reed turned and started for his car, but his ears were still tuned in, listening for her to close the door, and lock it. Satisfied, once he heard the sounds he was waiting for, he hurried on to his car.

He needed a shower, a shave, and a nap. She wasn't the only one who needed rest.

After she closed the door, she watched through her front window as he drove away. She wished he could've stayed. But she didn't know him well enough to ask, and she shouldn't be thinking of having his strong arms wrapped around her. Though sleeping with him holding her sounded nice, it wasn't his job to hold her, or to take care of her.

That didn't stop her from longing to be in his arms.

She glanced at the front door. She did feel better with it locked. Deciding to check the back door locks, she headed into the kitchen, and then moved throughout the house, checking all the window locks.

Now that she'd reassured herself she was thoroughly locked in, maybe she'd start to relax.

A hot shower, followed by sweatpants and a sweatshirt sounded good.

After that, she really did need to call Tanya. By then, it would be late enough on a Sunday that Tanya would be up.

Showered and dressed, Christie poured the last bowl of cereal in the house, and the last of the milk, then sat on the couch, and looked at the dark screen of the TV. Contemplating turning it on, she decided against it.

Every local channel would be talking about the shooting, and she'd been there, lived through it, and didn't need to listen to the newscasters talking about it repeatedly.

The police had kept the reporters and their cameras far from the theater and parking lot, but she'd seen the news vans, camera lights, and reporters hovering as they waited to pounce.

She needed her life to get back to normal, and to think of things other than the shooter.

Taking a bite of raisin crunch cereal, a remnant of her childhood, she closed her eyes, and forced her thoughts away from the theater, back to when she was ten, and she and Tanya were having a sleepover.

Good memories got her through the cereal, and then she picked up her phone to call her best friend.

She'd have to tell the story again, but she was ready now.

Tanya had always been there for her, and she would be there for her again.

Dialing, she waited for Tanya to answer.

"Christie! Tanya answered the phone right away, as if she'd been waiting for it to ring. "Are you all right?"

Tanya's stress could be felt through the phone line, and heard in her voice.

"I'm okay," Christie said. "It just scared me really bad."

"I bet," Tanya said. "What happened? Where are you now?"

"I'm back home," Christie said.

"Do you want me to come over? I can leave now," Tanya said.

"No, I'm going to try to sleep, after I get off the phone, but thank you," Christie said.

"Okay, if I'm not coming over, I want you to tell me what happened," Tanya said. "tell me everything. My God, I was so worried. I saw it on the news, and they said there'd been a live shooter and two people were at the hospital, but I called the hospital, and no one would give me any information on them. Then I drove over to the theater, but the police wouldn't let anyone near it."

"I'm so sorry you went through all that stress and worry," Christie said. "They took our cellphones when we went into the theater and didn't give them back 'til the police let us go. Then I had to get gas on the way home, and it was late, and I was not in a good area."

"The whole night sounds horrible," Tanya said. "I know you're glad to be home. What about the live shooter? Tell me what happened."

Christie knew she'd been dancing around it, talking about everything but that. "We were all watching the movie, everything was normal, except for the cellphone thing, and then this man stood up and just started shooting."

"Oh my God," Tanya said. "What did you do?"

"Well, I was already on the ground, crouching behind my seat, because I'd sat next to a Navy SEAL."

"You what? Sat next to a SEAL? Holy cow," Tanya said. "You got lucky, girl. He was the military guy who stopped the shooter, right?"

"Yes. He saved everyone," Christie said. "He pushed me down to the ground, before the first shots were fired, and told me to stay down. So, I did what he told me to do."

"Wow. That's incredible! He saved your life."

"Yes, and the lives of everyone in that theater."

"He sounds amazing," Tanya said.

"Oh, he is." Christie curled up on the couch with a throw pillow, and hugged it to herself, thinking how brave he'd been.

Even more of a real movie hero than Cole Kennick.

"He called the police, and then he gave his phone to me, and had me talk to them while he checked on the wounded."

"Wait," Tanya said. "You said they took all your phones."

"Well, he must've not told them he had one, because he had it on him," Christie said.

"And he had a gun! You're not supposed to have guns in theaters either," Tanya said. "There are signs up."

"I know. He had both," Christie said.

"Oh, he's a rule breaker then. A bad boy," Tanya said.

"I don't know about that," Christie said. "He got along with the police. They didn't even arrest him for having a gun."

"Huh."

"And when he put a tourniquet on the one man, I watched him and listened, and I put one on the other man."

"Wow, really? That means you're a hero, too," Tanya said.

"Oh," Christie felt her cheeks heat at her friend's words.

She hadn't felt particularly heroic.

"I don't know about that. I was just doing what he told me to do. Doing what needed to be done."

"Yeah, I'll bet that's the kind of thing he says too," Tanya said. "Heroes always say that. Unless they have big egos."

Oh. Tanya is right.

"Well, yeah. It is," Christie agreed.

"See?"

But that didn't make her a hero. She wouldn't have even known what to do, if Reed hadn't told her.

Maybe that needed to change.

A man could have bled out right next to her, if Reed hadn't been there with the right tools and the right instruction.

Do they have classes for that, like they do for CPR?

Another class I really ought to take.

She didn't want to be in a position of standing by helplessly when there was something she could do to save a life.

5

After she ended the call with Tanya, Christie wandered into the kitchen and opened cabinet doors to find something to eat.

She'd planned to stay in, but she really did need to run to the grocery store. That had been on her original "To Do" list for today.

Her stomach growled as she stared at the limited contents of her cabinets.

For the past few weeks, she'd paid for the new dress, the new shoes, and the new purse—basically an entirely new outfit from head to toe. So, she hadn't exactly been buying extras to stock her kitchen. In fact, she'd been eating what she'd already had stored.

Her cabinets held a variety of spices and sauces, pasta with no sauce to put on it, brown rice, pancake syrup, peanut butter, but no bread or crackers, and a yellow cake mix.

She'd had nothing to offer Reed the other night, when he'd escorted her home, except coffee. And it appeared she had little for lunch, or for dinner for herself today.

Last night she hadn't been hungry, but she was paying for that now, because the small bowl of cereal she'd just eaten for breakfast wasn't enough.

Despite what she'd told Reed about staying in today, she had to go out to buy food.

Taking a small notepad, she started jotting down a quick grocery list, thinking of foods her ex-boyfriend used to like. Salsa and chips, frozen pizza, and mixed nuts. All were good to have on hand to offer a hungry man. The next time a man came by to visit, she needed to have something on hand to offer him besides coffee.

It had been a year since she'd broken up with Mitch, the last man to sit at her kitchen table until Reed.

She paused, wondering if she was ready to start dating again. The answer to that question didn't really take much thought. If he was as nice as Reed, she most certainly was.

She wondered if Reed drank alcohol, and if so, what he drank. Her ex drank every night, and many nights he drank a lot. That was one major reason Mitch was an ex. Though he'd been gone a year, she still didn't stock alcohol. It hadn't been possible to keep drinks in the house when she was with Mitch. He'd finish off anything she brought home.

Over the last few months, she'd bring a bottle of wine home to enjoy, but that was it. Mitch had changed her. Made her wary of enabling someone prone to addictive behaviors.

Now Mitch was gone. It was time to let go of her fear. She wanted to be prepared the next time she had male company. It wouldn't hurt to have a bottle of wine if the occasion arose.

Finishing her list, she changed into jeans and a T-shirt, slipped her feet into her most comfy tennis shoes, and ran a brush through her hair. Glancing in the mirror, she tried to ignore the dark circles. She needed sleep, but she also needed food, and choosing one meant forgoing the other.

Not until she was behind the wheel of her car, easing into the parking space at the grocery store, did she realize how nervous she was to go out in public again. The live shooter had changed her view of the world.

She sat in the car, watching people come and go, trying to get her nerve up to get out of the car and go grocery shopping.

Everything looked calm. Seemed to be staying calm.

Finally, she opened her door, and then got out. After scanning the parking lot again, she headed toward the front† doors. She found herself glancing at faces, trying to read expressions and intent. She'd never been so aware of her surroundings in her life. In fact, she was hyperaware.

Inside the store, she gathered the things she needed, then hurried to check out.

By the time she got home with her purchases, and carried them into her house, she was exhausted.

Lunch was egg salad on a croissant that she'd picked up at the grocery deli. She opened the plastic box, and ate it without tasting it, while at the same time, putting everything away.

Afterword, she curled up on the couch, beneath the Afghan Tanya had made for her. Exhaustion took over, and she fell asleep.

Her cellphone rang, waking her.

She reached for it and squinted to read it.

The house was pitch dark, so it was obviously nighttime, and the only light came from her phone.

Tanya's name appeared on the screen.

Christie answered. "Hello?"

"How are you doing?" Tanya asked.

"Okay, I guess," Christie said. "I went to get groceries, ate lunch, and then fell asleep on the couch."

"Oh, did I wake you?" Tanya said, her tone full of regret.

Christie ran a hand over her face and sat up. "Yes," she said, and then cringed because she'd sounded a little sharp.

"It's eight o'clock. I wanted to call before you went to sleep, and make sure you're doing okay. Sorry about waking you."

"It's all right, Tanya, really. I need to get up and put my pajamas on and go sleep in my bed, not this old couch." Christie rolled her neck and stretched. "Thanks for checking on me."

"You're welcome. Is there anything you need?"

"No. I'm all set. I've got to get caught up on sleep before I go to work tomorrow morning."

"Have you talked to Mrs. Brown? I think you ought to take tomorrow off. You've been through something traumatic. I know she'd understand."

"No, I haven't talked to her. I don't want to take tomorrow off. There's no reason to. I'm fine."

"Okay," Tanya said, sounding doubtful. "Well, call me if you need anything or want to talk."

"I'm fine Tanya. Quit fussing." Eager to change the subject, Christie asked. "How are your fur babies?"

"Well, like I texted you, the vet says they ate begonia plants," Tonya said. "It was in the stuff they yakked up."

"I bet your neighbor's somehow responsible. She planted begonias last month, didn't she?"

"Yeah, but her plants always look great," Tanya said. "She wouldn't allow Miss Priss or Brutus in her yard long enough for them to eat them on their own. She hates both of my fur babies. Yells at them to get off her lawn before one paw even touches her precious grass."

"You need a fence," Christie said.

"Yes, I do." Tanya sighed. "I don't understand how they ended up eating the plants. They've never done anything like that before, and for both to suddenly start that behavior, it just seems odd."

"Maybe she poisoned them," Christie suggested. "Put it in their food."

"How would she do that? She's never been in my house, and she doesn't have a key."

"You think she doesn't. But what if she still has a key from before you bought the house? Maybe the previous owner gave her a key. If she had one, then she could sneak in while you were away."

Tanya gave a little chuckle. "I think your imagination is running away with you. You need to get more sleep."

"Yeah, I do need sleep. But still, think about it. She could so sneak in if she had a key from before. Did the vet say what begonias do to them? Is it lethal?"

"It makes them throw up and gives them diarrhea," Tanya said. "But it won't kill them; it just makes them very sick."

"I'm glad they'll be okay now. How are they doing tonight?"

"Fine, just clingy. I had to put Brutus in the other room, and he's in there, whining with his bunny rabbit."

"Poor baby," Christie said. "You know he must still feel bad if he's whiney and carrying Wabbit."

Brutus, Tanya's German Shepard never whined unless he was sick. Then the big strong guard dog was the biggest baby and wanted his Wabbit.

Christie loved to go visit and watch Brutus bark at the mailman, and then turn when the man was gone, and bring her his fluffy pink Wabbit to play with. He could turn off his fierce dog face quick, and then his tail wagged like a happy puppy.

"Maybe I need a dog," she murmured.

"What brought that on? I agree you should get a dog, and we've had that conversation before," Tanya said. "More times than I can count. Are you feeling lonely? Or scared?"

"No, not lonely," Christie said. "I just think having a good guard dog, like Brutus, would be nice."

"Well, you've got to train dogs," Tanya said. "Let them know you're the alpha. Are you ready to be the alpha?"

"I don't know."

It was an honest answer. Taking on an alpha role was not something Christie normally did. She didn't like overseeing people.

But, she realized, if you had a dog, you'd have to be in charge and be the alpha.

Brutus is a big dog. Could I handle a dog that size?

"I've pictured you more with a lap dog," Tanya said. "You get the cuddling, as well as the guarding then."

Christie chewed on her lower lip as she thought about that. "Yeah, but if there's a prowler, a German Shepard would be better protection."

"True. Look, if you're serious, I can take you to where I found Brutus," Tanya said. "You can talk to them about their next litter."

"Yeah, I might want to do that," Christie agreed.

"All right. You get some sleep, and we'll talk about it later this week. I'll call them to see about a visit."

"Okay. Thanks, Tanya."

"Night, girlfriend. I'm real glad you're still here to talk to. You'll always be my bestie. I love you."

Christie smiled. "Love you, too." Tanya was her oldest and best friend. It felt good to be loved and appreciated. She didn't know what she'd do without Tanya either. "I'm glad you called."

"Me, too."

"I'll call you after work tomorrow," Christie said.

"Sounds good," Tanya said.

"Good night," Christie said.

"Good night, bestie," Tanya said.

They both hung up, and Christie sat for a moment, smiling, and thinking how lucky she was to have Tanya in her life.

Christie had a job she loved, a home that was finally decorated just the way she'd always wanted, and a great best friend. Now, she just needed a dog companion, to cuddle with, and to scare away bad guys.

Life was good, and it was good to be alive. But it was awfully quiet here. Tanya was right. Sometimes, Christie did get lonely.

Maybe I'll look at dogs this week. Then I'll have companionship and be safer.

Monday morning came like every other Monday morning, yet not. This one came with the happy realization she'd be working with the flowers she loved so much a thought she had every workday morning. But this time she had a new thought added.

What if some crazy person comes into the florist shop, and starts waving a gun around, or worse, starts shooting?

This was something she'd never thought of before, and the realization that a live shooter could pop up anywhere shook her comfortable familiar world.

There was no going back.

No way to return to innocence, and the days of thinking everyone coming into the store was a nice man or woman. There were crazy bad people in the world, and they'd pop up when you least expected it. When you weren't ready. When you didn't know what to do.

If there was a fire, she knew what to do.

If someone tried to rob the store, she knew what to do. She'd hand over the money and hope that no one got hurt.

But a crazy person, someone who wants to kill people? Who wants to shoot them in cold blood? That she wasn't prepared for.

She felt different now. Changed.

Now, she expected violence. Knew it could happen. No longer did she live with a naïve mindset that believed nothing like that would ever happen to her, or to anyone she knew.

Because now, it had.

She didn't know what to do with all these new thoughts and feelings. The shooting had happened, and now she didn't know how to be.

Her life now fell into a split of what had happened before the live shooter, and what had happened after.

But the "after" part of her life story wasn't written yet, and she was standing on the page, not quite knowing what to do.

At least she'd slept last night, but her sleep had been restless. She knew she'd dreamed but couldn't remember what the dream was about.

Which was likely just as well. She had enough dealing with what was going through her head in her awake moments, without adding in the dreamtime thoughts, too.

Usually on her way to work, she'd turn on the radio and listen to music she liked, and sometimes she even sang along. But today, she didn't even turn the radio on.

No radio, like no TV, meant no news. It meant she wouldn't have to hear them talk about the shooting.

She drove in silence, until she pulled into her parking place behind the shop, and then sat in the car for a few minutes before turning it off.

Everything was quiet. In the car and outside of the car.

It was early. She usually came in an hour before they opened to the public to start working on the arrangements needed for the week's orders.

The silence in the car was a new thing, and a needed thing.

Then she opened the door, took her keys out of the car, and walked to the back door. Unlocking it, she cracked the door a bit, and peered inside before pushing it open all the way.

All was quiet. She was the only one here.

Good.

She pushed the door the rest of the way open and walked into the shop, quickly locking the door behind her.

No one can get in while both doors are locked.

For the first hour, the shop remained quiet as she worked on a silver arrangement with blue and purple flowers for the grand opening of a new hair salon. When that was done, she made three red rose arrangements for wedding anniversaries and one pink rosebud arrangement for a sweet sixteen birthday.

The hour went by fast, and she'd just finished the arrangements when Mrs. Brown opened the front door.

"Good morning," she breezed in past Christie and the beautiful arrangements standing on the long table. "Oh, these are lovely."

"Thank you," Christie quietly answered.

Mrs. Brown, always perceptive, slowed down to look at Christie more closely. "Something's happened."

"Yes," Christie replied.

Mrs. Brown's kind and concerned blue eyes watched her. Like a sweet, caring grandmother, she was easy to talk to.

Christie's hands dropped to her sides. "You probably

heard the news... That theater shooting. I was there. Inside, watching that movie."

"Oh, Christie, no!" Mrs. Brown gasped. "Oh, I'm so glad you're all right." She reached for Christie's arm. "Come over here and sit down." Taking her by the elbow, she moved Christie toward the small table and two chairs in the corner of the room where they took their breaks and meals.

Christie let herself be guided, and once they both sat, she said, "It was frightening."

"Why yes, my dear girl, that would have been," Mrs. Brown patted Christie's hand. "Terribly frightening. Now, tell me what happened."

Christie blew out a deep breath, before starting to share her story. "We were just sitting there, watching the movie, when this crazy man came in with a gun, and started shooting."

Mrs. Brown nodded. "I saw on the news it had happened, but they didn't name any of the theater patrons."

"No,' Christie shook her head. "I believe they'll keep our names private."

"That's good," Mrs. Brown said. "What happened with the Navy SEAL? I heard he saved everyone."

"He did," Christie nodded vigorously. "He stopped the shooter, shot him, and then he helped two wounded men who'd been shot. I helped him."

"You did?" Mrs. Brown's eyes widened with surprise.

"I did." Christie nodded. "Put a tourniquet on and everything."

Mrs. Brown gave her hand a squeeze. "Christie, I'm so proud of you. I didn't know you had any sort of medical training."

"I don't, but Reed talked me through it."

"Reed." Mrs. Brown smiled. "What a nice name. He sounds like quite the hero. Is he handsome?"

"Oh, very," Christie said, and felt a blush suffuse her cheeks.

"Built, too, I'll wager," Mrs. Brown said, arching one eyebrow.

"Oh yes. Very built." Christie nodded, remembering the way his muscles flexed when he moved. The power he held in his body.

"Handsome, built, and a hero. A Navy SEAL. Is he married?"

"No. I don't think so." Christie shook her head. "I didn't see a ring."

Ever the romantic. her employer held a hand to her heart. "I think this was meant to be. Not just chance that brought you two together."

Christie shrugged. "Maybe."

"It's time you started dating," the older woman nodded.

"Well, he hasn't asked me," Christie said. "And I may never see him again."

"I wouldn't be so sure. When it's fated, there is always a way." Mrs. Brown nodded.

Tuesday passed quietly, much like Monday, but on Wednesday, when the bell over the door of the shop jingled, and Christie looked up from watering the flowers, she saw Reed entering the florist shop.

"Hello," she said, her heart suddenly skittering faster.

"Hello, Christie," he said. "How are you doing?"

"I'm good. Been working with my flowers." She beamed at him. "I'm glad you found the shop. Are you here to place an order or pick up a bouquet? We have some lovely ones today."

"Actually..." He stepped closer, until he was standing

near enough to touch, his gaze never leaving hers. "I came in looking for you."

Christie blushed and dipped her head, feeling the heat rise in her neck and cheeks. "You did?"

"I did," he said. "I thought I'd invite you to the range for date night, if you're interested."

He'd come in looking for her, to ask her out.

She wanted to pinch herself.

Wait. Date night. Range?

She squeaked out the last word, before realizing she'd spoken out loud.

"Yes, the gun range," he said. "They have a couples' date night. We'd be able to shoot and have dinner there. Saturday night, if you'd like to go."

The concept was boggling her mind.

People do this. This is a date thing.

"This Saturday," he said. "If you're free."

Oh, he keeps talking because I haven't answered him.

He was waiting for an answer.

Her mind was in a spin. "I-I've never been to a gun range," she said. "I don't know anything about guns."

"That part's easy," he said, "I'll teach you."

"Teach me to shoot guns?" Her voice was doing that squeaking thing again.

Oh, why can't I answer him normally without sounding like a frightened little mouse?

His lips twitched. "Yes, teach you to shoot guns. You can learn to shoot handguns, or long guns, if you like rifles better. Anything you want to start with."

"Oh. Wow." Her eyes wide, she tried to wrap her head around the idea of this handsome Navy SEAL teaching her how to shoot guns. Images of old western movies where the hero taught the heroine how to shoot guns flooded into her head.

The hero would put his arms around the heroine, to show her how to shoot, and he'd be so close.

Reed would be so close.

Longing wrestled with fear, her long-standing fear of guns. She stood silent while they wrestled.

6

———————

Reed watched the range of emotions that slid across Christie's face like a continually changing kaleidoscope, a mesmerizing show that had begun the moment she'd noticed him walking through the door.

Quite simply, she fascinated him.

Clearly, she was entertaining many new thoughts.

He'd have to try harder to convince her. "The dinner special Saturday night is meatloaf, mashed potatoes, and green beans. It's country-style food there, and they usually have a few fresh pies to choose from for dessert. So, wear jeans, a comfortable shirt, closed-toe shoes, and bring your appetite." He gave her his warmest smile. "Sound like fun?"

She blinked. "Yes."

"Good. I can pick you up after work. You pick the time, and I'll make the arrangements," he said.

"Oh, okay, yes. Well," she said. "I usually get off work at five on Saturdays."

A short, white-haired lady, who must've been the Mrs. Brown Christie had spoken of, poked her head out of the back room. "You'll be off at four on Saturday, my dear. Plenty of time to go shooting."

Surprised, Christie swung her head to look at Mrs. Brown. "An hour early?"

"Don't think I haven't noticed more than a bit of overtime happening lately, my dear, which hasn't shown up on your time sheet," Mrs. Brown said. "And we don't have any big orders to work on until next week."

"Oh, all right then. Thank you, Mrs. Brown." Christie smiled at her.

"You're welcome, dear," Mrs. Brown said cheerily.

"Oh!" Christie turned back toward Reed. "I haven't introduced you. Reed Tindal this is Mrs. Brown. Mrs. Brown, this is Mr. Tindal."

"Nice to meet you," Mrs. Brown said.

"Pleased to meet you as well," Reed said.

"Well, since I'm off early," Christie said. "You can pick me up at five—if that's not too soon—or five thirty."

"Not too soon. That's perfect," he said.

He smiled his thanks at Mrs. Brown.

She winked at him and ducked away into the back room again.

"I'll pick you up at five," he said.

"I'm looking forward to it," Christie said.

Reed scanned the colorful flowers, wondering which she would like and said, "Which is your favorite? Roses?"

Every woman likes red roses.

"It's hard for me to choose," she replied. "There's a language of flowers, you know."

"There is? I didn't know that." He watched her, thinking, *she's full of surprises, and things to learn.*

"It can be complicated," she said. "But I could teach you."

He tilted his head. "Sounds fair. I'll teach you how to shoot, and you teach me the language of flowers."

"It's a deal," she said softly, blushing.

"But if you had to pick a favorite today?"

"Today, I would pick lilies," she pointed to a selection of lilies in various colors. "White lilies with some greenery and babies' breath."

He nodded. "Very pretty."

"I'm making an arrangement for a twenty-fifth wedding anniversary tomorrow," she said. "White lilies and baby's breath. They're having a dinner party and a pianist."

"Sounds elegant."

"Oh, yes," she smiled. "Very elegant. I'm looking forward to doing their arrangement."

"You love your job."

"Yes, I do." She nodded.

It's a nice change to meet a woman who loves her job. One who is happy with her life. A nice change of pace.

"I should let you get back to work," he said, surprised by how reluctant he felt leaving her. "I'll see you Saturday."

Her smile was wide and sweet. "Yes! See you Saturday."

He let himself out the door, the image of Christie surrounded by a profusion of colorful flowers staying with him.

~

Christie moved about her kitchen, watching the clock. Reed would arrive in twenty minutes, and then they were going shooting.

She still couldn't believe she was going to a gun range.

Reed was the only person who could have talked her into it. Though that's not how it had happened. She'd said yes so fast, she couldn't exactly remember how it had happened. Now, she was going to a gun range to learn how to shoot.

I wonder if he makes a habit of taking women on first dates to the gun range. It certainly is an unusual way to start a dating relationship.

She ran her hands down her best jeans and fussed with her new T-shirt.

Tuck the shirt in or wear it out?

Tucking it in showed off her figure. Wearing it out was more comfortable. She opted for out. The T-shirt was pale pink and decorated with embroidered purple violets with the saying, *Flowers are my superpower*, beneath them.

Absentmindedly, she checked her fridge and freezer again. This time, she had a frozen pizza, chips, popcorn, colas, and a bottle of red wine. Much more than coffee to offer him, if they ended up back at her house, hanging out. Though this date did include dinner, and they might not end up here afterward, or be hungry if they did.

At least she was now prepared for a man's visit and could offer him something besides coffee.

Reed rang the doorbell, and she hurried to the door.

She opened it to see his smiling face looking down on her.

He read her T-shirt. "Nice shirt. It suits you."

"Thank you," she said. She took him in from head to toe. His tanned face, dark hair along with a smile, which reached his eyes. Broad shoulders beneath a plain brown t-shirt, and his leather jacket and blue jeans showed his toned and muscular physique in a sexy yet understated way. "You look nice too."

"Are you ready?" he asked.

"As ready as I can be," she said. She grabbed her purse, then stepped outside her house, and locked the door.

"Nervous after the shooting?" he asked.

"Yes," she said. "Very nervous."

Placing his hand on the small of her back to guide her to his car, he said, "I'll have to see what I can do to ease your fears. Were you afraid of guns before the theater shooting?"

"Yes, I was," she nodded.

He opened the car door for her, and said, "Have you ever been around guns? Maybe growing up?"

"I'll tell you about it on the way," she said.

"Sounds good." He closed her door and went over to the driver's side, opened the door, and got in.

After starting the car, he turned the radio off, and turned his full attention to Christie.

She sighed, and then began to tell him. "My dad used to hunt," she said. "And he had guns. Shotguns and rifles. I can remember them being in a large wooden case with glass doors that mother and daddy kept locked. So, in a way, I was around guns. But I was always told not to touch them."

"And when you got older?"

"Daddy died in a car accident when I was ten. He was in his truck on the highway. A semi went out of control, and daddy didn't live long after he was hit."

"Sorry to hear that." Reed's face showed concern. "That had to be hard, losing a father so young."

"It was. Mother did something with his guns. I'm not sure what, but they went away, and I never saw them again. She remarried, but my stepdad didn't shoot or go hunting. He's a businessman, and he works and golfs."

"I see." Reed glanced at her, before looking back to the road.

He was a good driver and made her feel safe. But then his very presence did that.

"So, for you," he said, "Guns were big scary no-noes."

"Right."

"And you still see guns from a child's point of view."

She wrinkled her nose. "Probably."

"Did you ever see your dad handling the guns? Loading them or cleaning them?"

"Once, he had them on the kitchen table cleaning them. He'd started to show me what he was doing, but mother returned from buying groceries, freaked out, and told me I wasn't ever to touch them and to leave the room."

"So, you've picked up your mother's fear of guns," he said. "They wouldn't have hurt you, because he would have had to unload them to clean them."

She nodded. "Yes, he said they were unloaded. They argued about it, and I heard him tell her that."

"Okay. I'm going to start you off with learning the parts of a gun. I'll show you a shotgun, a rifle, and two handguns —a revolver and a nine-millimeter. I'll show you how the guns are put together and how they work. Somewhat like what your dad was trying to teach you before your mother walked in."

"That would be great. He did want me to learn about them." She smiled. "I think he'd approve of this part of our date."

He raised an eyebrow. "Good, but let's not get into the habit of bringing along what your daddy would approve of, on our dates. That could get uncomfortable."

She laughed. "Oh yeah, it could."

"I'd have had the father and teenage-boy talk, if I'd dated you in high school, I'll wager," he said.

"Oh yeah, you would've." She agreed. "Daddy was real protective. My stepdad? Not so much. With him, it's all about the money. How much a dress for the prom would cost. I always felt like he saw me as a burden. He didn't like paying for someone else's daughter."

"Are he and your mother still married?" he asked.

"Yeah. They still live in Pennsylvania, so I don't see them much. I stopped going to visit, after they never came here. I mean, the 'it's too expensive and too far' works both ways. But I still call mother, once a week. That's what works best, for everyone. He keeps her real busy."

"So, you get along, you just don't see each other."

"Something like that," she said. "I have real good memories of my dad and we were close. It wasn't like I needed a new dad. Sometimes, I miss him and start getting sad, but then I remember how he always hated to see me or mother sad, and he'd say something to cheer us up. So, I remember those things until I'm not so sad anymore. And it's gotten better with time."

"I hear you. Grief isn't an easy thing at any age. Sounds like you learned how to deal with it young."

"Yes" she said. "I did."

"I've lost family members, and I've lost men on my team who were like brothers. It's never easy, but we can't let it pull us down. We have to keep living. That's what they'd want us to do."

"Yes. We do," she agreed. "I'm glad we're going shooting today."

And she was. Somehow, he'd taken her fear, and by talking about it, had made it a faceable and beatable thing.

He's so easy to talk to.

That was rare and even rarer in someone she'd just met.

When they reached the shooting range, he parked the car and then got out to come around and open her door.

The range was a long, one-story building with a sign on the front, stating the name, with no other decoration. There was some greenery by the front door entrance, but that was it.

She'd never have guessed there was a restaurant inside.

He opened the door for her, and she got out. Then he went to the trunk and opened it.

Inside were two long gun cases, which he pulled out before closing the lid. "I brought a shot gun, a rifle, and two handguns. We'll have to let them check the guns, once we enter, and then I can show you how they work, before we go onto the range."

"Okay." She'd be doing far more than she'd thought she'd be doing when she agreed to this guns and dinner date. And she wasn't sure she'd remember everything after being introduced to so many kinds of guns, but so far, it sounded all right.

Reed was making it easy for her, and she was comfortable around him, if not the guns.

They walked inside and over to the counter.

The man working the counter asked for their IDs, and for them to sign a sheet. He had to put her into the computer, since she'd never been there, but Reed had been many times.

Once they'd registered, and Reed had paid for the dinner date, they headed toward a room in the back.

Inside the room were picnic-style tables, and the room looked onto the firing range, which they could see and hear through a glass window. It was loud, busy, and smelled funny.

In sensory overload, Christie's nerves were on high alert.

Bang.

Christie jumped.

Bang.

She jumped again. *Bang.*

With each bang, she jumped and now, she cringed and wanted to cover her head. She sank onto the picnic table seat to do just that, dropping the targets and the ammo onto the table.

Her hands went up over her ears. Her arms curving over herself protectively.

Bangs and pops kept coming, just like in the theater.

She huddled on the picnic table seat, like a frightened mouse. Not aware of anything else, but her fear, and the noises of the guns, her heart raced. Her thoughts raced.

Oh my God, oh my God, oh my God.

7

———

Shit. Reed's heart sank when he saw her reaction to the noise of the guns.

What the hell was I thinking? Bringing her here. I should've predicted this. Maybe this isn't the best idea. I thought she'd be okay.

He was on the other side of the table with the guns, but he quickly placed them on the table, and moved around to her side.

Sitting beside her, he put his arms around her and said, "Christie, hey, it's me, Reed. You're okay. We're just at the range. Nobody is going to hurt you. It's safe here. I got you."

He kept his voice calm, knowing he needed to help her realize where she was, and that she was safe, before this got any worse.

Then he heard her small whisper. "Reed?"

"Yes, sweetheart. I'm here. You're safe. We're sitting on the picnic table at the range."

"I know."

Good. She hasn't drifted. She knows where she is.

"You know you're safe, right? I wouldn't let anything happen to you."

She nodded.

Affirmative. Good.

"I was going to take these guns apart and show you how they work, remember?"

"Yes."

He waited to see what she'd do next. He stayed quiet, not asking her yet if she wanted to continue.

Finally, she raised her head, and he pulled back a little, still holding her in his arms.

She looked up at him and blinked twice.

He saw tears starting to form.

"I'm sorry I'm such a big baby," she said. "I'm ruining our date."

"Naw. You're not a baby," he said. "You're a woman. And you're not ruining anything."

She sat up a little taller and sniffled. "Okay, if you say so." She shrugged. "I'll watch, if you still want to show me."

"Of course, I do." His tone brushed it off in a 'don't be silly' kind of way, and he stood again to refocus her attention on his guns. "Okay, so we'll go over the rifle first, then the shotgun, and then the handguns. We'll start with the kinds of guns your daddy used."

She smiled at him, probably remembering her daddy. "Okay."

He showed her his guns, talked to her about them, and asked about her dads' guns, and about her dad, until she finally started to relax.

"Thank you," she said. "You brought memories back to me that I'd long forgotten, and I've learned a lot about guns today."

"You're welcome," he said. "Now, I'll let you shoot them. First, we'll start with the rifle. I'll have you try each gun, at least once, and then we'll figure out what you like to shoot."

"Okay," she agreed.

"When we go onto the range to shoot, we'll wear ear protection and eye protection," Reed said. "You can tell from here, how loud it gets in there."

"Oh, yes," she said. "It is loud, even through the glass, before we have to put on ear protection."

He unzipped one of the cases and took out a shotgun. "We'll start with this one. Have a seat."

She sat at the table and watched as he took the shotgun apart. Once apart, he put it back together, naming the parts and showing her how the gun worked.

He repeated this process with the rifle, the revolver, and the nine-millimeter. By the time he was done, she was no longer afraid of the guns like she had been before they started.

As she watched him pick the guns up to carry them into the range where they would shoot, thoughts ran through her head.

Guns are nothing without bullets. With them, they're lethal. Without, they're like a car without gas. Nice to look at, but useless without what it takes to make them go.

"Okay, you carry the targets and the ammo," he said. "I've got the rest."

She picked up the paper targets and boxes of ammo and followed him.

Before they entered the range, he made sure she donned eye and ear protection, and then motioned for her to follow him.

He spoke to the range master, and then headed toward number four lane, where he placed the handguns on a small table along with the long guns. He raised his voice, so she could hear and said, "Put the ammo here and hand me the targets."

She put the ammo down and handed over the targets.

He pushed a button, and a metal piece connected to a

track in the ceiling sped the metal piece toward them, until it stopped right in front of him. Then he attached the paper target with the picture of a man pointing a gun at them. Finally, he pushed the button again, and it sped back to twenty yards where he stopped it.

He showed her how to shoot the shotgun, and then it was her turn to shoot.

Placing it high against her right shoulder, she put her cheek next to the gun like he'd told her to, and then lined up the target and squeezed the trigger.

The gun pulled up as she shot, and her shot went wide up and to the right.

"I missed him," she said. "The gun jumped."

"You jumped," he said. "That's typical with new shooters. They jump. It's not the gun."

"I don't like this one," she said, rubbing her shoulder. "It's too much."

He eyed her small shoulders and nodded. "You don't have to shoot that one if you don't want to. Or you can finish out the bullets. Then we'll move on to the next one."

"I don't want to shoot that one anymore," she said. "It hurts me."

"Okay, I'll shoot." He reached for the shotgun, and she gladly gave it to him.

She watched as he fired off the rest of the shots, each one making a bull's-eye, all shots right through the hole the first shot had made.

"Wow," she said. "Do you ever miss?"

"Yeah," he said. "I'm not perfect. So, I do miss. But not with a shotgun, and not at twenty yards. If I miss, this close, someone might die."

She scrunched her nose. "This probably seems like nothing to you. Easy as child's play."

"It's not nothing," he said. "I enjoy shooting. And I'm enjoying teaching you. Next up, the rifle."

She eyed it. "Is that one going to hurt my shoulder too?"

"No," he shook his head. "This one doesn't have the recoil that shotguns have."

She tried it and found that she enjoyed shooting the rifle. It reminded her of her dad's rifle.

Her dad had gone shooting nearly every weekend. She wished she'd been allowed to go with him, even once.

"On to handguns," Reed said. "Which one do you want to shoot first?"

"The revolver," she said. "It looks like those guns in the wild west."

"It is," he said. "These are fun guns to shoot. First though, do you remember how to load it?"

"Yes," she nodded.

"Okay," he said. "Go ahead and load."

She loaded six shots into the revolver, and then looked at him expectantly.

"Now, go ahead and shoot," he said. "Just the way I showed you."

"Okay." She stepped up and aimed. Then she fired.

This time this gun only jumped a little.

She glanced over her shoulder at Reed.

"Hold on," he said.

She waited, while he corrected her position, moving her fingers.

"Try to relax. You've got a death grip going on. And remember to breathe. You're stressing too much."

"Yeah," she admitted. "A little."

She fired the gun again, and something hot flew up and landed on her head, making her jump. She laid the gun down on the table, and touched her head with her hand, feeling where the hot thing had landed on her. She looked at Reed.

"It's just a shell casing," he said. "Sometimes they do that."

She glanced down at the ground where shell casings lay.

"It was hot," she said.

"Yes," he said. "But it didn't hurt you."

She gave him a nod. It hadn't hurt her. Just startled her, scaring her enough to make her jump.

Reed pushed the button, and the metal thing holding the target came sliding back to him. He unclipped the paper, and then handed it to her, so she could see her shots close.

"Good job for your first-time shooting," Reed said, encouraging approval in his voice.

"I did okay?" She wasn't so sure.

Some shots had gone wide of the target, not even hitting it, while others had hit the target, but not in the center.

She was showing her insecurities, but she didn't care. She was just being herself, which was so easy with him.

"For your first time shooting a gun, you did," he said. "More than okay. Did you enjoy yourself?"

She thought for a minute, trying to decide if she'd enjoyed herself.

He'd made it easy for her. Being with him was easy.

"Yes," she said, surprised the answer was true.

"Good," he said. "I'm hungry. You ready to eat?"

"Yes." That, she had an answer for right away. She was hungrier than she'd thought she'd be.

"Okay," he said. "Let's go." He picked up the guns, and she held the targets, and picked up the remaining ammo.

Once outside the range, they removed their eye and ear protection, and then he put the guns in their cases.

"Okay, before we eat, you'll want to wash your hands." He glanced down hers. "Gunpowder."

"Oh! Right," she said. "Yes, I'd like to freshen up."

"We passed the restrooms on the way in. I'm going to put these back in the trunk, and then I'll meet you in the waiting area."

"Okay." The waiting area she'd seen had leather couches, and that must be where he meant. "I'll wait for you there."

She entered the ladies' room, washed her hands, then used the facilities, and washed her hands again.

She wasn't sure if she smelled like gunpowder, or if the scent was only in her nose, but the soap in the ladies' room had a nice scent, so that helped.

How does one remain pretty, and sweet-smelling, when on a date at the gun range? The soap, I guess. I like to smell good when I'm on dates. But maybe that isn't as important to men as I thought it was.

Christie thought about the primping she'd done after work to get ready for her informal jeans and T-shirt date and laughed to herself.

He probably didn't even notice. His mind is on the guns.

Coming out of the ladies' room, and around the corner to where the waiting area was, she saw Reed already standing and waiting for her.

Had she taken that long? Or was he just fast.

He gave her a wide smile, and then placing his hand at the small of her back, escorted her into the restaurant.

It was an informal, 'seat yourselves' restaurant, and it was getting busy.

He sat them at one of two tables left.

"Does the special sound good to you, or would you like to see the menu?" he asked, pointing at the blackboard.

"Oh, I'm fine with the special. I like good old-fashioned foods, like meatloaf and mashed potatoes."

"Great!" He signaled for the waitress, who came over with pen and pad.

"Ready to order?" she asked.

"Yes, ma'am. We'll both have the special," he said.

"And to drink?"

"What do you have?" Christie asked. Maybe she'd needed that menu after all.

The waitress rattled off a list of soft drinks, until she hit one that sounded good to Christie.

"Root beer," she said. "I haven't had that in a long time."

"Good choice. It's from a local bottling company," the waitress said. "Everyone likes it."

"I'll have tea, unsweetened, and bring sugar," Reed said.

"You're a sweet tea drinker," Christie said.

"Texas, born and raised. We drank it like water down there, with nearly every meal," he said.

"Oh, that makes sense," Christie said.

"So, Christie," he said, leaning back in his chair. "How did you like shooting those four guns for the first time?"

"I didn't like the shotgun," she shook her head hard, "because it hurt my shoulder, but I do like the twenty-two."

"Those are fun guns to shoot. Lots of kids start out shooting twenty-twos with their dads when they're young."

"So, it's more of a child's gun," she said. "Not really a useful gun?"

"No, it's just an easy gun to learn. And if you're good with it, you could shoot rabbits and other small game. So, it can be useful. For an intruder though, reach for a shotgun over a twenty-two. More stopping power."

"I don't think I want a shotgun," she said.

"For home protection, I'd suggest a handgun over a shotgun, for you. And you can carry a handgun, but you can't go walking down the street with a shotgun. A handgun is the first gun you should buy."

"I'm not ready to buy a gun," she said, shaking her head.

"Of course not. It's too soon," he said. "No one here is going to pressure you to buy a gun. But what did you think of the handguns? Do you have a preference?"

"I liked the revolver, at first," she said. "But I didn't like the hot bullet part landing on my head!"

"I can understand that" he said. "Bullet casings can be hot. That wasn't the good first experience I'd hoped for you."

"Do you have a lot of guns?" she asked.

"Heh." He grinned sheepishly. "To a civilian, the answer would be yes."

"And to your Navy SEAL buddies?"

"Not as many as some. More than others," he said. "Though I have a knife collection some of them drool over."

"Wow. So, you collect guns and knives."

"Guns, knives, tactical flashlights."

"Flashlights?"

"Yeah. And that's a thing we can get you now, whether you decide to buy a gun or not. A good tactical flashlight is a thing everyone should carry." He reached and pulled a black, heavy-looking flashlight off his belt. "I can show you once it's dark, but this is what I carry."

She looked at the flashlight but made no move toward it.

"It won't hurt you," he laughed. "You're not in a James Bond movie. It does what it does, no Hollywood spy stuff added. Though it's very versatile, if you know what to do with it."

She picked it up. "It's heavy."

"Yep." He watched her wrap her hand around it, and grinned. "Do you know what you've got there?" he asked.

She started to let loose, but his hand wrapped around hers, holding her fingers closed around the flashlight as he leaned in to speak quietly to her. "Like brass knuckles, you hit a guy while holding that flashlight, like this, it's going to hurt. Far more than your soft hand would."

"Oh!" His warm, strong hand holding hers, and her thoughts moving into a more intimate range now, had her flustered.

His mind isn't on that; it's on me, fighting to defend myself! Get your mind out of the gutter, Christie. He's trying to help you!

She blushed an even deeper red.

Thankfully, her root beer came.

She put down the flashlight and reached for her drink.

Their food came soon after. She looked at the large helping of meatloaf and mashed potatoes with the little bowl of green beans on the side.

"Hearty country food. What did I tell you?" Reed said.

"Yes, it sure is," she said. "Looks good."

"But save room for pie," he said. "They have apple, and pecan tonight."

"I'll be wanting apple," she said. "Of the two, I like it the best."

"That's my favorite, too," he said.

"My favorite is blueberry, but apple runs a close second."

"That's a good one, too," he said.

She nodded. Hungrier then she'd thought she'd be, she dug into her mashed potatoes. "These are one of my comfort foods," she said. "When I've had a bad day, or I'm not feeling so good, I like mashed potatoes."

"With gravy?" he asked.

"Yes, unless my stomach is upset," she nodded. "Then I just eat them plain."

"I don't have a comfort food," he said. "I mostly eat to fuel my body, unless I'm hungry for something in particular."

"Wow," Christie said. "I keep chocolate on hand, for

when I'm stressed. But at the theater the other night, I didn't crave it. Usually I do."

"That was an extreme situation," Reed said.

"It was," she agreed. "I'm sorry about my reaction to the loud guns in the shooting room."

"On the range," he corrected her. "And don't be sorry. You got through it okay, and it will get easier."

"I quit watching TV," she said. "The live shooter was all they wanted to talk about."

She'd stopped watching the news after the live shooter incident, exhausted by having to listen to the story over and over. There was never anything good on the news, and who needed all that negativity?

"I never watched it much to begin with," he said. "The reporting is not always accurate."

"I just can't handle it anymore," she said. "I'm going to start listening to music instead."

"What kind of music do you like?" he said.

"Oh, jazz, swing, big band, old time country." She grinned at him. "I like old music, old cars, and vintage anything."

"Sounds interesting," he said. "You'll have to share your music with me some time."

"I'd like that," she said.

As they ate, she asked about Navy SEAL training.

He explained many of the things he'd had to do to reach his current rank and skills.

Mostly, she listened, fascinated by it all.

She was on a date with an honest to God Navy SEAL and he was talking to her as if he were just another guy, describing his day at work.

It left her in awe. She couldn't help it. She'd never met a Navy SEAL before Reed.

Reed didn't miss how rapt she was over every word he

spoke about his SEAL training and anything to do with the SEALs. He was used to that but hoped she wouldn't go into a state of hero worship where she didn't see him as Reed the man. He hoped that, with time, she'd reach that point as they continued dating.

Over pie, Reed brought up the question he'd been deciding all night whether to ask her.

He liked Christie, a lot. But he'd wanted to get to know her better, before asking her out again.

Christie was the first girly-girl he'd dated. He hadn't expected her to take to the guns, wanting to shoot everything, and to be excited about all of them, like his other girl-friends.

She didn't have enough tomboy in her to do that. But he hoped she'd at least enjoyed shooting one of the guns, so they could go to the range occasionally, and she could learn how to protect herself.

It seemed like she had.

Maybe this could work, the two of them. Opposites did attract. And they were opposites.

But beyond attraction, could they stick?

He needed a woman who could be a team player, who could be a partner, not just a pretty face who was good in bed. And it wasn't easy being with a SEAL.

SEALs could be called away any minute, with no notice and might not be able to tell their women where they were going, or even after they got back, where they went. It took a special kind of woman to be with a SEAL, long-term.

He'd thought he'd found that once. But she couldn't keep her pants on when he was out of town and had run off with some other dude. Breaking it off with no explanation.

Christie, though, was like no woman he'd ever known. She intrigued him, and he enjoyed her company.

Not to mention the chemistry between them, which he'd

had to ignore tonight, so he could focus on the guns and on teaching her. Maybe it wasn't the most romantic date, but he would make that up to her. He had a plan.

They'd been thrown together, might never have met otherwise, and maybe there was a little bit of good luck and a little bit of fate in that.

Whatever it was, he wasn't going to examine it too closely.

He'd enjoy her company, keep getting to know her, and see where it went.

Now, it was time to plunge in, and ask her out again. This time, there'd be romance.

"In two weeks, my best friend, R.T., is getting married," he said. "And I'm in the wedding party. I don't have a date yet. Would you like to go?"

Christie watched his face, stunned.

Reed held his breath.

Was this date too much for her? Am I too much for her? Maybe she can't handle dating a SEAL. Will she say no?

8

———————

Christie sat stunned.

Two weeks until the wedding and Reed said he doesn't have a date yet. Does that mean he isn't dating anyone else, right now?

"Yes, I'd love to go." She tried to answer quickly to make up for the time lapse after being stunned.

This was moving fast, she and Reed.

"Excellent." Reed smiled.

He drove her home, thinking of how much he was looking forward to kissing her.

Finally, they were at her front door, and he was watching her use her key in the lock. When she stopped and looked up at him, he moved in, bending down to kiss her.

His lips met hers, in a gentle, testing way.

She responded, sweet and letting him take the lead.

His tongue teased her lips until they opened, letting him in. Then their tongues touched, and it was electric.

Their chemistry was off the charts, as they explored each other, and she was both sweet and eager.

He could have kissed her all night, but it was a first date, and he could tell she was an old-fashioned kind of girl with traditional values.

As he pulled away, his gaze met hers.

She smiled. "I had a good time tonight," she said.

"I did too," he said. "If you enjoyed going to the range, we'll have to do it again."

"I did enjoy it," she said. "And I would like that."

He made sure she was inside her house with the door locked before he walked back to his car.

Now that Reed had a date for the wedding, he needed to get on over to Chicks Oyster Bar and Marina, where the grooms meeting for the wedding was taking place.

Most of the guys were already there when Reed arrived.

Diesel waved him over. "Hey man, glad you could make it," he said, with a grin.

It was clear he was excited about the wedding.

"Wouldn't miss it," Reed said. "Just had to stop by and ask a lady to be my date."

"She say yes?" Cutter asked.

Reed just gave him a look.

"Of course, she did," Kik said, then he laughed.

Since Cutter was waiting for an answer, Reed nodded.

Cutter laughed.

All the men were in good spirits and enjoying a draft beer. Diesel's treat.

Sheri, their waitress, paused beside Reed and said, "What are you having?"

"A Frogman Lager," he said. He reached for a French fry that had fallen onto his chair from somebody's plate, and tossed it to Fred, the resident seagull, who sat in his usual spot on the railing by the docks.

Fred caught it and ate it, then watched Reed, to see if he

would toss him anything else. He was always on the lookout for more.

"Coming right up," Sheri said with a sweet smile between her two dimples.

"Shari," Diesel called. "Seen your pilot lately? You could pair up with one of the guys here and attend my wedding. There will even be swing dancing."

Now that Diesel had found the love of his life, he'd stopped flirting with Sheri, and instead had started trying to fix her up with one of his teammates.

"As much fun as that sounds," she answered with a smile. "We're still together." She picked up an empty glass in front of Rich. "He's flying on an Australia route for one month."

"A month can be a long time," Diesel said. "Just saying."

She shrugged. "He calls me." She turned to Rich, as she held his glass. "Refill?"

"Just one more," he said. "On my tab this time."

"You've got it." She beamed at him and then walked away.

The men all watched her go, enjoying the bounce of energy in her step, and the way her hips moved.

"Nice view," Cutter said.

They all agreed.

Even Diesel nodded with a grin.

"On that note, Diesel," Cutter said, "Are you sure you don't want to go see Mermaids or the Minx Kittens for your bachelor party?"

"Naw," Diesel said.

A fan of strippers, Cutter knew every stripper in town.

"I can set up a sweet deal, at either club," Cutter said.

I'm good," Diesel said.

He'd settled down after finding Pippa, and their son Bryce. He still enjoyed looking at the waitresses at Chicks, but now he was all about being a good dad to his little boy, and soon, to being a good husband.

"All right, man, but if you change your mind …" Cutter said, "Just give me the green light, and it's done."

"I'd rather party here, with the team guys who are coming into town for the wedding," Diesel said. "And I can't get too shitfaced. I've got to be ready in time for the wedding, and I need to help Pippa get Bryce ready. Wait till you guys see him." He grinned.

"Yeah, I saw him with Pippa last week at the commissary," Chris "Fen" Fenner said, grinning back at Diesel. "Little shit kicker looks just like his old man."

Diesel grinned deeper. "Okay, guys," he said. "Now that we're all here …"

The men quieted to listen to the groom.

"First," Diesel said. "Pippa and I want to thank you for being in the wedding party. We both really appreciate it."

"No problem, bro," Kik said. "That's what family is for."

SEAL Team XII was indeed a family. A tight one. They watched each other's backs and looked out for each other's wives and children.

"Okay, so since Pippa only had immediate family at her first wedding," Diesel leaned back, so Sheri could replace his beer with a new one, then continued. "Because her ex was a controlling ass wipe, she wants the whole nine yards this time," Diesel said. "In her words, a big romantic wedding."

Most of them knew what was coming, as this was not their first rodeo.

"So that means everybody in dress whites' uniforms," he said, "Six swordsmen and a sword arch," he said.

Several of the men groaned.

Reed knew what they were thinking.

Nobody wanted to put on a uniform and get a haircut.

Even for a wedding. But they would honor the brides wishes as SEALs always did for their women. Reluctantly, but they would get the groaning over with before the wedding and would ensure the bride had that special romantic day she dreamed of.

"We'll even have a small ring bearer," Diesel said. "Pippa ordered a special suit for him."

As he was speaking of Bryce, his three-year-old son by Pippa, who had been rescued by several of the SEALs Team guys when Pippa and Bryce were taken by her crazy ex, this lightened the general mood considerably.

Everyone on the team had met two-year-old Bryce, that day or shortly afterward, and he had quickly wrapped his little fingers around their hearts.

"How is little man?" Kik asked.

"Excited to be the ring bearer," Diesel grinned. "Pippa has had him practicing with a cookie on a pillow."

"He doesn't try to eat the cookie?" Daniel "Tractor" Edwards said.

"Only if he drops it, and it breaks," Diesel laughed. "Then he says, 'Oops' and pops half of that cookie into his mouth as fast as he can."

They all laughed.

"Okay, Rich is going to take it from here," Diesel said.

Rich, the Officer in Charge, said, "I need five volunteers. Each swordsman to carry a sword and form the arch with me."

James "Slim Jim" Slater raised his hand. Sam Valente, aka "Sammie the conductor, also raised a hand. Sawyer "Pipes" Ferguson was the third, and "Cutter" Antonius Cutter was the fourth. Daniel" Tractor" Edwards was the fifth.

"Good," Rich said. "I'll borrow the swords from some

other officers. And I want those swords locked up before the heavy drinking starts. Need I say more."

"No sir," many voices replied.

"On to your hair," Rich said, looking around the room at the men in their dark beards and long hair. "Either get a haircut or push your hair under your hat and use hair gel."

"Yes, sir," they replied.

~

This was in Reed's mind when Christie asked, "What's the dress code? Are you wearing a tux?"

"White dress uniform," he said.

"Ooh." Her eyes widened. "I've seen those on TV, and I can just imagine you wearing one. "Very formal."

"Yes," he said. "The reception is formal."

"You'll look so handsome in your Navy SEAL white dress uniform. I can't wait to see you in it."

He gave her a tolerant smile, still not thrilled to have to dress up that much. Give him a wedding on a beach, or in a forest, any day, without all the frills and non-essentials.

"Oh, I have just the dress," Christie exclaimed.

Excitement filed her as she thought of the one hanging in the closet.

Silver, with a low halter-style V and an open back. Like something a movie star would wear.

The special dress she'd never had a place to wear, because her ex would never take her anywhere fancy.

She loved dresses, and dressing up, and weddings. All the fancy things.

"Will there be dancing?" she asked, hoping.

"Yes, ma'am, there will be dancing," he said. "There will even be Swing dancing."

"Oh, good," she said and gave him a big smile. "I love swing dancing."

Our second date will be perfect. And I can't wait.

~

Two weeks went by fast.

Christie shopped for shoes, to match her dress, and had her hair touched up in the bombshell blonde shade she preferred.

The week of the wedding, Tanya came over to help her do a dress rehearsal, before the big date.

Christie's hair was swept into an up do with curling tendrils down her back that tickled just a bit.

Tanya put the last finishing touches on the hairdo, and then said, "If he doesn't want to undo this up do, he's not the healthy red-blooded male I think he is. Girl, this tempting hairdo looks like it might tumble down at any moment, though we know it won't. Maybe he'll want to tumble you, before the evening is over."

"I'm not sure I'm ready to be tumbled," Christie said.

"Reed isn't Mitch," Tanya said. "He isn't even close to being like Mitch." She moved in front of Christie and placed her hands on her shoulders. "Reed and you meeting was meant to be. Reed is your fresh start. Don't get cold feet now."

"Cold feet? This is just a date," Christie said. "Not a marriage. Not a moving in together. Not even a 'we're not seeing anyone else'. This is just a date and it's only our second."

"Just a date?" Tanya pulled back her head and made a face. "This is more than just a date. This is him introducing you to all his SEAL buddies; it's his best friend's wedding. This is where he sees if they approve of you, and if you approve of them. And you know how you get at weddings. Guys know how emotional we get at these events. Girl, this is far more than just a date."

Christie grinned sheepishly. "Okay, so maybe it's more than just a date. But we're still getting to know each other. And it is still only our second date."

"Yes, but *it's a wedding*," Tanya said. "You'll be meeting his friends, and that means he's letting you closer into his inner circle. He may make a move after the wedding. Lots of guys want to get laid after weddings. And they know we're feeling all emotional and wanting the romance. Just know what you want and, if you want him, go for it."

"Okay, okay." Christie put her earrings on. The long dangling earrings she chose swung when she moved her head.

"Now, those are some sexy earrings," Tanya said. "They're perfect. Go look in the long mirror."

Christie opened the closet door and looked into the full-length mirror. "Wow."

"Yeah, wow" Tanya said. "And that's just what we want him to think, when you open the door to greet him."

"I think this will do it," Christie said.

"Yeah, I think it will, too." Tanya nodded. "Okay. I'll be here an hour before, to help with your hair and makeup, and then I'll skedaddle before it's close to time for him to arrive."

"Thanks, Tanya."

"You got it, girl. Now, go shed your glamour, and then let's get a pizza."

"I think I'd better skip pizza this week," Christie said. "The dress is already form-fitting, and if I gain more weight..."

"There will just be more of you to love, and you'll fill out the dress a bit more," Tanya said. "It stretches, you know."

"I know," Christie said. "But it fits perfectly right now."

"Okay, then we'll order a veggie pizza and drink water," Tanya said. "Because we need to leave enough room for the brownies I made."

"Brownies!"

She loved Tanya's brownies, which were the triple chocolate kind and bound to add a few pounds to Christies curves.

Tanya grinned. "Yeah, I've been craving chocolate. Needing it bad."

"Why?"

"Oh, girl," Tanya sighed. "You have no idea how bad I need that chocolate. Wait 'til I tell you about Mrs. Vendt."

"Oh no, what's she done now?" Christie turned and grabbed Tanya's forearm. "Wait. Are Miss Priss and Brutus all right? She hasn't poisoned them again, I hope."

"No, they're fine," Tanya said. "But she's bought herself a huge water gun supposedly to rinse off her porch. Then when she sees either of them outside, or doesn't see me, she blasts them with the water gun."

Tanya had planted a border garden between her yard and Mrs. Vendt's yard, on Tanya's side of the border, and Miss Priss liked to wander through the plants. When she did, Brutus would follow her, sniffing around.

"Are they on your yard, or are they on – "

"On my land of course!" Tanya interrupted before Christie could finish. "I try to keep them off her lawn, so they hardly ever go over onto her side anymore, but it doesn't seem to matter. Just seeing them outside makes her mad. Miss Priss has come in soaked three times this week! And Brutus twice."

"So, they're staying on your side, but she's still soaking them anyway, even if though they're not in her yard?"

"Yes!"

"I hate the way she picks on them as much as you do," Christie said. "I know you worry about them."

Tanya shook her head. "I'm going to have to do something about it. This can't continue."

"Yes, and you can even call the police and press charges if she breaks the law," Christie said. "If you could catch her on video, being mean to them, then you'd have proof, and she couldn't play innocent. I'll talk to Reed about getting a security system for you. With a video camera. SEALs probably know about things like that."

"Thanks, Christie," Tanya said. "I'd appreciate it."

"You're welcome," Christie said. "Thanks for helping me get ready for this big date. Hey, go ahead and order that pizza, and I'll get changed. I'll bet your brownies are delicious."

9

———————

When Reed knocked On Christie's front door, to pick her up for the wedding, she was in front of her bathroom mirror again, fussing with her hair, double checking that she'd flossed her teeth, and that her makeup looked good. It still felt as if she was forgetting something.

Everything is in place. Must just be my nerves.

"Coming!" she called, as she hurried down the hallway on new silver high heeled shoes which made her taller.

She opened the door, a bit breathless, and still had to look up at Reed, despite the heels. "Hi!" She smiled, taking in how handsome he looked in his white dress uniform, his hair neat, and his face freshly shaken.

He was the most handsome man she had ever seen, and to Christie, looked better than a movie star. Soon they'd be dining and dancing together, and she could not wait. She kept taking him in with her eyes, hardly able to believe this evening was really happening.

As Christie opened the door, she took Reed's breath away, the way she gave that wide eyed breathy welcome, and the way she looked, filling out the sexy silver dress.

"Wow," he said. "You are a knockout." He gave her a deep grin. "Hi."

She blushed, charmingly, and dropped her eyelashes, suddenly shy.

The sight of her cleavage, and the way that blush spread across her skin, made him want to uncover the rest of her, to see where else he could make her blush.

But they had a wedding to go to, and since it was his best friend's wedding, they couldn't be late. He would not let R.T. down. Best friends, they always had each other's backs.

"Are you ready?" he asked.

"Oh, yes," she breathed, looking up at him again, her eyes meeting his. "I'm ready."

The moment hovered between them, full of what she might be ready for, before she broke that connection by saying, "Let me just get my purse."

She turned and went over to the couch, where a small silver purse sat, and picked it up. Putting the tiny silver chain over her shoulder she turned to him and smiled. "All set."

"It's supposed to get cool, later this evening," he said. "You might want to take something." He gestured to the halter dress that left her back and shoulders bare.

"Oh, yes, that's a good idea," she said. Then she opened her closet and pulled out a silky white shawl.

Reed placed his hand on Christie's lower back, to guide her out the door, and then turned to lock the door behind her.

Soon they were in his car on their way to the wedding.

"What's the bride like?" Christie asked. She looked forward to getting to know his friends. But she knew little about them.

"Pippa is a sweetheart," Cutter said. "And they have a son, Bryce, who is almost three. He'll be the ring bearer."

"Oh!" Christie said. That changed the idea she had in her head about the couple. "That's unusual."

"Everything about how Diesel and Pippa got together is unusual," he said.

"How so?" she asked.

"Diesel and Pippa met, at a masquerade party, on Halloween night," Cutter said. "They had a one-night stand, which gave them their son, Bryce. But since they were wearing masks, and didn't exchange names, or phone numbers, they lost contact again, until two years later, when Diesel's dad was visiting and saw his grandson in the park. He looked just like Diesel when he was that age. So, he told Diesel and Diesel started to search for them."

"Oh, wow," Christie said.

"There's more," Cutter said. "Christie had a violent ex-husband who was in prison. And when Diesel went to see Christie and Bryce for the first time, they'd been taken by her ex. So, Diesel called the team, and we went and got them back. Happy family reunited. Now today, they're making that little family official. Diesel and Pippa will marry and he's officially adopting his son."

"Oh!" Christie gasped and placed her hand over her heart, tears glistening in her eyes.

"That's real life," Christie said, "But it's also like some-thing out of a movie. What an amazing story."

"It is," he spoke quietly, not unmoved by the little fami-ly's story himself. Diesel, Pippa, and Bryce gave him that heart feeling too. "And now they've got another on the way," he said. "All Diesel can talk about it how he is determined not to miss the birth."

"Oh, my goodness," Christie said. "When is she due?"

"She's about three months along," Cutter said. "And Diesel is more excited than I've ever seen him. He missed the birth of his son, but this time he can be part of the whole thing. Unless he's deployed."

"Oh, he could miss the birth?" Christie asked. "I thought the red cross got you guys and brought you back home when you had a baby being born."

"Sweetheart where they send us, we may not even be able to tell our own mothers. The Red Cross aren't the ones getting ahold of us," Reed said.

"I see," she said.

"It's not easy being a SEALs wife," he said.

"That would be hard," she agreed. "For both. He'd be missing his child's birth."

"Yes," he said. "It would."

"I hope he can be there this time," she said.

"I do too," he said.

❧

Once inside the church, Christie stood with Reed in the entryway taking in the decorations and especially the floral arrangements. Red roses and white lilies. These weren't flowers she had done. These were done by a competing florist shop.

They were lovely.

"R.T.," another man in uniform said. "Hey man, Diesel is looking for you."

"Be right there," he said. "Christie, this is Osprey." He slid his arm around her back and looked at Osprey. "This is my girl, Christie." He directed his attention to her again. "He'll see that you are seated, and if you need anything, let him know. I'll see you after the service," he said.

"Yes, see you then." She smiled at him as he left to join the wedding party.

After he walked away, she glanced at Osprey.

Tall, dark skinned, with dark hair, and likely native American, his dark brown eyes watched her quietly.

"Nice to meet you," she said. "I don't know anyone else here, yet."

He nodded. "I'll look after you tonight when R.T. is busy."

"Thank you," she said. "Why do you call him R.T.?"

"Short for railroad tracks," he said.

"That's an interesting nickname," she said.

"A lot of our guys have interesting nicknames," he said. "I'll seat you on the groom's side since you're with R.T."

"That would be fine," she said.

He held out his arm, and she placed her hand on it, for him to escort her to be seated in one of the pews. Like Reed, his arm was warm solid muscle.

She realized once she was seated, that many men there were in white Navy dress uniforms.

Everything inside the church from the stained glass to the flowers, to the men in uniforms was visually stunning.

The organist started to play.

Reed and all the male members of the wedding party stood at the front of the church with the pastor, waiting on the ladies.

One by one, they came down the aisle.

Reed was paired with Pippa's sister, Jeanie Magic Smith, a full breasted woman wearing a dress which she appeared close to spilling out of.

The dresses were a deep red which matched the red roses. flowers were red roses and white lilies. Soon everyone was up front except the ring bearer and the bride.

The moment everyone turned to see three-year-old Bryce carrying the pillow with the rings on it, Christie got misty eyed.

The little boy who was the spitting image of his daddy,

was adorable in his little suit and tie, as he walked and looked around at everyone.

He spotted Diesel halfway down the aisle and said, "Daddy!" He stopped and waved, then he lifted the pillow up, "This is for you, daddy!" then he ran down the aisle toward Diesel.

Everyone laughed.

Diesel took the pillow from his son and handed it to Reed, who removed the rings, to ready them for the ceremony.

Pippa's mother got little Bryce to sit with her, on her lap and handed him a cookie.

Then it was the brides turn to come down the aisle, and the wedding march began to play. When she neared the back of the church everyone stood and turned to look at her.

In her long white wedding dress, and lace veil, the bride was stunning.

When the ceremony was over, the bride and groom came down the aisle and out the front doors of the church. Everyone stood outside watching them.

Just ahead of the newlywed couple, six SEALs stood lined up on the steps, three on each side, with swords touching overhead, making a sword arch canopy the newly-weds would walk beneath.

According to the program, Richard "Rich" Irvine, James Slater "Slim Jim", Sam Valente "Sammie the Conductor", Sawyer "Pipes" Ferguson, "Cutter" Antonius Cuttino, and Daniel "Tractor" Edwards made up the group of men with swords.

"Now may I introduce Mr. and Mrs. Tanner Taylor," the pastor proclaimed.

Everyone cheered.

The couple began to walk toward the first two SEALs

who lowered their swords to waist level, preventing the couple from passing.

"The first rite of passage is a kiss," Rich said.

A sweet quick kiss followed.

Everyone cheered. The swords were raised again, and the couple moved forward.

But the next two SEALs had now lowered their swords.

Sammie the conductor said, "The price of passage is one kiss."

Diesel kissed Pippa again and everyone cheered.

The swords were raised again, and the couple took a step forward, but the last two SEALs had lowered their swords, making everyone laugh.

"Laddie, ye must do better than that kiss," Pipes said.

Everyone laughed.

"The price of passage is a real kiss," Pipes continued. "Now sweep her off her feet, man."

Diesel took Pippa into his arms and dipping her in a romantic swoop, kissed her deeply.

Christie sighed. This was the most romantic wedding she had ever seen.

Diesel and Pippa stood back up, and the final swords were raised.

The couple took a step forward, and Slim Jim lowered his sword to swat Pippa on the butt, making her jump with surprise and rounded eyes.

Everyone laughed again.

"Welcome to the U.S. Navy, Mrs. Taylor!" he said.

The cheers were even louder now, as every SEAL present raised his voice to celebrate the newly wedded couple.

Bryce who'd been released from his grandmother's arms, went racing over to Diesel yelling, "Daddy! Play swords now!"

But the SEALs had immediately returned their swords to their holsters, and all the swords were now safely put away. Soon to be collected by the officer in charge before the reception got underway.

Diesel picked his son up as the photographer constantly moved around, taking candid pictures.

Christy couldn't help but smile.

The little boy was adorable, and the new family looked so happy.

Reed and the other SEALs were handsome and fit. She'd never seen so many handsome, fit men gathered in one place.

Being with him, here, felt like something out of a dream. And the happy little family before her appeared like every young girl's dream. A strong, handsome, protective husband, an adorable little boy who that husband clearly loved. A beautiful bride and a baby on the way. What a blessing.

It didn't get better than that.

R.T. was by her side now. "Come back inside, while we finish the pictures and then we'll head over to the reception."

"All right," Christie said as he placed his hand on her back, to guide her inside.

She quite liked all these good manners, and the way he was protective and considerate. The way he touched her. It warmed her inside; in a way she'd never known.

Though Reed had said SEALs did not make the best husbands, the little girl she had been, could only see the fairy tale perfection of this ceremony today and the brave, handsome men of SEAL team XII.

Today she found herself disagreeing with him and believing that one day she might also have that fairy tale.

A perfect husband, a healthy family, and a happy ever

after. It was all she'd ever dreamed of.

~

On the way to the reception, Reed watched the road and the way his date seemed to glow when talking about the wedding.

"It was the most beautiful wedding I've ever been to," she said. "Thank you so much for inviting me. I loved the flowers, the dresses, the music, and the ceremony made me cry. But then the sword ceremony," she clasped her hands together. "That was just amazing! Do they do that at every SEAL wedding?"

Reed had not seen Christie so animated before. She hadn't been kidding when she'd said she loved weddings.

"Not every wedding," he said. "Only if the bride wants a more formal wedding and requests it."

"You all are so handsome in your SEAL uniforms," she said. "And your dress whites are elegant."

"Pippa requested we all wear them," he said. "Otherwise, we wouldn't have."

"Oh," Christie said. "Why not?"

"They're uncomfortable as hell," he said. "None of the guys are going to volunteer to wear one." He shrugged. "But for Pippa, not one of us would have let her down. We all got haircuts and trimmed our beards too."

"Wow," she said. "That's really nice of you."

"We're a family," he said. "That's how we are."

"A Navy family," she said.

"SEAL family," he corrected her. "That's very different. Very tight. The men and the wives. You'll meet most of them at the reception."

"Your SEAL family," she said with a smile. "I'm looking forward to it. Do you think I will fit in okay?"

10

———

"They will love you," Reed said.

He had no doubt of that. Especially the way she looked tonight. He wasn't a jealous man, but this woman was special. No way was he letting any of the other guys get too close to her tonight. They hadn't been dating that long, and she seemed very caught up in the romance of the military wedding. She had that dreamy look in her eyes again, as she looked out the window.

He cleared his throat and she looked at him. "We're here," he said as he pulled into the parking lot. He gave her a long look.

She quietly watched him back.

"Be sure to save most of your dances for me." He winked at her. "I've been looking forward to that."

And the thought of holding you in my arms.

"I can't wait," she said, joy in her eyes. "Dancing is one of my favorite things to do, especially slow dances."

"I've got things as best man that must do," he said. "But I will dance with you as much as possible."

"I promise to save all my slow dances for you," she said. "I can wait for you."

177

Can you, sweetheart? How long can you wait for me when I'm overseas? When you don't even know how long I will be gone?

That 'Dear John' letter he'd received from Becky, though he'd finally burned it one night at a bonfire, while drinking with his SEAL buddies, was burned into his memory. He'd wouldn't think of it now, so he pushed it back.

But it was still behind everything, creating the doubt that would creep in.

"That would be great," he said. "But you don't have to."

He wasn't expecting anything. That way he wouldn't be disappointed in her, or any other woman.

"I want to," she said.

"Ready to go in?"

"Yes," she said, reaching for her shawl, which had slipped down, off one sexy bare shoulder. The way she reached for it and pulled it back up, as she glanced down, reminded him of how beautiful she was.

He got out and came around to open her door. He scanned the parking lot, helped her out, and then closed the door and locked it. Placing his hand on her back again, he guided her into the building, always aware of their surroundings.

With this many SEALs on the property, nothing was going to happen, but the habits were ingrained in him. Protection was a way of life, situational awareness a constant.

The bride and groom were just inside in a receiving line with their parents and their son. Christie thought the little family was the picture of perfection as she watched them. Little Bryce was wanting to shake hands with everyone, just like his daddy. It was clear he looked up to and adored his dad, who had picked the little fellow before he could run about the room, getting into trouble.

"Mr. and Mrs. Taylor, may I present my date, Christie Anderson," Reed said, when they got to the newly married couple.

Diesel took her hand. "Pleased to meet you, Christie," he said with a warm smile. "Glad to see R.T. has a good lady with him to keep him in line."

With that twinkle in his eyes, Christie wondered what kind of mischief Reed would have gotten into, if she wasn't here with him.

"Thank you," she said. "It's a pleasure meeting you as well."

Moving on to Pippa, Reed said, "You two share an interest in common."

Pippa smiled at them both, waiting to hear what it was.

"You both enjoy dancing and costumes," Reed said. "Christie likes everything vintage from the 40's and 50's."

"Then you will have a great time tonight," Pippa told her. "We're going to be swing dancing. It's something I had always wanted to learn. Diesel and I go swing dancing on date nights."

"Oh, that will be fun," Christie nodded.

It was time for the line to move along, so Reed and Christie moved toward the tables to look for their names. As he was part of the bridal party, their seats were near the newlywed couple, with a great view of the dance floor.

Soon dinner was served, and Christie was careful not to eat too much. She didn't want anything to interfere with her being able to swing dance. She wondered, did Reed know how?

Well, she would find out soon enough.

As the dinner plates were being cleared, the music

switched to dance music and Diesel and Pippa took the floor for their first slow dance as a married couple.

As soon as the floor opened for other dancers, Reed held out his hand to Christie. "Would you like to dance?"

A smile beamed across her face. "Yes, I would love to."

She placed her hand in his and stood.

He guided her to the dance floor, turned to face her, and pulled her into his arms.

The music, a slow song, suitable for waltzing, was one Christie hadn't heard before, but she liked it.

Later in the evening, after everyone had several cocktails, they all moved to the dance floor instead of watching the other dancers. This was totally unlike the last wedding she had been to where most of the guests preferred watching the others dance and rarely got up from their seats.

It was clear to Christie that SEALs were doers, and tonight what they were doing was dancing and celebrating with their SEAL brother and his new bride.

Little Bryce had fallen asleep, as all the excitement had worn him out, so his grandmother had told the couple good night and taken him with her to put him to bed.

Now the couple only had eyes for each other. It appeared to Christie that Diesel was wooing his new wife. The romance of this made Christie smile.

Christie was enjoying the dancing. All twenty SEALs from Reeds team were on the dance floor having a great time. Matt Hunt, Diesel, Cutter, Rich Irvine, Osprey, Kik Garcia, Big Mac, Martin Lopez, Chris "Fen" Fenner, Daniel "Tractor" Edwards, Davinci, Tom Campbell, Casper, James "Slim Jim" Ryder, "Pipes" Ferguson, "Sammie the Conductor", "Buzz" Horne, "Numbers" Lewis, Jake Summers. Reed was dancing with her.

Jeanie Magic Smith, Pippa's sister, barely fit into the front of her bridesmaid dress, and was really into the dance.

A ring of men had formed around her as they all danced and encouraged her, everyone having a good time.

Now that the music had changed from swing dance to a modern pop tune, she danced and sang to the tune. As she bounced up and down, singing the lyrics, her breasts bounced.

Nearly all the men's eyes were on her, as if they couldn't look away.

"It's like they're waiting for her to bounce out of that dress," Christie said.

"They are," Reed agreed, and sent her a grin.

Him too?

Christie just shook her head.

Men. They just couldn't help but look.

Changing the subject, she said, "I noticed you hung back from catching the garter."

"I'm in no rush to get married," Reed said. "I'm busy with deployments, or training. Not enough time to give. Most women can't handle that."

Good thing I'm not most women.

Christie kept the thought to herself. For a man like Reed, she wouldn't mind waiting.

"Did you want to catch the bouquet?" he asked.

"No, I would have been embarrassed if I had caught it," she said. "I don't really know any of these people. Someone closer to the bride should be the one to catch it."

"Her sister sure wanted it." he said.

"I think her sister likes all the attention of wearing that dress and bouncing around," she said. "So, she probably liked the thought of the attention she'd get if she caught the bouquet."

"Maybe so," he said.

The music changed to a slow song she and Reed could dance to, and he swept her into his arms and across the dance floor.

It was a night she wished would never end.

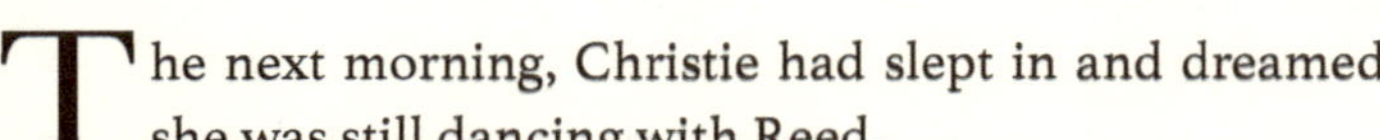

The next morning, Christie had slept in and dreamed she was still dancing with Reed.

She woke wishing she could return to the dream.

Padding into the kitchen on bare feet, Christie started her coffee, and then got out eggs to cook, and bread to toast. She'd just finished scrambling the eggs, and her toast had popped, when her phone rang.

She saw it was Tanya and answered. "Hello?"

"Hey girl, are you alone?"

"Yes," she answered slowly, wondering why Tanya was asking.

Christie was still getting to know Reed. It had only been their second date, and she had to make sure he wasn't a heavy drinker, before she could get serious with him.

"I've got an errand to run, out your way, and thought I'd stop by after," Tanya said. "But I wanted to be sure you weren't still entertaining your man."

"Nope, not entertaining," Christie said. "Just home relaxing. I'd love it if you stopped by. Have you had breakfast?"

"Heck yeah," Tanya said. "Had my usual bagel, and then walked the dogs. I'll be around in about an hour."

"Sounds good," Christine said. "See you then."

"Great! I want to hear all about your date with Reed! See you soon."

Christie hung up, and her thoughts returned to Reed.

Would he turn out to be her long-term boyfriend?

He doesn't seem to be dating anyone else.

The first time they'd gone out, he'd asked her out before the first date was even over. This time, on their second date, he hadn't asked her out again; he'd just brought her home.

Should I have invited him in?

The date had been wonderful. The dancing, the beautiful setting, that kiss he'd left her with. She'd hoped he would ask her out again. Maybe he would, soon.

If he wanted to be her long-term boyfriend, she was ready.

Long term though, that meant sex. And he's so fit. Super fit. Muscular with very little fat.

She glanced down at her curves.

Whereas I'm all curves and not very muscular. I'm not exactly the uber fit, hang out at the gym, kind of woman.

Prior to meeting Reed, that hadn't been a concern.

She was happy with herself and her life. She didn't look in the mirror and see one hundred things wrong with her, the way she had done when she was younger.

She saw curves, and her bright shining eyes, and her smile. She hoped that was what Reed saw when he looked at her.

Maybe he did. He'd asked her out twice, in a short period of time. He'd been making an effort to get to know her. Which meant he must be interested in things going further.

She wanted that too.

Why does that thought make me so nervous?

11

———

Christie stood at her closet, eyeing the red and white checked dress that she'd worn to the movie premiere. She'd worn it for only a few hours, and later despaired that the blood stains might have ruined it.

She'd worked hard on the dress, soaking it, and then scrubbing it, to get the stains out. It wasn't as white as it had been, but she'd taken a brush and painted bleach on it, and then had rinsed it out again, until the stains weren't noticeable.

Maybe I could wear the dress again.

Her phone rang.

Reed.

She answered it. "Hello?"

"Hello," she said. "How are things?"

"Busy," he said. "I wanted to check on you and see how you are doing."

"Good," she said. "It's really nice to hear from you."

"I'd like to take you to dinner," he said. "Saturday night if you're free."

"Yes, I'd love to have dinner with you, Saturday," she said.

"Great," he said. "I'll make reservations and surprise you."

A thrill shivered through her. "Oh, I like surprises."

"That's good," he said. "Now, I have a request."

"You do?" She hoped it was something she could accommodate. "Okay, what is your request?"

"That red and white checked dress you wore, the night we met. Was it ruined? Can you still wear it?"

Her eyes widened. It was as if he'd been reading her mind. Now he *wanted* her to wear the vintage dress.

"Yes, I can wear it," she said. "I'd be happy to. I didn't know you liked it."

"Yeah, I liked it." His husky voice sent a feeling through her that warmed her inside.

"Oh, I'm so glad," she said, her voice lower now, and breathy.

"You looked hot in that dress," he said.

He'd said hot. He must be thinking of sex. So, he is interested in me that way.

"Thank you," she said.

"Wearing a dress like that," he said. "Someone should be taking you out to a nice dinner."

"That would be lovely," she said.

"Great," he said. "I'll pick you up at seven Saturday."

"Perfect," she said. "I'll be ready."

Reed watched Christie moving in the red and white dress. She was like visual candy.

Thoughts of her in that dress, and then her stepping out of that dress, had become his new favorite fantasy.

They were seated, and then the waiter took their drink order.

He returned with a bottle of red wine, and then offered Reed a taste.

Reed took a sip and okayed it.

The waiter poured them each a glass, took their orders and then left.

Christie took a sip of her wine and began to speak. "It's nice to relax," she said. "I haven't really done that since the shooting. Being around you relaxes me. And I haven't ever had lobster ravioli before."

"I'm sorry to hear you're not sleeping," he said. "But glad you can relax with me. I think you'll like the ravioli, but if you don't, I'll share half of my lasagna. The portion sizes here are generous."

She took another sip and smiled at him. "Thank you." She set her glass down and put her hand in her lap to smooth out her napkin and her nerves.

Christie looked up at him again and brought up the first topic she'd wanted to talk to him about.

"I'm thinking about getting a dog. Well, a puppy really. Because I live alone. I think I'll feel safer with a dog. I've been wanting to get a puppy for a while anyway."

"A dog would be good." He nodded. "What kind?"

"German Shephard," she said.

"Good choice," he said.

"My friend Tanya has one. He's the one her neighbor, Mrs. Vendt, tried to poison, along with her cat."

"You're sure the neighbor poisoned them?"

"Well, we don't have proof, but I'm sure it was her." Christie frowned. "She hates them."

"Hmm," he said. He watched as the waiter brought them bread to munch on, before speaking again.

Once the waiter left, he said, "Has your friend told the police?"

"No, because we have no proof," Christie said.

"That's one thing police do," he said. "Look for proof. They have the training that you and Tanya don't have."

When she continued to frown, he changed the subject.

"Have you thought about getting a handgun?" he asked.

"Yes, I have," she said. "I ought to buy a gun for my protection at home. But I've no idea what to get. I don't feel comfortable with the big guns. I'd get a small handgun, but that won't do any good against a man with a big automatic gun like the theater shooter. I wouldn't know what to do against someone like him."

Reed watched and listened, waiting until she'd finished speaking. "Let's talk about that. Why do you think the shooter wasn't able to do more damage?"

"Because you stopped him," she said.

"That's part of the reason," he said. "He had the bigger gun. I had the handgun. Why did I win?"

"Because you're a Navy SEAL."

He liked the way she said that, so instinctively, because it made him feel like Superman. "One thing SEALs do constantly, is train. I know my guns like I know my own hand."

"You won with a handgun, a smaller gun, because you were trained," she said.

"Right. Training is key to winning." Reed nodded. "The other thing is, these idiots who want to shoot up a theater, or any other public place full of civilians, think fully automatic will cause more damage, so they don't bother aiming, and they end up causing less damage than if they'd used a pistol more carefully. Big gun doesn't always mean big win."

She frowned. "But they have more bullets."

"Having more bullets, and rapid fire, does not mean accuracy." He tilted his head. "You like vintage things. Think back to the 1920s. You've seen movies with the tommy guns, right? Thompson submachine guns?"

"Yes," she nodded. "I have. I love the 1920s dresses, but those guns are scary."

"Those are some of the most inaccurate guns ever made," he said. "They were heavy and pulled up when you shot them. The shots would spray." He moved his arm in an arc up and over. "Like this."

She watched as he demonstrated.

"So, if you're aiming at a guy, you might hit him," he said. "But if you didn't hit him at first, already the gun would be moving, and you'd be fighting to control its aim. It's not an easy gun to shoot. Modern guns are more accurate, but the same principals apply."

"So, I'd need to go to the range and train," she said.

"Absolutely," he said. "I'd be happy to train you."

"Okay, so maybe I can try some of the other handguns and find one that is easier to use." She glanced down at her small hands. "I might need one of those tiny guns, like women used to hide in their dresses."

His large, warm hand closed over hers. "We'll find you one that fits your hand but isn't too small to be effective."

"Okay." She smiled.

"Would you like to go to the range next week?" He asked. "Tuesday night I'm free."

"Yes," she said. "I would like that."

He continued to hold her hand, and then gave it a squeeze before letting go as the waiter placed their plates in front of them.

Their Italian food all looked delicious, the music was restful, and the restaurant was dark and romantic.

To Christie, it was a perfect date.

And when he brought her home, walked her to the front

door, and bent down to kiss her, she wanted to freeze the moment in her memory forever.

Their first kiss. It was everything she'd ever dreamed of. He gently claimed her lips as if he was the only one meant to kiss them, as if he treasured her, but underlying that was an intensity he held back.

It was a wooing kiss, and she wanted more. Oh, so much more.

She wrapped her arms around his neck and pulled him closer.

His tongue slipped between her lips to meet hers, and their tongues touched, tentative, and then, dancing together, and moved faster. The intensity ramped up until they broke apart each needing air.

"Wow," she said.

He was thinking the same thing. He'd kissed a lot of women. But none of them were Christie.

Sweet, sexy, delicious Christy.

He could have kissed her all night.

She seemed a little dazed, and maybe that was the wine. She took a step and wobbled a little on her heels.

He reached out to hold her, keeping her from falling.

"Oops," she said. "Maybe I'm a little tipsy. Either that or you made me dizzy."

He looked at her closely. "Tipsy, probably," he said.

"I'll be okay, once I sit down," she said.

He helped her unlock her door, and then guided her inside.

She sat down on the closest chair. Not the couch, he noted. He couldn't tell if she wanted him to stay, or if she was ready for him to leave.

"Thank you for taking me to dinner," she said. "And to the wedding, and to the range to learn to shoot."

"My pleasure," he said. "So, next Tuesday I'll take you shooting again."

"Yes," she nodded, then leaned back against the chair and closed her eyes.

That was his cue.

She must be sleepy. Maybe she'll sleep well tonight.

"All right, sweetheart, I'll let myself out, and lock up for you. Good night."

"Night," she murmured.

He bent to kiss the top of her head, and then turned to let himself out.

〜

Early on Tuesday morning, before the sun was even close to rising, Christie woke, groggy, and with a feeling something was wrong.

She heard a strange noise in the other room, which must have awakened her.

She had to lie very still and silent, listening.

Someone is moving in the other room.

Who is in my house? The burglar on the news, who'd been breaking into houses? It had happened in a different neighborhood, and those people weren't at home.

Oh my God, I bet it's him. What will he do if he knows I'm home? What if he has a knife or a gun?

She reached for her cellphone and dialed Reed.

He didn't pick up, but his answering message did.

She whispered into the phone, "Reed, someone is in my house. In the other room. I don't know what to do."

The sounds were getting nearer.

She pulled the phone under the covers, and placed it face down, so the light wouldn't show. Turning the phone to mute, it would now be silent, and Reed would be able to hear.

The door to her room started to open.

Frozen in her bed, Christie closed her eyes and stilled her breathing, trying to appear asleep, and waited for what would happen next. Her heart raced.

Maybe he'll think I'm asleep. Please God.

The door to her room started to open.

12

———————

Not daring to peek, even a little, Christie stayed as still as she could, hoping that the thumping of her heart didn't give away the fact she was awake.

The intruder moved to her dresser and opened a drawer. The telltale sound of the drawer scraping as he pulled it open told her what was going on. She tried to control her breathing; sure that he could hear her.

Rummaging in the drawer, he then moved on to the next one, doing the same. Other sounds came then.

Maybe he's taking something.

Suddenly the sounds stopped.

She heard nothing but silence and her own breathing.

Oh my God. Where is he?

Her heart thumped doubly loud in her chest, and she prayed he didn't hear it, and guess she was awake.

Then she heard him breathing.

He was standing at the foot of her bed, breathing. Not moving.

Oh my God. He's looking at me. Watching me.

She felt it. Sensed it. Pinpricks of fear spread across her body, raising goose bumps.

Would he see them?

Or see her breathing and know she wasn't asleep?

He stood watching and listening for what felt like forever. And then he moved toward the door.

Still praying, she waited. And waited. Until her bladder felt like it would burst.

Is he gone?

The house was silent. No one was in the bedroom. He hadn't closed the door all the way, and she peeked at the door.

A crack showed the hallway. She eyed that crack, and then dared to glance at her phone.

Thirty minutes had gone by. No response from Reed. He must not have received her message.

Slowly she crept out of bed, into her bathroom and closed and locked the door. Then she dialed 911.

How did he get in?

She needed to find out, but she didn't want to leave the safety of the bathroom until the police got there.

Dialing 911, she was determined to wait until the police arrived before coming out. She just hoped the burglar wasn't still in the house to come in.

The wait seemed to take forever.

When the police arrived, with light and siren, she came out of the bathroom, to answer the front door after grabbing her robe to wrap around her pajamas.

It felt safe to go back into her bedroom to get it because the bad guy wouldn't stick around if the police were there.

The lights would've scared him off.

She let the officers in, after they both held up their badges for her to read, and then a kind officer named Tom O'Malley took her initial statement, while Officer Skip Teagan looked around for any evidence.

Officer Teagan found an open window, in the living-room on the side wall, with the lock and the glass broken. "This is where he gained entry," Officer Teagan said.

"He could have hidden behind those bushes, and no one would have seen him breaking the window from the road," Officer Tom O'Malley said, then he turned back to Christie. "You might want to have that tall, wide bush on the corner trimmed, Miss."

"Please call me Christie," she said. "I don't know how I slept through that window breaking! I don't like to think what he might have done to me if he'd known I was awake!"

"From the pattern of the break and the glass, it may not have made much noise," the officer said. "It looks like a professional broke in. The same pattern you've likely heard about on the news. Don't beat yourself up over this, Christie. You did the right thing playing possum." He gave her an encouraging smile.

"My boss told me about the break-ins," she said. "I haven't been watching the news, since the live shooting in the theatre."

"Where you there?" Officer O'Malley asked.

"Yes," she nodded. "I helped put the tourniquet on that other man."

"That was a fine thing you did, Christie." He nodded, smiling at her.

She blushed red, and shifted on the couch, uncomfortable by the attention.

"Well, Miss Christie, can you look around, and see if anything is missing? If so, we'll need a list from you."

"Oh, yes, of course," she said. "Oh, and I haven't even offered you both anything to drink yet. Where are my manners? I can make coffee."

"Your manners are just fine, and we thank you for the offer, but we don't need any coffee." He waved the coffee off with his hand. "Just concentrate right now on seeing if anything has been taken."

She went into her bedroom and opened the top drawer in her dresser, where she usually stored her jewelry.

"All my jewelry is gone," she said looking up at Officer O'Malley.

The jewelry box was empty. It appeared the thief had grabbed everything in it, her costume jewelry, and the good jewelry she'd inherited from her grandmother. Tears filled her eyes.

Everything from grandmother is gone.

"I need you to try to remember everything that was in your jewelry box," Officer O'Malley said. "Jewelry, money, keys."

"Keys?" she asked.

He nodded. "Many women store keys with their jewelry. Car keys, house keys, keys to safety deposit boxes."

"Oh." She wrinkled her forehead. "No, I never put keys in there. But grandmothers' jewelry was. I'd better list that. Some of mine was costume though. I doubt he could resell any of that."

"List everything that's been taken," Officer O'Malley said. "The insurance company will sort the values out. And a good description will help us if it turns up at a local pawn shop."

She started a list of everything she could remember being in the drawer.

Once the police were done taking her statement and had written down everything, they were ready to go.

Officer O'Malley stood. "Christie, I hope if you're ever in a situation again, that you'll call 911 first, not your SEAL friend. Even Mr. Tindall called 911. Our dispatchers are always on the job, twenty-four seven, and will stay on the line with you."

"Oh, yes, I see what you mean," she said. "In the theater he stopped the man and then called 911. They stayed on the line, talking to me, until I had to help him put a tourniquet on the other man. I guess I should've thought of calling you first when the thief broke in."

"Hopefully you won't have any more problems, but here's my card if you do, or if you have questions about the robbery." He handed her his card. "And if any of your jewelry turns up, we'll let you know."

The card had Officer O'Malley's number on it.

"Thank you," she said. "I really appreciate that."

Once they'd left, she locked the door behind them, and then went back to bed and tried to sleep.

It was impossible to relax enough to sleep.

Finally, she got up, and fixed herself a bowl of cereal, then fired up her computer.

By morning, when the sun rose, she'd already looked up places that could come out and repair the glass, and she started calling them as soon as they opened.

The sooner she could get the window repaired the better.

After she'd found a man who could come out that day to fix it, she hung up and called her best friend.

"Hey, you're up early," Tanya said.

"Yes. Well, I haven't slept. I may never sleep in my own bed again," Christie said.

"Oh no. Why not?"

"A burglar broke in last night and stole all my jewelry while I was in bed asleep."

"Oh, my God," Tanya said. "You're kidding."

"Not kidding. I stayed in bed, not moving, while he robbed me, and then waited until he left and called the police."

"Oh, girl, you must've been terrified."

"I was," Christie said. "Literally could not move. Frozen like an ice sculpture, under the covers. And the creepiest, scariest part? He stopped at the foot of my bed, and stood there, and watched me."

Tanya gasped.

"I didn't know what he would do!" she said. "It was terrifying! He watched, probably to make sure I was asleep, and then he left."

"Thank God for that," Tanya said. "I'm so glad you're okay."

"Me, too," Christie said.

"Oh my God, girlfriend!" Tanya said, "You have the worst luck, with crazy stuff happening, and the best luck, at coming through without getting hurt."

"Right?!" Christie said.

"I'm coming over," Tanya said. "No arguing with me. It's what I should've done the last time. I'll bring chocolate covered donuts, and a great big hug. You make the coffee."

"Okay. That sounds good." Christie wasn't going to argue with Tanya. This time she knew she really needed that hug.

13

Wednesday, the window was repaired, and Tanya spent the whole day with her, after Christie called into work and explained the situation.

Christie stayed in her pajamas, wrapped in her grandmother's quilt, on the couch. and watched old movies. She didn't feel like going anywhere, but also no longer felt safe in her own home.

Her phone rang, but it wasn't Reed.

By Wednesday night Reed still hadn't called her back. Something she was trying not to think about because she didn't understand why he'd gone silent. Especially given the message she'd left on his phone Tuesday night.

Tanya called Thursday morning.

Christie answered. "Hello?"

"If you still want a German Shepard puppy, you'd better move fast. I just called the breeders this morning to ask about puppies for you. They have four eight-week-old puppies, and one has already been sold. They sell fast. So, we need to go today. Are you ready?"

"Yes," Christie said.

If she'd had a puppy to bark at the intruder, he might

not have entered her house. He wouldn't have been able to stand at the bottom of her bed, watching her.

"Good. I'll call them back and tell them we'll be there in an hour. Throw your shoes on and be ready to go," Tanya said.

"Okay." Christie thought about her plans for the day and mentally went down her list. There was nothing that couldn't be rescheduled. This was important.

"Bye."

"Bye." Christie hung up the phone and started looking for her shoes, as excitement started to run through her.

I'm going to get a puppy! This is better than Christmas.

Even if the recent scare was now part of her motivation. She was getting a puppy!

She found her shoes, her purse, and her car keys. Though it sounded like Tanya was driving.

Christie could hardly wait. She loved animals, dogs especially, and now she'd have one of her own. A German Shepherd like Tanya's sweet dog, Brutus.

Two hours later, they were home with eight-week-old Lacey. Tanya had put one of her dog crates in the back seat of her car, and the puppy had ridden in it.

They'd stopped at the pet store to get food and water bowls, a new collar and leash, doggie shampoo, treats, and several toys. The pet store was one where you could take your dog inside with you.

Lacey wagged her tail at everyone and sniffed nearly everything in the store.

Her excitement was contagious.

Now at home, the puppy was free to sniff everything in the house, and the tail wagging and sniffing commenced.

Tanya went into the kitchen and came back out with paper towels and cleaning spray. "She's going to pee all over the place until you get her trained and she settles down. With all this excitement, she's going to have accidents."

"Oh, I know puppies do that." Christie nodded. "We had a couple of dogs when I was growing up and got them both as puppies. I remember. I also remember they don't sleep much at night at first."

"No, they don't," Tanya agreed. "I hope you're prepared for all that."

"It can't be any worse than when the burglar broke in," Christie said. "That was nearly as terrifying as the shooting at the theater. Honestly, I haven't been sleeping well since that happened."

"I'll bet," Tanya said. "I'm so glad you decided to get Lacey. She'll bark and scare any burglars away."

"Yes, she will." Christie smiled. "And she'll be my constant companion. Except when I'm at work."

"Remember what I said about crating her. If you let her have the run of the house, she'll chew up things while you're gone. Puppies love to chew."

"Yes, I will. Do you think I should look for a pet sitter, or a doggie day care? She'll be home by herself when I'm at work."

"Can you come home for lunch to let her out?" Tanya asked.

"I'm pretty sure Mrs. Brown will let me go a few minutes over, if I explain what I'm doing," Christie said. "I often stay late, when we have big orders, and she knows the work will get done."

"Okay, good," Tanya nodded. "Then I don't think you need a dog sitter."

They played with Lacey for a while, and then Tanya left.

Christie couldn't wait to get settled into her new routine, just her and Lacey.

She still hadn't heard for Reed, but now she had a new puppy to keep her busy.

Who needs a man, anyway? The two of us will be just fine.

He needed to call Christie and explain he'd been called away on a mission and he needed to ask if she was willing to reschedule their date.

The minute he was able to use his cell phone again, Reed pushed the button, to listen to voice messages, and then frowned. His frown grew deeper the longer he listened.

Immediately, he dialed Christie's number.

No answer.

"Christie, are you all right? I just got your message. Damn, I hope you're okay. Call me."

He hung up the phone and scowled. It had been four days since she'd called, terrified that someone had broken into her house. First was the message, then the long pause, and finally the breathing, and the hang up. Anything could've happened.

It was Saturday and he'd received no other calls since the first one.

This is not good.

He had to find her as soon as he left the base.

If she wasn't home, he'd try the florist shop.

It was dark when he pulled up to her house and saw her lights on.

She's at home. Why hasn't she called me back?

He got out, walked to the front door, and knocked.

Inside, a dog started to bark.

She opened the door with a German Shepard pup at her feet who stood furiously barking at Reed. She was safe.

Relief flooded through him.

She appeared safe. But pale.

"Come in," she said, without smiling, her voice brittle, unspoken anger in her tone. "Meet Lacey."

His stomach tightened. This wasn't the greeting he'd expected. So few words. Not even the trace of a smile. And she was angry.

They hadn't seen each other in over a week.

Is she even glad I'm back? Things were fine when I left.

Frustration coursed through him.

Damn it.

He had to fix this.

"Lacey," he said. "Can I come in?"

She picked up the puppy and stepped back, to let him in, but she still didn't speak.

The puppy barked at him as he stepped inside.

"Nice dog," he said. "When did you get her?"

"After the break-in," she said with a shrug.

"So, you did have an intruder. Damn."

He closed his eyes for only a second. When he looked at her again, he noted she was watching his face.

She was so reserved, tonight. Not the smiling, happy woman he knew. She was upset. Upset enough to get a German Shepard puppy.

Has she moved on? Can she see my regret?

"I got your phone message only an hour ago," he said. "I couldn't use my phone before then."

"Yeah, I heard your message when I got home from the pet store," she said.

He shook his head. "Why didn't you call me back?"

She shrugged.

He raked a hand through his hair. "I was worried."

Her tone brittle, she said, "Well, you're a little late to be worried. The break-in was days ago."

His shoulders fell. "I was deployed."

"And you couldn't say, 'Hey Christie, I'll be away'? Don't wait for me Tuesday night. I can't go to the range?"

"No, this time I couldn't," he said. He had to make her understand. "Sometimes . . . we can't. The order comes, and there's no time. We must leave right away."

He wanted to reach for her, to hold her, but this was important. They needed to straighten this out. He wanted to work things out between them, but if she couldn't accept this part of his life, there wasn't any point trying. Because it would never work long term. And the headspace she was in right now would be stuck on repeat.

"That's a Navy SEAL's life, Christie," he said, his voice roughening. "Not every woman can handle that. It's especially hard on wives and children."

She was silent for a moment, her narrowed gaze still studying his face.

But then she squared her shoulders. "I can handle it. I have a dog now, and I'm going to get a gun. I don't need a man to protect me."

Is she saying she doesn't need me? Doesn't want me around? Is it over between us? What we have is good. Worth fighting for. If she'll fight for us, with me.

He watched her, assessing.

The defiant way she'd spoken, made him wonder.

She wasn't the fighting type, and she'd had no training, just one visit to a gun range.

He noted the way her jaw, jutted just a little, as she stood there, holding her dog.

Despite what she'd said, it didn't look like she was handling being a SEAL's girlfriend very well. She had that 'my feelings are hurt' look some women got.

"Tell me about the break in," he said, wanting to know, and wanting to straighten things out between them. "You sounded terrified, being in the house with an intruder."

She put the dog down.

Lacey started sniffing his feet, but she had stopped barking at him.

They both watched her for a moment.

"I was terrified," Christie finally admitted, opening to him to share her story. "I stayed very still under the covers and hoped he didn't know I was awake."

Froze, he thought. *What she did was freeze.*

He'd seen how she reacted to danger. Hunker down and hands over her head was her go to. He would bet she'd had those covers over her head, shaking. That was not good.

But he could train the freeze out of her . . .

"So, you stayed real still," he said. "Then what happened?"

"He stopped at the foot of my bed and watched me."

He sucked in a breath. Fought the surge of anger that rose swiftly inside of him. He'd been holding it back, trying to listen.

It was always harder to listen when you got angry.

"How do you know it was a man? Did you get a good look at him?"

"No, but most burglars are men," she said.

"Don't be so sure," he said. "It could've been a woman."

She crossed her arms. "Well, this burglar, whatever he, or she was, stared at me."

Damn. She had to have been terrified.

"Then what happened?"

"He left. With all my jewelry. Most of it was costume, but he got a few nice pieces that were my grandmothers that could bring money."

"That really sucks, and I hate that it happened to you.

But I'm glad you weren't hurt."

"He got in through a window, but I had it replaced. And I got Lacey."

"Good. Sounds like you handled things well, and she's a great pup." He held out his hand to Lacey.

Lacey, done with sniffing Reed's shoes and barking at him, came near to sniff the hand he held down for her.

When she started licking his hand, Christie uncrossed her arms, and chuckled softly. "She likes you."

"Dogs always do."

Christie smiled, some of her hurt feelings over his desertion soothed now that she understood the cause.

He seemed genuinely regretful over the fact he hadn't been able to warn her.

Reed hadn't been playing mind games, he really had a job which didn't allow him to tell people where he was going and what he was doing, or when he would be back.

She believed him and trusted him. With her life. And he'd been nothing but honorable since she'd met him.

Reed sat on the couch, playing with the puppy while she watched.

If she'd thought he was handsome before, watching him play with the puppy made him even more attractive. Then it hit her.

I am head over heels in love with this man. Everything about him.

"I'm glad you have a guard dog now," he said. "You'll need to train her."

"I plan to," she said. "I already signed up for obedience lessons on Saturdays. Mrs. Brown was nice enough to agree to give me Saturdays off, starting next week. For several weeks in a row, which is a lot in the florist business. But she agrees I need to train Lacey. So, I'll be working late, on some Friday nights when she needs me."

"How late?"

"However long it takes to get the arrangements done."

"Sweetheart, it's time to get serious about getting the handgun you were thinking about. Since you can't take your new guard dog everywhere you go. And since I'm often called away, out of the country, I'd feel better, knowing you were taking measures for your safety."

Oh, he's worried about my safety. He must care for me.

The thought made her feel warm inside.

"I was scared when the guy broke into my house," she said. "I froze. What if I do that when I have a gun? The bad guy might take it from me, and then I'd be even worse off."

"That's true, you would," he said. "This is why we train. So, we don't freeze, and instead, go into the moves we've practiced. I can train you past the freeze point--if you're willing."

"I'm willing," she nodded.

"Good. Now let's talk about getting you set up with a security system. I could install it for you."

"Oh, that's a great idea. Thank you. My friend Tanya needs one too. Because of her crazy neighbor, Mrs. Vendt, who hates Tanya's cat and dog."

"I could put one in for her," he said. "After I set yours up."

"That would be great," she said.

"Turn on your laptop," he said. "And we'll look at some different set ups for security."

They spent the rest of the evening looking at things she could do to be more secure, and they talked late into the night.

It was good to have him back in her life, and to know he'd never really left her. But he had been deployed. And that made a big difference.

He was right, it would be hard when he deployed, but

she had Lacey now, for protection and companionship, and he was focused on making sure she would be safe when he wasn't around to protect her.

When he was with her, she was very happy, and he was present and attentive with her.

Before he left that night, they had a plan for her security. He would put up camera's, he would take her shopping for a handgun and would continue to train her on it. And she had Lacey, who had been very protective at first, when he had arrived.

At the door, before they said goodbye, he said, "I've missed you. The whole time I was gone."

"I missed you too," she said. "I'm glad you're back."

He dipped her into one of those sweeping kisses, like Diesel had swept Pippa at their wedding.

Oh my. He really did miss me, she thought. Then she forgot everything else but the kissing.

After two months of dog training, firearms training, and self-defense training, the woman Reed picked up for their Tuesday night date at the range looked the same, and yet different.

Christie still walked out the door in one of those sexy retro outfits, after punching in the code on the new alarm on her house, but instead of stepping tentatively on those high heels, she strode.

She strode in, wearing her new boots, like a woman who had confidence, who would look a man in the eye, instead of blushing and looking down. She was a perfect mix of feminine and aware. Not the first female a predator would target.

And that gave Reed great satisfaction.

She didn't have a victim's mindset.

After what had happened in the theater, and then the break in at her house, she could so easily have gone the other way.

He was glad she hadn't, and he was prouder of her than he could say.

She stepped into his car, and he waited until she was settled, before closing her door.

He could envision doing this for the rest of their lives, and soon, he would tell her so, and see what her thoughts were on that.

Driving to the restaurant for dinner, he asked, "Did the police ever find your jewelry, at any of the pawn shops?"

"No, they didn't recover a thing." Christie shook her head. "It's just gone."

"That's a shame," he said. "Have you thought about replacing things?"

"Yes, but I just haven't yet," she said. "I probably look plain without any jewelry."

She did look plainer, when he was used to her wearing her sparkling things, but she looked beautiful to him, without all of that. And he would make sure to tell her so.

"You look beautiful," he said.

"I just feel so bare without my jewelry," she said.

"Open the glovebox," he said, looking forward to seeing her reaction.

She gave him a puzzled look but then she reached for it. Opening the glovebox, she looked inside.

A small box sat inside.

"Open it," he said.

She pulled the box out and lifted the lid.

Inside were gold hoop earrings.

"Oh, wow! I love them!" she said, her eyes sparking.

"I had to ask the jewelry clerk for help," he said. "I told them retro style or vintage. I'm not up on all that. I told her you liked 40's and 50's style. Then she showed me a whole line of 1950's jewelry."

"You did great!" Christine said, "This is the style Marilyn Monroe wore! I could show you pictures."

He grinned. "I'm glad you like them."

"Like them? I love them," she said. She was already putting them on. "Wait till I tell Tanya!"

"I thought you could wear them to the cookout next weekend," he said.

"There's a cookout?"

"Yes. Now that Diesel and Pippa are back from their honeymoon and his deployment, they want to throw a big party. He's got a new grill to try out."

"Oh, that will be fun. I didn't really get to talk to her much at the wedding, but she seemed nice."

"She is," he nodded. "You can invite Tanya if you'd like."

Tanya kept telling Christie that she wished she could meet a hot Navy SEAL and Christie had finally mentioned it to Reed.

"Oh thanks, she would love that," Christie said. "Wait till I tell her. Is it next Saturday?"

"Sure is," he said.

"Perfect."

Christie moved her head from side to side, looking at her new earrings in the mirror over the dash. "These earrings are perfect too."

"I'm glad you like them," he said. "They look great on you. It's good to see you looking so happy."

She beamed at him, and he smiled back.

"I wish every day would be a perfect day like this one," she said. "I love it when we have a day together."

He would be away from the base, training soon. SEALs were always training, somewhere.

"I like spending my days with you, too," he said.

He was almost ready to talk to her about their future, but still he held back. That old dear John letter had done a number on his head. He knew it but hadn't kicked it yet. Another week or two couldn't hurt, if he wasn't deployed before they talked about it.

"Picnics are one of my favorite things," she said, still beaming.

Learning her favorite things gave him satisfaction because then he knew how to surprise her and bring that sunny smile more often, which was rapidly becoming one of his favorite things to do.

~

Tanya rode with them to the barbecue and was attending as their guest. Reed introduced her to Diesel and Pippa, their hosts and then to a few of the guys. It was clear she loved meeting all these SEALs, but she appeared thunderstruck now and she stood looking past him and Christie.

Someone had arrived and she was frozen to the spot.

Reed turned and saw "Casper" standing near the gate to the back yard. He should have known. The man had a way of entering a room and leaving it without anyone knowing he was there. It was a rare and valuable skill set which saved lives. He should have been in the CIA, but maybe he had been, or still was.

Christie turned to look too, after seeing the reaction of her best friend. "Oh, that's Casper," she said to her.

"Casper," Tanya whispered. "Is that his real name?"

"No, that's his nickname," Reed said. "Given because he can enter a room without you knowing he is there."

"How cool," Tanya said, clearly in hero worship mode.

"His real name is Scott Roberts," he said. "Come on, I'll

introduce him to you."

Eyes wide, Tanya just nodded, then she walked with him to where Scott stood.

Christie stayed where she was, watching them.

I've never seen her like this. Tanya must have it bad for Casper. The last thing she needs is another female nearby when they meet for the first time.

It appeared that Casper was as delighted to meet Tanya as she was to meet him.

Soon Reed was back by her side. "Those two hit it off well," he said.

"I could tell that from way over here," Christie said. "Is he a good guy?"

Reed gave her a look. "I wouldn't introduce her to one who isn't," he said.

"Good, because I don't want her to get her heart broken."

"I wouldn't want him to, either." Reed gestured to the tables full of food. "Ready to fill a plate?"

"Yes, more than ready," she said.

They enjoyed burgers and brats on buns, potato salad, coleslaw, baked beans, corn on the cob, and sliced wedges of watermelon for dessert.

When they finished, Reed said, "Want to go for a stroll?"

"Yes, of course," she said.

He gave a signal to Diesel, and they headed for the gate.

"What did you tell him?" Christie asked.

"That we'd be back shortly," he said.

"It's fascinating the way you guys can talk to each other without speaking," she said. "Do you use that all the time?"

"When it's needed," he said.

She smiled at him, and he threaded his fingers through hers. "Have I told you how pretty you look tonight?"

She shook her head no.

"Well, you do." He made a note to himself to tell her that

more often. He wasn't used to a girly girl for a girlfriend, but Christie lit up his world in a way he had never known, and he needed to make sure she knew it.

"It's the earrings," she laughed. "Have I told you how much I love them?"

"Only about twice a day since I gave them to you."

"I've been wearing them everywhere, even to the grocery."

"Then I must have done something right," he said.

"You do more than something right," she said. "You do all the things exceptionally well."

He got that grin in the corner of his mouth that she loved to see. It went with the assurance he had, being a SEAL.

Giving her hand a squeeze, he stopped and turned to face her. "I'd like to talk about our future."

Our future?

She stood still and caught her breath, holding it.

"I'd like you to be my woman on a more permanent basis, if you're comfortable with that. Sort of a pre-engagement period. Let's try it for a year and see where it takes us. No pressure, just more of what we've been doing."

"So, you won't see any other women, like in other ports, the way some of the guys do," she said.

"I would not. For me, there would be only you," he said.

"And I wouldn't see anyone else either," she said.

"Good," he nodded. "If you decided that you wanted to, you would tell me and only then would we see other people. It's going to take good communication to make a long-distance relationship work, and with a SEAL that's what you will have. I'll be there when I can, but sometimes, I can't."

"I understand," she said. "Yes, this is what I want, too. Let's try it."

"Excellent," he said. Then he bent down and kissed her,

deep and long.

When they came up for air her heart was racing. They would have to walk back soon. Tanya had ridden with them, and they would need to take her home.

Reeds cell phone buzzed. He looked at the text. "Casper is giving Tanya a ride home if that is okay with you," he said. "Though I don't know why he would need your permission."

"It's our code thing," she said. "Ask him for her word."

He typed in... Code word.

In a minute he got back... girdle. He showed the screen to Christie, and she laughed.

"Why girdle?" Reed asked. "Or is it a secret."

"That's her code for cut me out of my girdle now, I want to get naked with this man."

Reed laughed. Then he paused, looking at her and asked, "Is that a code word you use, too?"

"Not me," she shook her head. "That is all Tanya. My code is lipstick when I want to kiss a guy, and slow dance when I want to make love. I'm more of a make love than a get naked kind of woman."

"Slow dancing. I like it," he said. "So, Christie, now that we have the evening to ourselves, how about a little slow dancing?"

"Yes," she said, her smile spreading over her whole face. "I have been dreaming about slow dancing with you."

"Then by all means, let's make that dream come true." He winked at her.

Then hand in hand they walked back to say goodnight to their hosts, moving faster this time as both were rather impatient to get to that very special dance.

THE END

ACKNOWLEDGMENTS

Thank you to all who helped make this book possible.

To USMC veteran Jacob Romo for the class on situational awareness, and self defense classes. To USMC veteran Charles "Tazz" Welshans for advice on Marines and gunfights. To Army veteran, Robert Arrow, aka Bobby, my gun instructor, friend and sometimes co-writer. I could not have written these gun scenes as well, without you.

To Navy SEAL veteran Bill Hellman, for advice on SEALs and guidance with developing my new Green Brotherhood: SEAL Team XII series.

To all previous editors and early readers of my novella, *Split Screen Scream,* which was the seed for this revised story, *Real Movie Hero*, and the new series. You wanted to read more of the story and now, here it is, with a SEAL Team of twenty men and many more stories to follow.

To Sheri L. McGathy, my cover artist, for all the covers for the new series and the series logo.

To my assistant, Melissa Ammons, who helps me with numerous things, so I can write.

Thank you to my family, and especially my husband, for love and support through all these years together, for the adventures and journeys we have taken and are still taking, and for making it possible for me to write so many books. May the adventures continue.

Special thanks to my readers.

I love you all.

SAVING THE BELLYDANCER

*For "Sabeya" aka Francesca Sabeya Anastasi, founder of
International Shimmy Mob,
and for all my Shimmy Mob bellydance sisters.*

It has been an honor, to found Shimmy Mob Memphis, in the inaugural Shimmy Mob held on May 1st, 2011. Each year, I get goosebumps, seeing my sisters all over the world dance. Each of you are a shining light and together we light up this globe. I thank you with all of my heart.

*It is to each of you, my dance sisters, shining your lights, along
with Sabeya, that I dedicate this book,
Saving the Bellydancer.
May your light always shine*

1

2011

Little Creek, Virginia

Navy SEAL Antonius (Tony) "Cutter" Cuttino slid his six-foot frame behind the wheel of his red Corvette. Starting the car up and then shifting gears, he pulled the car out of the garage, and down the driveway, before backing into the street.

As he headed to Chicks Oyster Bar, he thought about his buddy's upcoming wedding.

Cutter getting married will change everything.

Change, however, was a part of life.

Chicks Oyster Bar, located at the Marina, was a big SEAL hangout. This was where the guys would throw the bachelor party. Many SEALs married bartenders or waitresses they'd met there, and women looking to meet a SEAL knew it was a possibility that one of the fit, handsome guys who frequented the bar was a SEAL.

Cutter had met his share of women at the bar, but none

of those get togethers had lasted more than a month. He hadn't been looking for anything long term. He'd entered the Navy, wanting to see the world first, without having to worry about a family, or a permanent girlfriend.

His grandmother was still living, and other than a large group of cousins, she was the only family he had in the states to come back to. His job as a SEAL suited his adventurous soul.

Still fit, and mentally sharp, his grandmother had her circle of friends and stayed busy, though she was always happy to hear from Tony, or be surprised by his visits.

Thinking of her, he reminded himself to call her tomorrow, before the day was over.

Reed Tindall "Railroad" aka "R.T." would soon be getting married to Christie Anderson, a cute little floral designer who worked at Floral Blessings. R.T. had lucked out meeting Christie. With her blonde hair and curves, she looked like a gorgeous pin-up girl, and wearing 1940's style dresses and heels which was her big hobby.

If Cutter had been as lucky as R.T., and met a woman like Christie, he might have considered a permanent relationship too. He wouldn't want her to get away.

Glad he hadn't met the woman of his dreams yet; he was happy for his friend.

After Becky, the girl who'd sent him a chickenshit Dear John letter, Cutter made sure none of the girls he dated lasted longer than a month. He had fun, he treated women right, but he wasn't about to get tied down. He made it clear that their fun was for a short time only. Anything else was a deal breaker. He wasn't about to get his heart broken again by another damn letter.

It was easier for a SEAL not to have a girl to worry about back home. There were women to be found in every port in the world. It wasn't as if he lacked female companionship.

Being a SEAL, and a tall dark and handsome Italian American, he drew women like a magnet.

R.T. had been a carefree single man too, until meeting Christie. Then no other woman caught his eye. That was a sign, if anything were, that they were meant to be. But the couple had an unusual first meeting story.

They'd met at the movie premiere of the Cole Kennick movie, Stand and Deliver, when they'd sat next to each other. A live shooter had entered the building.

R.T. had taken out the shooter, and then had to apply tourniquets to two men, before they bled out.

He'd saved Christie's life, and then talked her through applying the second tourniquet, to save the second man's life. The way she'd handled herself, had him seeing a side to her that drew him in, beyond her blonde bombshell looks.

Afterward, he'd seen her safely home. From that night on, they'd dated constantly, and she became the only woman Railroad was interested in.

Christie kept saying it was the worst and the best day of her life. While it wasn't R.T.'s worst, he never talked to her about the worst day of his life, he agreed with Christie that it was the best day of his life too.

Cutter had been with R.T. on the worst day of his life, and had been one of the ones to save R.T. One of the team. They'd been on that mission together, and all come home together, which was nothing short of a miracle. It had knit them all tighter together then anything else would, or could have, and that bond of brotherhood was now unbreakable.

Each man would be celebrating this wedding with everything a SEAL had in him, because each knew how short and precious life could be. This meant it was going to be one hell of a party. For many reasons.

First was the theme. The bridal party would all be wearing 1940's style clothing.

Cutter looked forward to seeing the ladies dolled up, and to swing dancing which sounded like fun. He'd never done any swing dancing, but Christie had arranged for an evening lesson for the whole wedding party.

Cutter was a quick learner, like most SEALs.

He'd have yet another skill to add to the ever-growing list of things he knew how to do. Watching his grandmother in her thirst for learning, he knew it was a lifestyle, and a way of thinking, that would keep him young. She seemed younger than her age, and her high spirits had a youthful way to them.

Tonight, he was meeting the guys at the bar, and getting the scoop on what else was planned for the bachelor party they were all looking forward to. It would, of course, be at Chicks, and involve shots, stories, and maybe a challenge or two.

Partnered with one of Christie's 1940's group friends, Cutter looked forward to dancing. He watched as the first couple, who taught the dances, demonstrated the dance they'd be learning.

Swing dancing was well named.

He watched the couple swing around the floor, the man swinging the smaller woman, as if she weighed hardly a thing.

R.T. had a great big grin on his face, as he looked at his fiancé.

She wore a glow which was undeniable. Anyone viewing the scene, could have picked out the bride to be, as they both were clearly in love, and she wore that glow that well-loved women often take on.

R.T. couldn't keep his hands off her, something Cutter

wasn't used to seeing. It made him grin. *They were like a couple of teenagers.*

Cutters dance partner was a dark-haired girl with blue eyes. He'd always been drawn to dancers, loved their legs, and the way they moved, so normally his dance partner would've held his attention and interest, but their chemistry was off, and her high-pitched laugh grated on his nerves more than a little.

But when the music started, he set that aside and concentrated on learning the dance steps and moves, so he could swing his partner around the room.

At the end of the hour, it hadn't been so bad. He'd kept her busy dancing, not chatting, and the hour was up. It had been fun.

Though he'd be paired with whoever Christie desired to pair him with from the wedding party, he wouldn't be escorting her as his date. He'd find a date.

There was time.

Too bad he couldn't be paired with Tanya, Christies best friend who was beautiful, and fun to talk to. But she already had a boyfriend, so that was a no go.

It wasn't as if he had trouble getting dates. He'd find someone.

Local belly dancer "Zarifah" entered the dance studio late. She'd missed troupe rehearsal, and was supposed to stay afterward, to practice her veil solo, where she could use the two walls of mirrors and the large space.

Her apartment was much too small to spin around in with a veil, without knocking things over, and she couldn't do that anymore. Not with the porcelain figurines Hassan had given her decorating the rooms.

The beautiful gifts were too expensive, and treasured by her, to risk them, so she no longer danced in her apartment, even without a veil. She missed dancing there.

Amina, the studio owner and troupe director, saw her coming through the door and said, "I wondered where you were," then she took a few steps toward her, a frown coming over her face as she took a closer look, and saw bruises covering the left side of Zarifah's face. "Honey, what happened to you? Are you all right?"

"He came back. Last night." She spoke quiet, though there was no one else in the studio to hear her. It was still hard, sharing what had happened, even with one of her closest friends.

"Oh no. Honey, who did that to you?" Their eyes met, and then Amina's eyes widened, as she realized who had done it. "Hassan."

"Yes." Zarifah nodded. "Luckily, my neighbor, Mrs. Dieter, called the police. Or I might not be here with you tonight. He was so very angry."

"Come in," Amina gently touched her elbow, to guide her in, and then pulled her hand back, as if afraid she might hurt her. "Was that okay? I don't want to touch you where it hurts."

"Yes. I'll be fine. I'm just a bit beat up at the moment." She gave a slight shrug.

Though this was a different kind of bruising, Zarifah had grown accustomed to bruises left by gymnastics, when she was young and still learning. Her sights set on the Olympics, she and her coaches had pushed her hard back then.

Bruising happened. You got over it.

She set her jaw, summoning that determination which she'd learned at a young age while training for the Olympics.

Amina pulled a chair around for her. "Sit. Rest. I'll make us some tea. Then I want you to tell me what happened."

"Okay." Zarifah sat, but didn't relax in the chair. She hadn't relaxed, since the night the man she'd thought she loved, who she thought had loved her, had turned into a monster. She wondered if she would ever relax again.

Amina loved tea, and any excuse to make it. Tonight was no exception. "Chamomile this evening, I think. It's a soothing tea. Sound good?"

Zarifah nodded, and then watched her friend, as she readied the small, portable tea maker, pouring water into it, before starting the water to boil. Once the tea was ready, Amina would want her to tell everything that had happened with Hassan.

Hopefully the bruises will be gone before our next performance. If not, I'll have to bow out. Hassam will get his wish, if I'm not dancing. I don't want anyone taking photos, or video of me looking like this.

She had to tell Amina, and she also needed to tell her that Hassan was dangerous, in case he ever showed up near any of the other dancers.

They were used to him, and wouldn't see him as dangerous, so everyone needed to be told. It wouldn't be right to keep it private, and keep them in the dark.

Security at the venues in their dance schedule wouldn't have seen him before. She'd run through the list of places in her head, on the drive over, to remember if he'd ever come to watch her dance at any of them. He hadn't.

She wished she hadn't burned all her pictures of him last night, and blocked him on social media, when she'd been too upset to think she might need one photo of him. She'd been thinking she never wanted to see his face again.

They would have to find a picture of him somewhere, somehow. To give to security.

Maybe Amina can help.

It was important that all their dance sisters be safe.

~

Cutter was running late, for the first half of the bachelor party, at the Sweet Kitty Kat Club, and didn't want to miss the main event. They would watch the girls, and then move on to Chicks, for drinking games and hot chicks.

Being on the SEAL teams meant you could be called away on short notice, for a good long time, and called away often. That made it hard on girlfriends, fiancés and wives. RT had worried that Christie might not be able to deal with the lifestyle. But she was sure she wanted this. Time would tell, but they had a good chance of making it last.

Christie was a good woman. R.T. had made a wise choice in her. She was a real cutie, with her retro pinup outfits, and good girl next-door good looks.

The wedding party would be in Navy dress uniforms for the men, and the women would be in vintage dresses, like Marilyn Monroe would have worn. The kind that showed off all their curves. Cutter was all for that look, and looking forward to all the eye candy at the wedding.

He couldn't have been happier for the couple. RT was happier than Cutter had ever seen him, and Cutter could envision the two of them as a happily married gray haired couple in their twilight years together. He wanted that too, when he grew old.

But that was far into the future. He was living in the now, the today. Because that was all anyone ever really had.

Tonight, Cutter was running late to the party, but with any luck, the headline dancer wouldn't have started yet. He enjoyed watching dancers, with their long legs that could

228

wrap around a man, and their toned bodies, which moved in ways that made him think of moving with them in a more intimate way across the sheets.

Dancers were hot. This first half of the party at the strip club should be good.

He sped up, his mind on long legged females stripping.

While he was glad for R.T., and their other buddy, SEAL Tanner "Diesel" Taylor who had a wife and two kids now, he wasn't ready to find his own wife and settle down. He was too busy having fun in between deployments. Dating strippers was part of that fun.

~

The next morning, Tony's cell phone rang, the vibration mode making it dance on the nightstand.

He reached for the phone. His eighty-year-old grandmother was calling, so he answered. "Good morning, grandma," he said, as he glanced at the stripper sleeping next to him in his bed.

"So Tony, when are you going to come home and see your grand-mamma?" his grandmother asked.

"Who's on the phone, baby?" Tawny asked. She ran her hand up his thigh. "Come here."

His grandmother kept on as if she hadn't heard the woman. "Nicki has three babies already, and you never even married."

He turned away from Tawny, stood up and walked away, holding up a finger to her to wait. "Yes, Grandma, I know. Nicki has a new baby every year. I'm happy for her. She deserves the best."

Nicki was a neighborhood girl he'd dated in high school.

Tawny got out of bed, and started pulling her clothes on.

He watched her naked body, as she covered it with clothes, while he listened to his grandma.

Tawny had a great body. Long, sexy legs. Big breasts that bounced. She'd also gotten drunk last night, after they got to his place, and had been wild, as strippers often were. One thing he liked about them.

He rolled his left shoulder, feeling the scratches she'd made across his back. Those long silver painted fingernails of hers were killer. He'd made her scream a few times. Noisy sex that could wake the neighbors.

He walked into the other room, to be further away from her, as he talked to his grandmother, so he could pay better attention to his grandmother as she continued to talk.

"When you gonna get married, Tony. I want to be holding my own great grand-babies, not somebody else's," his grandmother said. "You gonna get yourself killed, doing all that crazy stuff. I want you home soon. Marry. Have lots of babies."

He laughed. "Grandma, I'm not ready for marriage yet. The girl has to be the right girl, you know?"

"I know you're too picky," she said. "What one you have there with you this morning? Is she even Italian?"

Tawny was a hot blonde, with blue eyes, and was not the kind of girl he would bring home to meet his grandmother.

Definitely not Italian.

"Not Italian. I need to take her home, grandma. I'll call you later on today."

"Okay, Tony," she said. "But don't forget about your old grand-mamma."

"I would never forget about you, grandma. And you are not old. I'm planning to visit you soon. We can talk later."

"Okay, you go and take that one home. Then find one you can marry. I'm not getting any younger, you know."

"I love you grandma," he said.

"I love you too, Tony boy."

"Talk to you soon, grandma. Bye bye."

"Okay, bye bye." She hung up the phone, and then he hung up.

She was only person he knew that he said, 'bye bye' to. After his parents had passed, his grandma was all the family he had.

An only child, it was up to him to carry on the family name, and give his grandmother some grand-babies to fuss over. She was right; he did need to visit her. But not with a potential wife. He could fly home for a weekend, and then fly back. He had plenty of leave, and as she'd said, she wasn't getting any younger.

When he got back to Tawny, she'd crossed her arms, and was giving him the stink eye expression. Why, he didn't know, as he'd thought the sex was good last night, for both of them.

"So your real name is Tony?" Tawny said. "Is there a reason you told me your name is Cutter, not Tony?"

"That is my name. They're both my names. Call me Cutter," he said.

"But your grandma calls you Tony," she said.

"That's right."

She took out a cigarette and lit it. Something she hadn't done last night. But he'd realized once they were naked in bed, that she was a smoker. Because smoke wasn't just on her clothes from working in the club. Once she removed all her clothes, and he began kissing her skin and her lips, he could taste that she was a smoker.

He would never marry a woman who smoked. It was a real turn off for him. He regretted inviting her back to his place last night.

Maybe his grandmother was right, he needed to start dating a different kind of woman.

"I'm ready to go," she said. "You gonna buy me breakfast?"

"Sure." He reached for his keys. "Where do you want to go?"

"There's a waffle place, around the corner from the club."

"Okay." He nodded. "Let's go." He'd feed Tawny, drop her off at her car, say goodbye, and then, make sure she drove away safely. But first, since he needed a date for the wedding, and he was out of time, he'd ask her if she'd like to go.

She seemed to have a thing for SEALs, and had mentioned she'd dated a SEAL before. Then she'd peeled off her top, revealing those marvelous breasts, and walked toward him. Watching them bounce, he'd forgotten about her comment.

Now he wondered who the guy was.

~

"Here you go." Amina handed Zarifah a cup of hot tea. Sitting back in her chair, she put her full attention on Zarifah. "Now, tell me everything. From the beginning. I only knew that you had called off your engagement to Hassan."

"From the beginning." Zarifah took a deep breath. "Okay." She nodded. "The reason I called off our engagement," she frowned, paused, and then decided to start over.

Amina patiently waited for her to get on with the story.

"From the moment Hassan put the ring on my finger, everything changed," Zarifah said. "He changed. It was as if he was a different person."

"Oh no," Amina said.

"He did *not* want me dancing." Zarifah frowned.

"He didn't? I thought Hassan loved your dancing," Amina said. "He was always enthusiastic, usually clapping the loudest, and he came to all our shows, and was encouraging afterward." Amina's face showed her surprise.

Apparently, Hassan had fooled her too.

"Oh, he loves it all right. But only for him." Zarifah shook her head. "He said I would only dance in private, for him, from now on. And, from now on, meant, right this minute. Not after we got married, not after the shows I've already committed to."

"If you need to pull from a show, I will understand," Amina said. "It's okay. Just keep coming to the studio to dance with us. We would miss you terribly if you left."

"No, that's not what I need," Zarifah shook her head and frowned. "Hassan is unreasonable. *He* is the problem. He insisted I would not wear a belly dance costume, outside of his house, or ever dance in public again, after we were engaged."

"Ah. His Middle Eastern upbringing is coming out." Amina nodded. "That's how he was raised. Wives don't dance, except in private at home, or with other women. Not even at weddings. The only dancers there are the hired belly dancers. He doesn't understand it's different here, in the United States. These are cultural differences."

"Very true. He seemed more open minded when we were just dating. Never showed any signs of this kind of attitude before." Zarifah's forehead crinkled. "I had no idea he would change like he has. He couldn't seem to understand that I have commitments. That I'd agreed to do shows, and I'm on troupe contract. I can't just drop everything, because he snaps his fingers, and says right now." She shook her head. "And I can't marry a man who expects me to jump, just because he says jump."

"No, you can't." Amina shook her head, along with Zarifah, agreeing with her. "Wives are partners, not trained dogs."

Zarifah continued with her story, telling it for the first time, to a good friend. "So I knew I couldn't marry him. That was the conclusion I came to, about us, and I told him the next night, after he still wouldn't see reason and change his mind about my dancing. When there was no talking it out, I said, 'I can't do this any more. You won't listen to me, or discuss this reasonably. I can't marry you.' I called the engagement off."

"Well, you had no other choice. It's a good thing you called it off, before you were married," Amina said.

Zarifah remembered how she'd held out the ring to Hassan, to give it back, but he hadn't taken it.

He wouldn't even look at the ring.

"I took the ring off to hand it to him, but he wouldn't take it," she said.

"Oh no." Amina's tone held dread for what was likely coming next in Zarifah's tale.

"He said, 'You're just nervous. It will pass. Brides get nervous. You are my betrothed. My perfect jewel. I have been searching for you for years, and now that I have found you, I will never let you go'," Zarifah said.

Amina's eyes widened. "Never let you go. Oh that does *not* sound good. Not when you are calling things off, and *want* him to let you go."

"I was in shock. Speechless. I just stood there with my hand out," Zarifah paused, shaking her head. "He ignored my hand, the ring, my shocked expression, and he acted as if everything was normal. Then he kissed my cheek goodbye, told me to get some sleep, that I'd feel better in the morning, and he was out the door, before I could even think what to do next."

"Wow." Amina sat back in her chair, as if she too was shocked.

"It was as if he didn't see me, or hear me, beyond the role he wants me to be in. I didn't know what to do. He hurried out the door, and I was sort of stunned."

"Sort of? That would shake any woman. Especially after pulling a Jekyll and Hyde switch you weren't prepared for. Of course he took you by surprise."

"Maybe he's never seen me. I mean really seen me." Zarifah shook her head. "Maybe he never saw past the dancer, to see the real me."

"I think you are right," Amina said. "He sounds like one of those who wants the dream, not the real woman. He sees Zarifah, the dancer, his beautiful dream girl. Not Edith, the woman behind that image."

This was true.

Zarifah was her dance name. Dance was only a part of who she was. But it was a part that she loved, and which brought her joy.

He saw no problem with her dropping everything, and just walking away.

She would never do that. Besides being their troupe director, Amina was her friend. The other dancers were her friends. But even if they hadn't been, she wouldn't go back on her promises and her commitments. She wasn't that kind of person.

This major problem between them, which had made her step back to take a closer look at him, and where things were headed, had changed her mind completely about marrying him.

She was an American belly dancer, with American sensibilities, living in the United States of America. Freedom was on an upper rung of the ladder of importance in her life. She could never marry a man who thought he could order her about, as if he owned her.

"Did he want you to give up teaching gymnastics too?" Amina asked. "Or just dance?"

"He didn't pay much attention to me teaching gymnastics," Zarifah said.

"No? But that's your job, and also very much a part of you."

"True." Zarifah nodded.

It was very much a part of her, more than her dance persona.

Edith Smith was her real name, and the one everyone associated with gymnastics. Trained from a young age, she had competed with an eye on Olympic gold, until she began to sprout up, taller than the other girls her age, her arms and legs growing so fast and awkward, in just one summer.

The tallest girl in her elementary school class, Edith felt gangly and awkward, not graceful. She would grow tall, and be more suited to basketball, than gymnastics. That's what her coaches had told her, as they'd turned their attention to younger, shorter girls, while dashing cold water on her dreams.

Now she taught gymnastics to children, and was much kinder to them than her coaches had ever been to her.

Belly dancing was a fun hobby on the side.

Belly dancing was freedom.

Dancing, she competed with no one, while her gymnastics background gave her a unique style of dance, as the other dancers were not as flexible as she.

"It sounds as if you really didn't know him either," Amina said. "He didn't show you his true colors, until now. And he didn't want to know the real you. Marriage to him would've been a major disaster."

"Yes, it would have," Zarifah agreed.

Dancing was where she felt most free. And she would never have given it up for Hassan.

She'd kept her dancing separate, using her dance name in public, and few people connected the two sides of her life, unless they were close enough to her for her to tell them.

Hassan had fallen for the dancer side. He'd been completely uninterested in the other side. He'd never seen her at work, never wanted to hear about it. She taught small children, that's all he cared to know. All he'd said after he'd asked her what she did for a living was, "Good. That means you will be a good mother, when you have children of your own."

They hadn't discussed whether she wanted to have children or not. She wouldn't mind having one or two, but it certainly wasn't what drove her. She had a career and a hobby, and both took large chunks of her time. She'd been too focused on building her business to even think about having children of her own, and she loved what she did.

The driven, competitive, athletic side of a woman who'd nearly gone to the Olympics as a child, that strong, female businesswoman wasn't what Hassan wanted. He wanted a woman he could control.

Zarifah could not be anything but what she was. Nor did she want to. She was very much a gymnast, and she loved to dance with her troupe. If he couldn't love her for who she was, she knew she had to call the engagement off.

Amina had been silent, listening, but now she spoke again. "So he walked out, leaving you holding that beautiful one-karat diamond ring with two rubies. Then what happened?"

"I overnighted the ring to him the next day, so he'd have to sign for it and accept it."

"Good. Smart lady." Amina nodded.

"I couldn't keep it. I don't want anything he gave me. But listen to this," she pulled her cell phone out of her bag and hit play.

Hassan's angry voice message played. "Zarifah, you do not throw my gifts back in my face with your messenger. You do not send your messenger to me, making me sign. I do not accept this. We are still engaged. You do not treat me like this!" His voice rose with each sentence as he became angrier.

"Oh no!" Amina had a horrified look on her face.

"He kept calling my phone, but I started deleting his messages, after this one, and didn't listen to any more of them. Then it got real quiet, and I thought he was done." She took a sip of tea, and swallowed, for her throat had gone dry with what she had to tell next.

Amina said, "Oh no," and patiently waited for Zarifah to go on.

Zarifah took a deep breath and continued. "He showed up at my apartment, and somehow got in. There's no sign of breaking and entering, and I could've sworn I locked the door. I *always* lock the door. But he came in, some way. He had the ring, and insisted I put it back on." She paused, frowning, remembering.

"Did you put it on?" Amina asked.

2

———

"No." Zarifah shook her head. "I refused. The rest is a blur. After I refused him, he got even angrier. He was very angry. It, well, it escalated. He started pulling my hair, so I couldn't move away, and he started hitting me."

Her eyes gazed off, away from Amina, as she relived the events in her mind.

Hassan had grabbed her ponytail, pulling her close. His brute strength was too much for her long slender arms, more used to dance and gymnastic flips, then to fighting.

She'd never had to fight anyone before, had never hit anyone, so she didn't know how to fight. She'd tried to pull away from him, but his grip only tightened. The more she struggled, the harder and meaner he'd fought, hitting her.

It was her screams that had brought a neighbor pounding on the door, calling out to her to answer, asking if she was all right.

Lost in her memories of that night, and losing her story telling ability, she stopped telling her story, and looked down at her tea.

How do you explain what happened to you, when someone

you loved, who was supposed to love you, turned into a monster, and started hitting you without stopping?

Amina's hand closed over hers. "I understand. You don't have to tell me the rest, if you don't feel like it. I understand."

It was her kindness that allowed Zarifah to break through. The same way she pushed through with gymnastics training when she was bruised, and aching, and tired.

She told the rest of the story quick and flat, without emotion, to push through to the end.

That neighbor had called the police.

Luckily they had a patrol car just around the corner, and the police had arrived at her apartment complex within minutes.

Hassan hadn't stopped hurting her, until the police showed up, shouted 'Police!' and then kicked in the door, breaking in, and pulling him off her, taking him down, putting him in handcuffs to take him away.

He'd been charged and put behind bars. Now she had a restraining order as well.

"Oh honey," Amina squeezed her hand. "I'm so glad you're safe now. I'm so glad the police came in time to stop him and take him away." She held Zarifah's hand briefly, until Zarifah pulled her hand back, no longer needing the comfort.

She was usually quite independent. She didn't want to be pitied.

"I'm all right," she said. "The police came in time. He went to jail. I've pressed charges." She picked up her phone again, and hit the delete button on her phone messages. "I gave this to the police. I don't need to hear it again. Or read his texts. They have copies of those too." She looked up at Amina, who had tears of sympathy in her eyes. "I have a restraining order on him now. He won't be allowed to come near me again."

"I'm glad. And I'm so glad you're all right." Amina paused, peering at Zarifah closer. "You're sure you're all right?"

"Thank you." Zarifah nodded. "Yes. I'm sure. I talked to a counselor this morning, and she pointed me in the right direction."

"That's good." Amina nodded. "Do you feel up to dancing tonight? Or are you ready to go home?"

"Yes, I want to dance, and I *need* to dance. It helps to dance things out," Zarifah said.

"It does." Amina smiled. "I know how that can be. Is it all right if I stay and watch?"

"Don't you need to get home to the kids?"

Amina had three children, under the age of ten, at home. Remembering how Hassan had said she ought to be home with her children, not running a dance studio, Zarifah pushed the thoughts and memories of him out of her mind. They'd crept in, and she wasn't going to allow that any more.

"Not tonight, I don't." Amina said. "Grant has taken them to visit his mother, and he can put them to bed after they get home."

"Okay. Then stay and keep me company," Zarifah said. "I'd like that. You can critique, and point out all my flaws."

Amina just smiled and poured herself more tea.

Zarifah rose and then, taking her veil out of her bag, she set her music to play and began to move, ignoring the stiffness and pain as she warmed up, moving through her dance solo.

Moving through the movements, stiff parts of her body loosened, parts she'd been keeping still, after she'd been hit. Moving through the air with her veil, changing the dance, instead of sticking to her choreography, she added gymnastics moves as familiar to her as sleep. Moves that were strong and sure, movements as natural to her as breathing. Even the aching parts felt good, while somewhere deep in her soul, something released that needed to be let fly, something that spoke of freedom in body and in spirit. Caught up in the music and the dance, she forgot Amina was there, watching. She danced until she danced the memories out, along with the pain.

When she was done, she stopped; breathing hard, and then finally remembered her friend, who was still sitting in the chair, watching while silently sipping her tea.

"Perfect," Amina said, tears shining in her eyes. "Beautiful and perfect."

On a different day, Zarifah might have argued with her. She rarely thought of anything she did as perfect, and was good at finding flaws in herself, an attitude carrying over from her challenging childhood.

But tonight, she simply let those loving words from her friend sink in, soothing her, and sent her a soft smile with two soft words. "Thank you."

They collected their things, and started shutting down the studio for the night.

"There was something I'd wanted to talk to you about tonight," Amina said. "But then I wasn't sure if tonight was the time. I think now it is."

"What is it?" Zarifah asked, her curiosity now fully piqued.

"Have you seen the post about Shimmy Mob on the internet?" Amina's brown eyes shone with excitement as she pulled her long brown hair into a ponytail.

"No." Zarifah shook her head, her long black hair brushing her bare shoulders. "What's Shimmy Mob?" She reached in her bag for a big hair clip to pile her own hair up.

"It's an event to be held in May, on international belly dance day, all around the world. Everyone will dance to the same song, doing the same choreography, and there's a

Shimmy Mob t-shirt everyone will wear. Each city team who signs up, will be raising funds for our local domestic abuse shelters." Amina's excitement could be contagious, and today was no exception.

"That sounds fantastic. But I've never heard of it before." Zarifah wanted more information before she committed to this project. "And you say it's all over the world?"

"No one has heard of it before," Amina laughed. "Because this is the first year for it. It is brand new!"

"How cool!" Zarifah was starting to catch the excitement, but then she caught herself. "Wait. You said 'our'. Does that mean we are doing this Shimmy Mob?"

"Yes! I just signed our city up, and agreed to be team leader. Dancers will sign up to dance. It's less than fifty dollars, and you get the music, the dance moves, a hip scarf and a t-shirt. So, let's do this!"

"I'm in. Sounds like fun, and all for a good cause!"

"Great! Amina's smile spread even wider. "Will you be my assistant?"

"Sure." Zarifah nodded.

"This is going to be awesome. It will help lots of women and children," Amina said.

Zarifah nodded again, and her thoughts drifted back to the night Hassan hit her. "I hope we raise a lot of money, and can help as many women and children as possible."

"I do too," Amina said. "And we will!"

As they headed outside, both excited about the upcoming Shimmy Mob, Zarifah reached into her purse for her new key ring with the pink pepper spray tube.

"Oh how cute. Is that a lipstick case?" Amina asked.

"No," Zarifah smiled. "It's my pepper spray."

"Oh!" Amina's face showed her surprise, and then she smiled too. "That is a great idea, to carry one of those."

"I just bought it today," Zarifah said. She peered into the

darkness, hoping her ex-fiancé was still in jail, and not outside in the dark, waiting. She held the pink tube on her key ring, ready to spray anyone who came at her. She looked over both tense shoulders, heart racing.

"I'm glad the police took him away," Amina said, her calm voice helping to settle Zarifah's nerves, centering her in the present.

No one is waiting to jump out at me. Good.

But she couldn't help the feeling that Hassan would come back, angrier than ever, and hurt her again.

"I know you're nervous, honey, but he's behind bars now," Amina said.

"He will have made bail," Zarifah said. "He has plenty of money, remember? He could be out now."

"I'll watch you walk to your car, from now on," Amina promised. "We will all look out for you. And I'll have security at the show notified, and will show them his picture. Do you have a photo of him I could use?"

"No, I burnt them all, and deleted them off my phone. I blocked him on social media. I was so upset; I didn't think to save one photo to show anyone. I just wanted to never have to see him again."

"Well, if he is on social media, then I can find a picture of him. Call or text me, when you get home safe, okay?"

"Okay," Zarifah said.

"Thank you," Amina said.

Amina gave her a quick hug, and then they hurried to their cars.

Zarifah unlocked her car door, climbed in, closed the door, and then locked it right away. Only then did she exhale some of the tension she'd carried with her through the parking lot.

Maybe now that she'd had tea with Amina, and told her everything, she would be able to eat dinner. It had been a long day, and she was tired and suddenly quite hungry.

She could never eat before dance practice, so her dinners were often quite late, and her appetite quite large. But she hadn't felt much like eating since Hassan had attacked her.

Now it seemed her appetite was back.

~

Cutter stood inside the wedding chapel, taking it all in. The chapel was fully decorated with deep red flowers, delicate white baby's breath flowers, and dark blue ribbons. Against the dark wood of the chapel, it was tastefully elegant, and yet overflowing. Cutter had never seen anything like it. It was both patriotic, and very romantic and wedding like.

Christie worked at Floral Blessings Floral shop, and the owner, Mrs. Brown, who was sitting in the pew where Christie's mother and grandmothers would have sat, was the closest to family of anyone in Christie's life. The gray haired woman loved her like a grandmother. So, she'd done all the floral decorations as a gift, and they were stunning.

Cutter approved.

His grandfather had run a small nursery, and his grandmother loved flowers, so Tony had grown up with knowledge of them. Something he rarely talked about. Like a lot of things. He would however, make a point of letting the older woman know that the flowers were well selected, and well done. And he'd tell his grandmother about them. She would approve of the flowers. She would not approve of his date.

He glanced at Tawny, who cleaned up quite nicely, in a little black dress that showed off her curves. No one but he, knew she was wearing absolutely nothing beneath it.

She'd told him, the minute he'd picked her up, so she could tease him with it all evening.

For now, he had to keep his attention on his duties, as part of the wedding party. He was paired up with Lorrie, the hairdresser who'd done Christie's hair for the occasion. A thin white ribbon was part of that hairdo.

Lorrie saw him looking, and whispered, "Christi's garter is made from that ribbon. With a red bow added. I dare you to catch it."

He gave a brief shake of his head. No way was he catching any garter, or letting anyone think he'd be the next man to get married. That wasn't part of his immediate future game plan. And though he was a leg man, he really didn't need to watch his buddy's new wife hike up her dress, to show off her legs. Throwing the garter was one tradition that should've been done away with by now. It reminded him of stripping, and that made him think of sex.

Cutter liked women. A lot. And he dated lots of women. But he was particular about certain things. He was clear and up front about what he wanted. One reason he liked dating strippers, was that they could be up clear and up front too, and were usually sexually uninhibited.

Sex was never a problem for a SEAL.

Finding the perfect wife? That could be a problem.

R.T. had gotten lucky in that movie theater. Today, he looked like the luckiest man on the planet. Christie was a keeper. One look at the two of them, and you could see this was true love.

That's what Cutter wanted when he did marry. He wouldn't settle for anything else.

The ceremony was soon over, and pictures of the wedding party were next.

Tawny, who'd been waiting for him in the back of the church, slid her hand onto his arm when they were done with photos, and whispered, "I want a word in private with you. Don't let anyone see us."

Stealth? Oh yeah. I can do stealth.

He held back in the hallway, and then turned them toward a small room. "Go ahead," he called to Osprey. "We'll catch up with you at the reception."

Osprey nodded, watching Tawny.

Cutter gave him a short shrug, and then Osprey walked away.

Pulling his hand, Tawny tugged him into the empty room, and then hiked up her dress, showing him her bare body below her waist. "Let's do it here," she said.

"In the church?" he said.

She's a wild one. Not one to take home to grandma.

"Sure," she said, pulling her dress up enough to expose her breasts, which popped out with a bounce.

Despite his immediate reaction to the sight of her, he was not going to do it with her in the church. That seemed more than a little disrespectful.

"You know you like it," she said, and she wiggled her ass, which made her breasts bounce. "I'll be ready to go, any time. Keep that in mind, big guy. Weddings make me horny. Let's do it."

"Later," he said. "We've got to head to the reception."

She pouted. "Not even a quickie?"

He shook his head no, not amused by her little girl pout.

"Then find us a spot on the way," she said.

He pulled her dress down. "Later, Tawny. We've got to go."

Her pout grew bigger.

Losing his patience with her, he turned to head for the door.

As he'd expected, she hurried to follow him.

"Okay, okay, we can do it at the reception," she said. "Find us a spot."

He didn't respond to that, he simply said, "Come on."

She stopped pestering him about it, and grabbed hold of his left bicep. "I love your muscles." She squeezed his arm. "They feel so good."

None of this was having the affect she likely intended, as it had become very clear that Tawny was not the right woman. She was a 'for right now' kind of woman, and at this point he wasn't even sure about the "for right now" part.

They reached the reception, and Tawny was once again polite, and nice to everyone, with her sexual vibe tuned away down.

But for Tony, it was too late. He wasn't ready for sex at the reception. He wasn't ready for sex with her anywhere. He'd finish the date this evening, and then he was done.

Osprey and several of the other members of the team had eyed him, when he walked in, but nobody said anything to them about being the last ones to arrive. They hadn't been late.

Through the dinner and the toasts, everyone laughed and had a good time.

To Cutter, it was a visual delight, with many of the women in the retro theme, which included the ladies in wedding party with their dresses, and even some of the guests.

When the time came for the garter toss, Cutter reluctantly got in with the group, but toward the back.

He watched as R.T. slid that garter off his new bride's leg to a saucy tune and whistled, as she blushed becomingly.

Yeah, she's hot.

He did not want to get turned on by his buddy's girl. That would not be cool.

He caught Tawny's gaze.

She winked at him.

Then the toss was up, and the single SEALs, and other single guys were shouldering each other, some trying to get the garter, some trying to avoid it, and others trying to push their buddy to get the garter.

It was up, it was down, it bounced off one guy's hand, who maybe didn't want it, and then fell down into the crowd of men, which made them look down for it, as if they were looking for a rugby ball amidst all the pushing and yelling.

Crap it's on my leg!

Lifting his knee he attempted to soccer knee punch it up, toward someone else.

Not going to touch that thing.

One of the other guys grabbed it.

Whew. At least that's over.

Tawny had watched the whole thing with a smirk.

He was fairly certain she didn't want to marry anyone either.

She was taking a class during the day, and stripped at night to pay her bills. She claimed to love stripping.

He watched her run her tongue around her red lips, a signal that she wanted him, right here, right now.

Damn

He headed for the bar, needing a drink.

"I can see why you didn't want to catch the garter, with that one watching," Kik said to him, low enough no one else could hear, as they waited for drinks. "You know she's dated SEALs before. Before you came onto the team, there was a big stink over her. Bar fights, slashed tires. It got real ugly. She'll fuck any guy who's earned a trident. Sometimes in the same night."

"Damn," Cutter said.

"Yeah," Kik said. "Just thought I'd warn ya."

"Thanks bro," Cutter said.

"Always got your six," he slapped Cutter on the back.

Cutter wondered who all she'd slept with. Suddenly any desire to sleep with her again withered. He was done.

He went up to Kik again. "So, which ones?"

"What?" Kik asked.

"Which SEALs?"

"Amigo, you really want to know?"

3

———

"Yeah." Cutter said. "I want to know."

"Trevor, Bales, and Magnum, Team two. Oscar and Buzz," Kik said.

"Our guys?"

Kik nodded.

Oscar and Buzz were on SEAL Team twelve, but they weren't at the reception.

"Our guys fought?" Cutter wanted to know what happened, and why none of his team had said anything to him about her before.

"Fought back," Kik said. "They didn't start it. But none of them will touch her now. Field is clear, if you want her."

Cutter grunted.

"That wasn't a happy sound, bro," Kik said. "Woman trouble?"

"Nah. I'm done after tonight."

"Smart," Kik said.

"How come none of you told me about her?"

"Didn't know you were still seeing her," Kik said. "Figured after the show was a one-night deal. She don't stick with anyone long, bro."

Diesel and Pippa's two beautiful children were running around laughing and ran past them, followed by their dad.

Bryce at three years, and Julie at one year, were both pretty darn cute.

Cutter glanced over at their mother, who was talking with Christie and laughing.

Christie and Pippa were two beautiful women.

He glanced at Tawny. Eyeing her and the other women, and wondering how many other SEAL's Tawny had been with, made her now appear less attractive.

She couldn't match the inner beauty of the two women, which shone through everything they did, and said.

Tawny was down and dirty sex. With everyone apparently.

Christie and Pippa were the take home to meet mama, or in his case, grandma type of women.

Tawny was fast and exciting. Does she use sex to reel men in? If so, she's good at it. And she's fun. But there were other ways of having fun.

The way Diesel and Pippa carried on, the two of them were still having fun, after being married a few years, and having two kids.

RT and Christie certainly were, as newlyweds.

Maybe dating a good girl could be fun too, if you found the right one.

The thing was, he'd gotten used to having fun with wild girls, and wasn't sure how to find one of those good girls.

They wouldn't be hanging out in strip clubs.

He needed to stop getting distracted by all the long-legged dancers in the clubs.

Sitting back down at their table, he reached for his glass of bourbon, and finished it off.

"Did you find us a place yet?" Tawny asked low, her hand moving beneath the tablecloth to his thigh, her fingers caressing his muscle. "I need you. Watching all those sexy men, jumping for that garter, really turned me on."

"Some women find SEALs really hot," he said.

"Hot blooded women," she whispered in his ear, and then flicked it with her tongue as her hand kept searching. When she found what she was looking for, her hand squeezed.

Then she released him and sat back with a smirk. Her eyes watched him, like a cat watching a mouse, before she glanced around the room, cool as if nothing had just happened.

His mind was on what she'd just done, and what she might do for him now, if he wanted her to and now, he couldn't stand up and move away from the table, without anyone noticing his reaction to her.

He needed another drink. He handed Tawny his empty glass. "This SEAL is overheated. Get me a drink."

"Just the way I like you." She grinned. "Hot, overheated, thirsty, and bossy." She stood, and carrying the glass, walked toward the bar.

Diesel moved into her vacated seat. "I don't need to guess where you picked her up."

Cutter shrugged. "Yeah, she gave me her number at the club, so I called her after the party, and she came by my place after work."

"I should've warned you about her," Diesel said.

"Kik just did." Cutter shrugged. "It is what it is."

"You ever dated a woman who wasn't a stripper?"

"Sure," Cutter said. "Plenty of girls."

"Since you became a SEAL," Diesel said.

"Nope." Cutter shook his head.

"I sense there's a reason," Diesel said.

"I had a steady girl, when I was in training. We lasted until the week I graduated and earned my trident. She broke up with me the day before, and she didn't even attend the ceremony. She had a new boyfriend. One who could take her to the movies every weekend, not one she had to wait for."

"Damn," Diesel said. "So, she broke your heart."

"I'm over it." Cutter shrugged. "Good girls deserve attention. I get that."

"Yeah, it can be hard on them," Diesel said.

Both of them knew the odds on marriages with SEAL team members. Many didn't stick together, and those that did, often had problems.

Diesel and RT were lucky, and they knew it.

"We've worked hard on our relationship," Diesel said. "You don't see it, because we don't talk about it. We've even gone to marriage counseling, to get some things straightened out, to be able to communicate better."

"Wow. I'd never have guessed."

"Well, the night we met, we were both wearing masks, we didn't know each other's names, and though we'd had great sex, we hadn't talked much. Add in a couple years, and the son we share together, and we were starting from a very unusual position."

"Yeah, I can see that." Cutter nodded.

"But everything is great, now," Diesel said.

"That's good to hear, man," Cutter said. "Maybe one day I'll have that too. Kids, a house, and a dog. The whole deal."

"First thing to do, is stop dating strippers," Diesel said. "How about you try something else for a change? Pippa got tickets to an Arabian nights belly dance show next weekend. A friend gifted her with three tickets, but we're not taking Bryce. Three is too young to sit still through all that, and Pippa needs a night out, away from the kids."

"Yeah, I'd like to go, but are you sure Pippa wants you to invite me, instead of one of her girlfriends?" Cutter said.

"Yes, she just told me to come over here to ask you."

"Cool, then yeah, sure. Sounds like fun. The only belly dancer I've seen was at a strip club. She was hot."

"No way, bro." Diesel shook his head. "Pippa has informed me, that real belly dancers never take off their clothes. Those girls are just strippers wearing another stripper costume, with Velcro to play that character."

"Got it." Cutter nodded, just as Tawny walked back, with his drink.

"Here you go," she sat the drink in front of him.

"I'll get back to my table," Diesel said. "Chat with you later."

Cutter gave him a thumbs up.

When the dancing started, Tawny wanted to dance, so the minute the floor opened up to everyone, they headed to the dance floor. He knew she'd be a good dancer, and she was surprised at how good of a dancer he was.

Soon the floor was full of SEALs dancing with their wives and their girlfriends.

As the evening went on, Cutter realized that not only did Tawny like to dance; she was ready to dance with every guy there. He went to the bar for a drink, and she kept dancing. Not that he cared. He'd already decided this was their last date.

That nice little old lady, Mrs. Brown, who'd done the flowers, was sitting alone, smiling with tears in her eyes as she watched the dancers.

He walked up to her table and pulled out a chair to sit next to her.

"Quite a party, isn't it?" he said.

"It surely is," she said. "My Jeff and I, we used to really cut a rug." She dabbed at her eyes and then smiled at him, before putting her embroidered handkerchief away. "He passed several years ago."

"Mrs. Brown, I'm Cutter," he said, "Though my grand-mother calls me Tony. Just don't use that one around the guys."

"It's nice to meet you, Tony," she said. "Thank you for sitting here with me. I was falling into sadness, missing my Jeff."

"Any time, Mrs. Brown," he said. "I wanted to compliment you on the beautiful floral arrangements you designed. They're stunning."

"Why thank you." She beamed at him.

He noted how her face, now lit with happiness, was looking years younger than when she'd been sitting there with sadness creeping in. It made his heart happy to cheer her.

"Here's something the guys don't know about me." Cutter said. "My grandfather used to run a nursery, and they delivered to flower shops in several counties. It was quite a thriving business in its day, before he passed. I used to follow him around, helping, when I was a small boy. So I know a few things about flowers. I know you chose some very expensive, high quality roses for the arrangements, and you put a lot of love into them."

She'd sat listening to him, her happiness growing with each word. "Well, I love Christie like a daughter, you see. So she had to have the very best. She trusted me to surprise her. It's my wedding gift to her."

Being that Christie worked in the Floral Blessings Flower Shop with Mrs. Brown, she would know the value of the flowers, and the care that went into the display as well.

"I'm sure it touched her heart in a way that will be with her all her life," Cutter said.

"Thank you for your kind words," she said. "There's more to you than handsome, and strong." She tipped her head, and asked, "How does such a caring young man end up with such an uncaring woman?" She glanced over to Tawny, who was dancing with yet another SEAL, this time grinding her body in a dirty dance. "She's not behaving honorably toward you. Though you have toward her. You've been a gentleman."

"Well she's a stripper," he said. "Not my girlfriend. She's just my date for this evening."

"Usually it's the girls who settle," she said. "I see it all the time." She paused, and looked down at the wedding napkin, with the date and the name of the couple in silver across the top.

He knew she was implying that he was settling, instead of finding a good woman to marry. She and his grandmother would get along well.

"This one will last," she said. "I've been to many weddings, and can predict them well. It will last, because he is a high value male, and she is a high value female. And it will last, because they value each other, and don't pull on each other's value, bringing it down. That is the recipe for a long and happy marriage."

"I hope it lasts. They seem very happy," he said.

"It will," she said. "And you, young man, you just have to find your high value female. And then value each other, and lift each other up."

"I'm not quite sure where to find her," he said.

"Just like flowers," she said. "Look for the fields where high value flowers grow."

Watching Tawny embarrass herself on the dance floor, as she got drunker, Cutter decided he'd better go see if he could salvage the situation. The happy couple didn't need any scenes at their reception, and he was starting to suspect that Tawny not only liked SEALs, she liked them fighting over her.

"I'd best go see to my date," he said. "Thank you for your

company, Mrs. Brown." He took her hand in his, and gave it a gentle squeeze. "I've enjoyed visiting with you."

"Thank you, Tony," she said. "You find that high value girl, you call me, and we'll send her some flowers. Start you off on the right foot with her. Young men have forgotten how to send flowers to girls these days, unless it's a holiday, or they are apologizing. Simple bouquets seem to be out of fashion. My Jeff, he brought me flowers every Friday night, on his way home from work. Little bouquets usually. But oh, so full of love."

Now he was feeling emotional, and blinking moisture away from his eyes. "Thank you Mrs. Brown. I think your Jeff sounds like a great man. Reminds me of my grandfather."

She patted his hand. "I see it in you too. You're a high value man, and don't you forget it. Especially when rescuing that date over there."

He laughed. "I will."

She stood up to go. "I'm heading on home now. These parties get wilder, the more they drink, and then they get louder. I've had about all the loud my tired ears can handle tonight. Enjoy the rest of your evening."

"You too, Mrs. Brown. You too."

She made her way to the door, and he moved toward the dance floor again.

Tawny had a drink in one hand, and her other on one man's chest as she danced around him. For the first time since Cutter had asked her back to his place, he regretted that he'd asked. Not just asked her to the wedding, but asked her to go anywhere.

"Hey big man," she said to him when she saw him. "You took too long finding us a place to get it on, and I'm too turned on to wait, while you talk to some old woman." She started to run her hand down the other man's torso toward his crotch.

"You're drunk, Tawny. Are you ready to go?" he asked. He'd take her home, to her home; do the right thing, since she was his date. Be the gentleman. Even though she wasn't acting like a lady.

"No, I'm not ready to go home. I told you I wanted you to find a place here, and do me."

"Not going to happen, Tawny," he said.

"Well, if you won't, he will," she said, her hand patting the man she couldn't keep her hands off. "Jeff's a Marine. He can finish what you can't."

"That so."

There was no point to tell her that he didn't want to finish. She was drunk, and starting to cause a scene.

Someone needed to have a talk with Tawny, about being a high value woman. She didn't value herself.

Then it hit him what Mrs. Brown was trying to tell him.

By bringing Tawny to the wedding, he wasn't valuing himself.

"Cutter. You don't cut nothing," Jeff said, his chest puffing out. "Tawny needs a real man. So, I'm cutting in."

It sounded like Tawny wasn't the only one who was drunk. This was not cool to be happening at his friend's wedding, and it was his fault for bringing her.

"Everything cool, bro?" Kik had come up behind Cutter, covering his six.

Cutter was not going to fight over Tawny. "Yeah, it's cool. She isn't ready to go home. I offered." He shrugged.

"I don't want to go home with him," Tawny said, "I want to be with Jeff."

"You want to be with Jeff," he said, confirming what she'd said.

"Yeah, you heard me," she smirked, running her hand down to Jeff's crotch.

"Then be with Jeff," he said with a shrug. "Our date is officially over."

Her jaw dropped. "Wait. What?" She appeared stunned he wasn't fighting for her.

"I said our date is officially over," he said, and then nodded at them. "You two have a good evening."

Kik clapped him on the back, and the two of them walked away together.

"You handled it. I wondered at first, if Christie and R.T. were going to have wedding memories of a brawl on the dance floor," Kik said.

"Naw, man. She's not worth it," Cutter said. "I gave her the chance to stop acting like a slut, and go home and sleep it off, but that's not what she wants. And I'm not going to put up with a brawl at our brother's wedding."

"You okay, bro?" Kik asked.

"More than okay. I'd rather hang with you guys anyway. She requires a lot of attention."

Kik laughed. "Yeah, I could see that. Hey, there's a new bet going around the base, that you haven't heard about."

"What's the bet?"

"The bet is, who she's gonna do here, and in what room. They say she's got a thing for going at it in all sorts of places. Closets and rooms in busy buildings, empty houses in new subdivisions when there are tours, that kind of thing."

"Yeah, she does," Cutter said.

Kik gave him a look. "So about that church..."

"Yeah, she would have. But I made her wait," Cutter said. "Then I decided I'm done with her for good."

"You're doing the right thing." Kik reached the table where Fen, Big Mac, Matt, and Diesel were hanging out. "I'd hate to have to explain to our commander, why one of our best guys is ruining his career, by hanging out with the wrong chick, in the wrong places."

Cutter pulled out a chair. "Hey," he said to the others. "What're you guys jawing about?"

"You," Big Mac said. "Was wondering when you'd get fed up with her."

"You've never brought one of your girls to any of our events," Fen said.

"Mostly, I've taken them back to my place, or theirs for the night," he said. "But I'm done with all that."

"Stay out of the strip clubs, son," Matt said. "They are your downfall."

Kik spoke up. "Not any more they aren't. He's done."

Cutter shot Kik a glance, and Kik nodded at him, backing him up. Letting him know he supported the new choices Cutter was making.

"Good to hear, bro," Diesel said. "Pippa and Christie will be happy to hear it. They asked me if we had to invite her to the barbecue on Memorial Day. I told them hell, no."

"Yeah, she was out of line tonight," Cutter said. "Don't worry, I'm not gonna bring her."

He'd known he could do better. He just hadn't tried. Because the last high value girl he'd gone with had nearly ripped out his heart.

But was she a high value girl, or just a good girl? A high value woman would have waited. Would have come to my graduation.

They'd both been younger back then. Enough years had gone past. He very much wanted a woman with whom he could share parts of himself that he'd kept quiet about.

Like his grandparents, the nursery, other experiences and interests he had. It had been nice talking about them with Mrs. Brown tonight.

Sex was great, but when you were done, it was nice to be able to talk about stuff, and just enjoy each other's company.

That had been missing in his life for a very long time. He didn't want a woman who just saw him as a SEAL, and was only with him because she thought that it was hot to date a SEAL.

He had a new goal. To find a high value woman who would care about his heart, not just the hard body that housed it.

The rest of the evening he spent drinking with the guys, putting Tawny out of his mind, which it turned out, was quite easy.

4

―――――――

Two nights after Zarifah had shared her story with Amina, she was with the troupe again, in rehearsals at the studio, getting ready for their Arabian Nights show.

Student dancers who weren't in the troupe, were in the studio as well, and would rehearse after the troupe was done.

Zariah noticed other dancers eyeing her arm. She'd put heavy stage makeup on tonight, and had covered the bruising on her face, hiding most of it. But the biggest bruise on her arm was highly visible. Makeup wasn't going to cover a bruise that purple.

She rubbed at it briefly.

"Does it hurt?" Amina asked with concern.

"A little. But mostly it's ugly." She looked down at it. "I should get some of that makeup that covers tattoos. The kind actors use. But I'm not sure what it's called, or where to find it."

"It will soon be healed, and no one will see it by Shimmy Mob day," Amina put her arm around her. "There's time. It's one month away."

"I know. I just signed up last night," Zarifah said.

"That's great!" Amina's face lit up.

"One month isn't long to learn the dance," Zarifah said.

"It's not." Amina agreed. "But I only just found out about the event myself, and I signed us up as soon as I could."

"Well, we've learned other dances in less time." Zarifah shrugged. "So I guess I shouldn't worry. We can do it!"

"That's right, we have," Amina said. "And we'll all be learning the dance together. This event allows brand new dancers to join in, too, so we might be teaching some of them the moves. I'll probably need all of you to help the newer students learn one on one, since we don't have much time, depending on how new they are. It's hard for a brand-new dancer to learn from a video. They've got to learn the right posture."

"I remember my first class. You kept saying tuck your tailbone!" Zarifah laughed. "And I was a gymnast, so I didn't have posture problems. I remember what it was like to be new to this dance though, and I'll be happy to help the new students."

"Yes, you didn't need as much instruction as some," Amina said. "I'm so thankful for your help with Shimmy Mob and your help with teaching the new dancers. The first thing we have to do, is to get the word out to all the dancers in town, and ask them to sign up."

"Yes! Are you announcing it here, tonight?" Zarifah knew Amina hadn't told any of the troupe dancers about Shimmy Mob yet, and usually she told the troupe any news before she told the other dancers. This time she hadn't.

"Yes. I made up these fliers last night." Amina showed her a stack of fliers. "Can you hand them out, while I make the announcement?"

"Sure." Zarifah reached for them.

"Thank you." Amina handed her the fliers and then clapped her hands. "All right ladies! Attention please."

One of the women made the high-pitched "lelelelelele" zaggahret sound, and the eight women all hushed immediately.

"I have some exciting news!" Amina began. "We are holding the first Shimmy Mob event in our city. How many of you have heard of Shimmy Mob?

No one raised their hands.

"Shimmy Mob raises awareness of domestic abuse, and raises funds for our local domestic abuse shelters. It is an international event taking place all around the world on International Belly Dance Day."

"I didn't know there was an international belly dance day," Bayda said. "How exciting!"

"There is," Amina said. "And we're going to show the world what we can do. We'll be dancing to the same song, doing the same Shimmy Mob choreography, and wearing the same Shimmy Mob T-shirts, along with our dance sisters all around the world." she smiled.

"I just got goose bumps," Farrah said. "This is so wonderful."

Zarifah could see them on Farrah's light brown skin. She'd worked for the Peace Corps in Thailand, and had met her extended family on her mother's side. Her dark eyes shone with excitement at the news of Shimmy Mob.

"I got them too," Zarifah said.

Farrah sent her a happy smile.

Zarifah waited for Amina's nod, to hand out the fliers. She was excited to be involved in this new project, and so glad she hadn't given up her dancing for Hassan. If she had, she would have missed this wonderful event, and sharing the experience with her dance sisters. Her thoughts moved away from him.

This event would unite their group with their dance sisters all around the world. And they would be helping women all around the world to escape from dangerous situations, like the one she'd been rescued from. It was more than exciting. She had goose bumps, and a good feeling about the event.

How close she had come to being married to Hassan.

What if he hadn't changed until after the wedding?

She couldn't imagine what it would be like to live with a man like him. To be married to him. Horrible was one word that came to mind. Dangerous was another.

Too many women found themselves in dangerous situations. Now there was something she could do to help. They could all help.

"This is an important cause," Bayda said. "I'll do anything I can to help. I'm so glad we're doing this."

Amina nodded. "It is. I'm thankful for your help. I'm the team leader for the event, and Zarifah is my assistant team leader. One of the things we're supposed to do, is spread word about the shelter. Let women know what is out there for them in our area. Raising awareness for the shelter is one of our goals. But first, we need to know what those options are. Zarifah, can you research that info for me?"

"Sure. I'd be happy to. I already have a head start because the counselor I talked to gave me a brochure for one place."

"Excellent." Amina addressed the entire group again. "Ladies, I'm going to turn this over to Zarifah, so she can share her story with you. And she has fliers for you as well."

Zarifah started to hand out the fliers, and to talk about what had happened to her. When she was done, she realized her friend had given her something to keep her busy, while she talked, which had made it a bit easier to do the telling.

Now that she'd shared her story, she found that telling them had been easier than she'd thought.

The women's hugs, their tears, and their concern for her right now, told her how much these women cared. They were her dance sisters, soon to be her Shimmy Mob sisters.

Goose bumps covered her arms.

This seemed to be becoming a thing, getting goose bumps in connection with Shimmy Mob. It was pulling out her feelings in a deep way. She wondered if that was just her, or if any of the others were feeling it too.

Amina smiled. "Thank you, Zarifah." She turned to address the group again. "We have to get the music, and the choreography, and start practicing," she said. "Once you sign up as a dancer, and pay the fee, you'll get access to the website section for our team. The dance is on three videos there, broken down into three different dance styles."

"Three? Oh boy," Bayda said. "I only know one."

"Most dancers only know one," Amina said. "A few know two. So we're all learning at least one new style and moves. Parts one and three are Cabaret, and part two is ATS or American Tribal Style with Tribal Fusion. But don't worry. Everything is on the videos. The choreography is broken down so we can learn it a section at a time. Then there's a final video with the complete run through to the music. Once you've signed up, I'll set up a schedule for rehearsals."

She walked over to put music on for tonight's rehearsal.

"But now ladies, we have a show to get ready for, so we need to get started on our rehearsals. Please remember to take a few extra fliers at the end, before you leave, and hand them out to invite all your dance friends to dance with us. Post them up where you can. Shimmy Mob welcomes beginning dancers."

The circle of dancers around Zarifah began to thin, as they moved back to where their starting places where.

Amina started the music, and dancers glided out into the middle of the studio floor to begin to dance.

Everything went smoothly, and then the student dancers collected their things before leaving. Only the eight troupe dancers remained. Amina, Zarifah, Farrah, Latifah, Bayda, Nasheeta, Saba and Isis.

Her closest dance sisters.

Troupe dancers could each teach, and could take on paid gigs when those came in. They often met separately to talk about troupe business, and met socially as they enjoyed each other's company.

Zarifah hadn't been taking any paid gigs, since starting to date Hassan, because to him, paid dancers were like prostitutes.

The moment he asked her, "You do not dance for pay?" with that look on his face, and she'd said, "No, I only dance for fun. I like the music, and dancing with the other women." The expression on his face had cleared. That was apparently acceptable to him.

She wished now, that she'd said, yes, instead.

One small lie, though she'd justified it to herself, by telling herself that from that moment on she didn't dance for pay, so it wasn't really lying, had set up their relationship on a path she should never have been on. Maybe, had she fully disclosed then, she'd have seen the real Hassan in the beginning.

Neither of them had been fully honest. So neither of them could realize they were not suited for each other.

She would never make that mistake again.

One small lie, even a lie of omission, at the beginning of a relationship, is like building a house with a small hole in the foundation. All the pieces aren't there.

If she ever decided she was ready to date again, she wanted to make sure neither of them left any of the pieces out.

Both men and women should be fully themselves when

they were together. No veils between them, no acting, or playing games.

The next guy would have to be completely himself.

If she ever went out again. Something she wasn't sure about.

The guy had better be rock steady, all American, and never try to curb her independence.

Cutter had called things off with Tawny, and had already had to turn down her offers for a quickie three times in two days. He wondered if she was a nymphomaniac. Yeah, she was good at sex, but he needed more than that. Maybe he'd needed to meet a woman like Tawny, to make him more aware of that. His cell phone buzzed again and he looked down.

Tawny.

He wasn't going to answer her this time, and was done with being polite.

No contact. That's the best practice for cutting off anyone who is so persistent. Because they take any response as encouragement.

Likely some men would give in, if she tempted them enough.

But Cutter wasn't like most men. He'd proved that joining the SEAL team.

If she liked dating SEALs so much, then she ought to be used to this by now. He wasn't the only guy on the team with enough self-control to cut her off.

Once he did, he'd heard a few more stories.

She was trouble, once she got her hooks into a man.

He deleted her text message, and then called his grandmother.

When she answered the phone, he said, "Hey grandma. Thought I'd check in on you."

"Tony boy! I love hearing from you," she said. "You didn't forget your old grand-mamma."

"Of course not, grandma. I could never forget you."

"They're not sending you across the pond again, are they? To that desert of vipers?"

"No. They're not sending me anywhere, yet. I thought I might come out and visit you. You know, before they do send me somewhere."

"I would love that," she said. "Will you be here for dinner?"

He laughed. She always asked him that, when he said he was coming over, and she loved to cook for him. Even in her eighties, she still loved to cook for the people she loved. "No, grandma, not that fast. I'll get my flight schedule, and tell you soon. Just had my leave approved, and wanted to give you the dates first."

"Oh that is good. Let me sharpen my pencil. The led just broke from so much excitement."

He heard the whirl of an electric pencil sharpener and grinned. She was always breaking pencils because she pressed so hard.

Going to his grandmother's house was like stepping back in time with her old-fashioned utensils of all kinds. But she loved her electric pencil sharpener. Sometimes he wondered if she broke the pencil leads on purpose, just to use it, or if she really did press that hard every time she wrote.

"Now, it's sharp again, like you, my sharp grandson. Now, I'm ready."

"Okay grandma. I have a whole week. So I'll have plenty of days to visit with you, and to fix anything around the house that needs fixing."

"That's good. There are a few things."

"Make a list for me, so I can see it when I get there." She didn't know text, or write emails, but he could always count on her to write an old-fashioned handwritten letter. The letters were things he'd treasured over the years, and now filled a sock drawer in his bedroom, along with other mementos.

"Yes, I'll do that," she said.

He gave her the dates next, and then she told him about her day, the neighbors she'd talked to, what she'd bought at the grocer, what she was making for dinner. When she started in on the nice girl she wanted to introduce him to, he said, "Love you, grandma, but I've got to call the airlines now, and buy my ticket. I'll call you again tomorrow, after work."

She could sometimes be hard to get off the phone, but he knew it was just because she missed him, and was lonely. He knew what it was to be lonely. That was one reason he'd kept going out with strippers.

If he could have talked his grandmother into moving out to be near him, he would have. But she was stubborn, and she loved the home she'd lived in for years, while her health was still good, and she got around.

He understood stubborn, it was where he'd gotten that trait from, more than likely. A family trait. One that had helped him to get through his training.

She still drove herself, in her old white Cadillac, which would likely be a collector's item one day. While he was there, he'd check on her car. He started making a list of his own, of things to fix while he was staying with her.

After rehearsals were over, Amina gathered the troupe dancers together in the corner and said. "Remember, we're supposed to meet an hour before the Arabian Nights show, to try on the new costumes that are coming in this week."

She turned to Zarifah. "You can update me on what you've learned about our Shimmy Mob dance site options then."

"Sounds good. What color did you order for me?" Zarifah asked.

"Red, of course," Amina said. "Like always."

Zarifah smiled. She did like red.

Everyone said it went with her long dark hair, and pale skin. The right shade of red would set off her blue eyes.

Eyes that Hassan had told her were prettier than the sea. He'd been full of complimentary words at first, before he'd flipped his switch, totally changing his way of treating her. He'd told her that she was his jewel.

She needed to stop thinking about him and his pretty words, and move on.

The Hassan she knew and had fallen for wasn't the real man. She'd fallen for a dream, as he'd tricked her, and the dream wasn't the reality, so now the adjustment was something she was having trouble getting used to, for her heart wanted that dream man who didn't exist. Her mind and heart were still adjusting to that, and it was taking longer than she wished.

Focusing on the new costume was one way to move on. Getting rid of a few costumes that reminded her of him would be another.

"I have some costumes to sell," she said. "Can you put them on consignment for me?"

"Of course, honey." Amina smiled. "Which ones are you selling?"

"The white and gold dress, the black and silver dress, and the purple bra and belt with skirt. Put whatever price on them you think is best. I want them to sell."

Understanding filled Amina's eyes. The gold dress, Hassan had bought her, and the other two were favorites of his. All three outfits were expensively beaded and expensive. They were her showiest costumes. He had called her his princess Zarifah when she wore them. She didn't want to wear those outfits again.

"I want to buy your white and gold one," Bayda said. "It's hard to find costumes that go with my red hair."

"I'd rather not see them again, even on one of my dance sisters," Zarifah said. "Sorry, Bayda. Otherwise, I'd sell it to you right now."

"It's okay. I understand," Bayda said.

Amina said, "Time for a new start. If I list them online, they'll sell faster."

"Then that's what I want to do." Zarifah nodded.

"I understand. You've got it," Amina said. "Your new costume will be here, just in time for your new start."

"Did you get me the gold sequined costume, or the silver?" Zarifah asked.

"The gold," Amina said. "I thought that combination looked richer with the red, than the silver. And a red veil to match, instead of gold."

The show's theme this year was Arabian Nights, and they'd all been excited about it. But Zarifah was no longer enamored by Arabian things, though she knew the others were. She would never daydream about sheiks again.

What she needed was an American man who understood her. A knight who would fight for her, not one who would fight her and hit her, and hold her back.

She wondered if Hassan still had the Arabian Nights show ticket she'd given him, and if he'd try to attend the show. She hoped he didn't, but how could she stop him?

The show was open to the public, and anyone who had a ticket could get in. It was a theater Amina had rented to put on their show.

The troupe dancers had never had a problem at a show before, and this one didn't have security guards. For the first time, Zarifah wished they had. She'd have to ask Amina about it later. Maybe Amina would have an idea of someone they could get to be security for the show that night.

She was busy right now though, as they were getting ready to run through the troupe dances that would be performed at the show.

"Everyone ready?" Amina asked, as she took her place in the front of the room. "We need to run through Nile Streams again, and work on better synchronization after the entrance number. So I'm going to play the end of the first number, and we'll work on that transition."

Once everyone was ready, they began, and Zarifah thought no more of Hassan, as she was swept up into the complicated dances, giving herself to them.

When she danced, she danced with her body, mind, and soul. It was a freer expression for her than gymnastics had ever been, and the thing she loved most about it.

She let the music pull her into that state of graceful Zen which dance gave her.

❧

Zarifah looked up from her seat in the green room, where she was sitting, while Bayda applied gold glitter over Zarifah's eyelids to enhance her stage makeup. Her own hands had been shaking too much to apply it herself, as her tension around whether Hassan would use his ticket to come see the show had her twisted tight with nerves.

Amina had hired a bouncer to provide security at the event, and the man who'd just entered the green room was a big brute of a man.

But Zarifah wasn't frightened of him. Instead, she was glad Amina hadn't hired some skinny guy.

She knew Hassan's strength. It would take a big man to subdue him.

Hassan was the one she was afraid of.

The bouncer had been given a photo of Hassan, and he'd been watching the crowd fill the theater seats.

She looked up at him, holding her breath, waiting for what he had to say, afraid to ask him what she was thinking.

Is Hassan here, in the audience?

5

———

"No sign of him," the bouncer said. "I'll keep watching. Just wanted you to know, before you go on. Ease your mind."

Hassan isn't here. Oh thank God.

Her shoulders dropped down, as some of the tension released. Now maybe she could relax, and just dance. "That's very thoughtful of you," she said. "Thank you for letting me know."

"You're welcome," he said and stepped back out again, closing the door.

"A man of few words, and big muscles," Bayda said. Then she giggled. "Real big muscles."

"It was nice of him to come and tell me that," Zarifah said. "Very thoughtful."

"He's all business, too," Bayda said. "Isn't that sexy?"

"I'm not looking for a sexy man," Zarifah said. "I'm going to stick to teaching gymnastics and dance. And just be happy being me. Since men can't seem to handle all of me."

"Because you are just so much awesome in one package," Bayda said. "Few men can handle that. Only a very special man will be able to handle so much awesome."

Zarifah laughed. "If you say so."

"It's good to see you more relaxed." Amina said. "Everything is going to be fine."

"Well, I do say so," Bayda continued, "You're awesome, and we all know it. Men are stupid." She reached into her bag. "Here, try this new perfume I bought. It has jasmine, and tiare flower scents in a nice blend." Taking it out, she handed it to Zarifah.

Taking the perfume bottle, Zarifah spritzed her inner wrists, waved one in the air, and then the other to dry them faster, and then took a sniff. "Oh, that is nice," she said. "I'll have to get some of that. Thank you."

"You're welcome."

Amina said, "Okay ladies, it's show time!"

They heard the intro music starting. There would be two short musical numbers to prepare the audience to step into an Arabian Nights world.

The energy in the green room was up, the dancers ready to perform.

Zarifah stood and started rolling her shoulders, beginning to do small warm up moves, to get her body ready. She stood, moving her knees back and forth, fast, in the small movements of a shimmy freeze. The green room was crowded, so her movements were small, but this shimmy freeze she always did before she performed, was more than a warm up for her knees. It was also how she sent tension out of her body, before going on stage.

The excitement in the room was catching, and she felt it even more so than usual, now that she was worried.

Now if she could just stop worrying about him, and just dance. The flips she did, required her full attention, and a distraction of any kind wouldn't be good. That was the kind of thing that used to make her fall off the balance beam, missing a hand placement, because something outside of her threw her slightly off. She didn't want that kind of thing happening tonight, to ruin her dance.

She closed her eyes and shimmied faster, trying to visualize all her stress moving down through her knees, down her legs and feet, and into the floor.

~

Cutter stepped into the theater, behind Diesel and Pippa, as they moved down the aisle, to their seats. Finding their row, they moved into it, found their seats, and then sat.

The lights dimmed, and music filled the air. Sweeping violins, and what sounded like a full orchestra, set the scene for a romantic Arabian night in the desert.

Not exactly the way Cutter remembered his time in the Middle East. For him, this show tonight would be total fantasy, like watching an Aladdin cartoon movie, or an old rerun of that show about an astronaut and a genie. Despite his time in the Middle East, he'd never seen a real belly dancer dance. Since, as Pippa had said, the stripper didn't count.

Many dancers came out for the opening number, and he enjoyed watching them. They weren't what he'd expected at all.

None of them looked Middle Eastern, but appeared like a cornucopia of many types of women, of varying skin color and hair color.

He'd barely glanced at the program before the show, noted all the Middle Eastern names, and how many dances there were, but that was all.

The program showed dance numbers alternating between the eight group dancers in the troupe, and dances where the troupe and student dancers performed together.

In between those dances, were solos by each of the eight troupe dancers. The opening number and closing number contained all the dancers. Each dancer was named and the names were obviously dance names.

Zarifah would be the next number.

She entered to mysterious sounding music, with a red veil wrapped around her, even her head, so that Cutter couldn't see her fully, only that she wore a red and gold bra, a red and gold beaded belt with fringe, and a red skirt beneath the red veil, which she could see through, to her audience. Her eyes were lined with the dark kohl often seen on women in the Middle East, as they peered out from their veils.

The beginning moves of Zarifah's dance mimicked this, and the blue of her eyes and her pale skin struck him with how stunningly beautiful she was.

Then the music changed, and she burst out of her veil, her hands still holding it, and he saw her long dark hair, and the pale skin of her graceful arms and legs. Tall for a dancer, she glided, and then spun, using her veil, the veils movements as fascinating as the dancer herself.

Fascinated, Cutter took in her every move, every expression of her face. Her dance skill was amazing. He'd never seen anything like it.

She was beautiful, moving with both a dancer's grace, and with an athlete's power, in a way the other dancers hadn't.

He wondered what she did, along with her dancing, to give her that athleticism. Her movements alternated, some smooth and flowing, and some strong bursts of power. Her long dark hair flew out behind her, and her veil soared through the air.

She danced like a goddess. Like a queen. She had a

majesty he couldn't have put into words, but he saw it, and felt it.

Her dance pulled him to her, as if she'd wrapped that veil around him, bringing them closer.

Then she bent over backward, her long arms touching the floor, one foot still on the floor as she went into the flip, the other leg coming up to go over, followed by the other leg. Her long slender legs fully visible, all the way up her legs to red dance panties, her pale skin beautiful against the red.

His breath caught. Those long sexy legs and her movements, along with the music, were the most erotic sight Cutter had ever seen. They reached out and called to him.

Smitten, he knew he had to meet her.

Cutter knew a thing or two about meeting dancers, and getting them to go out with him. This one was no stripper though, and he didn't know if she was single.

He would take a different approach, and treat her like a high value woman.

Taking out his phone, he pulled up Mrs. Brown's information, and placed an order, paying extra for quick service and delivery. Then he put his phone back down and continued watching the dancers, who while good, were nowhere, in his opinion, as good as Zarifah.

She was in a class all her own.

Intermission came and the house lights went up again, for a ten-minute intermission.

"Everything okay?" Pippa asked, gesturing to his phone.

"Yeah. I just had to order something," he said.

"Here? Now?" she asked, laughing. "I thought you had a thing for dancers."

"Yes." He nodded. "I do."

She just shook her head at him, and then the three of

them went out to the lobby. They moved around looking at the colorful art on the walls, which was for sale.

He hoped Zarifa might step out of the green room briefly, but no dancers appeared.

Then, when intermission was almost over, they went back in and took their seats again.

The second half of the show was just as good as the first, and Cutter now looked for Zarifah every time the black curtains opened again. He thoroughly enjoyed her dancing. She was not only beautiful; she was mysterious, and intriguing.

When the show was over, there was a standing ovation, and then the director thanked everyone for coming.

Diesel's cell phone rang and he answered it. Their three-year-old son, Bryce was running a fever. After Diesel hung up, he said, "Hey man. Sorry to bail on you for drinks and snacks, but we need to get home to Bryce."

"No problem, bro." Cutter said. "I understand. I hope the little guy is better soon."

"Thanks," Diesel said. "Me too."

Everyone gave quick hugs, and then Diesel and Pippa were off, hurrying home.

Cutter wondered if the flowers he'd ordered had been delivered yet. He'd ordered half a dozen roses of varied colors, and some white baby's breath in a vase. Since he didn't know what her favorite flower was, or her favorite color.

Most men went for red roses, but Cutter had his own way of doing things. He knew the language of flowers, and wasn't sending any sort of message to a woman he hadn't met yet. Varied colors was safe and non-threatening and, with no undertone message attached to them, she could just enjoy the flowers.

Zarifah was in the green room, putting all her costumes

into the suitcase she carried them around in, when a delivery person knocked on the door ,and asked for her by name.

Farrah who'd opened the door, pointed over to where Zarifah knelt, and the delivery person came in, carrying flowers.

"What in the world?" Zarifah said as she stood up. "Who is sending me flowers? I'm not even dating."

Hassan had always sent red roses; saying only red roses were good enough for a beautiful woman. So it wasn't him. And he would have sent twelve, or two sets of twelve, if he were feeling extravagantly generous, as he often was.

This bouquet was beautiful.

"I've never seen one like this," she said. "With all the colors."

"There's a card," Bayda said. "Open it."

Zarifah opened the card.

Zarifah,

I enjoyed your dancing tonight. I hope you enjoy these flowers.

Cutter C.

"I don't know anyone named Cutter," she said. "Does anyone here know a Cutter C.?"

All the dancers shook their heads and said, "no."

"Well, they're lovely," Amina said. "And your dance was too, so I'm not surprised you have a new admirer. Just enjoy them."

"Oh, I will," she said. The relief that Hassan hadn't showed up, and hadn't sent the flowers, made her relax again.

It's going to be fine.

"Does everyone have everything before we go?" Amina said. "Someone do a quick walk through, across the stage, to make sure nothing was dropped. The stage lights are still on, but I need to tell the lights and sound guy that he can go."

They collected all their things, and were carrying them out of the green room, when Zarifah saw a tall, handsome, dark haired man, dressed in black pants and a blue shirt, by the doors which led outside, waiting for someone.

Something about him felt familiar.

How do I know him?

They stepped closer to the door, and she got a better glimpse of him.

He had brown eyes and was smiling at her.

The smile warmed her from the inside out, as if he'd lit a candle.

No, I don't know him. But it feels as if I do.

Though she'd never seen him before.

Their security guy was waiting, to escort them to their cars. She hadn't even noticed him until now, and he was a big guy. Quite noticeable with his build. How had she missed seeing him? She'd been distracted by that handsome man.

Oh, I do not need to get twitter pated about a man right now. Not with Hassan out there. I need to pay attention to my surroundings. Focus.

"Miss Zarifah," the tall dark haired man said. "I enjoyed your dancing."

"Thank you," she replied, a warm blush spreading across her cheeks and neck.

Why am I blushing? I'm used to people complimenting me on my dancing. Oh, but this man, he's more than hot.

His voice reached something deep inside of her, and the way their eyes now met and connected, this was hormonal attraction on steroids. Something she'd never experienced.

Part of her wanted to pull her gaze away. Part of her wanted to stay.

"I hope you enjoy the flowers," he said.

"Oh, you sent them?" The surprise nearly knocked her over.

He sent them? This handsome guy? Oh my.

"Yes, I'm Cutter," he said.

"Nice to meet you, Cutter, and thank you for the flowers," she said.

"You're quite welcome," he said. "I'm glad you like them."

"It's an unusual arrangement, all the different colors. I've never seen one like this."

"My grandfather owned a nursery, so I know a few things about flowers. It's limiting to choose only one color, when there are so many variations."

A man who understand flowers, and puts thought into floral selections, she thought. *How fascinating. But, oh, is he gay? Maybe he's into dance shows and flowers because he's gay.*

That thought was tossing water on her attraction to him. But he was so hot. As was this attraction. Even the thought of him being gay wasn't putting it out.

Oh, I hope he isn't gay.

"You probably have guys asking you out all the time," he said. "Your dancing is sensual and enticing. But there's more to you than that."

Now every fiber in her being wanted to hear what he had to say next.

"You're an athlete," he said. "You move like an athlete. You've had training in something beyond dance."

He sees me. He really sees me. All of me, not just the dancer. He sees past the performance. Oh God, I hope he's not gay. Please don't let him be gay.

Because every part of her being wanted to, shout yes!

Their meeting seemed profound, fated. The way his

voice, and his eyes, were making her feel, was like some-thing out of a movie.

But she remained cautious. She had no idea what this was, or where it was going.

"Yes. I was a gymnast as a child," she answered.

"Still are, as far as I can see," he said. "You're very good. Where did you train?"

"I was at the ..."

Amina interrupted. "Our table at the restaurant is ready, and we're all starving."

Zarifah was as well, but she'd momentarily forgotten. The handsome man had captured her attention, and she didn't want the conversation to end yet.

"Cutter, if you'd like to continue our conversation, why don't you join us?"

Amina's eyebrows rose.

"I'd love to," he said.

"El Patron, two blocks from here," Zarifah said. "We're going for Mexican for tonight. None of us eat, before we dance, so we need to get over there, and order. If you'd like to meet us over there?"

"Perfect," he said, and smiled. "I'll see you there."

His smile made her break into a huge grin. "Yes, see you there."

Everyone headed to his or her cars, and this time, Zarifah didn't look over her shoulders, to see if Hassan was anywhere waiting.

He hadn't come to the show, or tried to contact her lately, so it really must be over, and he'd likely moved on.

As Cutter went to his car, he was aware of their surroundings. Situational awareness at all times was a way of life for him, not something he turned on, and off. Being unaware could get you killed.

He noted a black Mercedes, in the back lot, next to the

theater's parking lot, with a man inside who sat, talking on his phone. There were no other cars in that lot.

When they each pulled out of the theater parking lot, the man stayed in his car, on his phone and didn't follow them.

Cutter drove to the restaurant, excited to be getting to know the beautiful dancer a bit more. He parked, and then went in to join the group, still wondering who the man was, and if he'd been there watching someone, or waiting for someone.

With eight troupe dancers, and four companions, they were seated for twelve.

Cutter had a chair on the right side of the table, on the end. Not optimal, as he had his back to the door, and the chatter of so many women was high pitched and noisy, but at least he was across from Zarifah, and would have the chance to get to know her a little bit.

And she'd invited him into her world, something, which had surprised her director.

Once the drink orders and food orders were in, introductions went around the table, as he was a newcomer to their party.

Zarifah of course he'd met.

Amina, the troupe director, was there with her husband, Thomas Ballantine, a slightly balding man, who looked like a businessman. Bayda, a slim, pale, redhead was by herself, and sat with the only blonde dancer, Saba, who was with her husband, Ken, a slim effeminate looking man. The two black dancers, Latifah and Nasheeta were cousins, though they didn't look like they were related at all. Latifah had a big bosom, and more curves than Nasheeta. And Isis, who appeared to be Chinese or Korean was with her husband.

Most of the dancers had changed into day clothes, but

all still wore their heavier stage makeup, and a lot of jewelry, which jingled.

Already he was finding belly dancers much more interesting than strippers.

Zarifah out shone them all.

"I'm Cutter," he said. "Nice to meet everyone."

Pleasantries now exchanged, the drinks, chips, and salsa had arrived and everyone began to snack and drink.

He noted, as Zarifah was looking away from him, and dipping her nacho chip into her salsa, that she had a lot more makeup on one side of her face, which looked like it was covering some bruises. And when her wrap slipped off her arm and shoulder, that her arm was badly bruised. He wondered what had happened to her, but kept a poker face, and glanced away acting as if he hadn't noticed.

Taking charge of the table conversation, redirecting things, he said, "I'm curious. Your dance names are mostly Arabic, obviously stage names. How do you select them?"

Amirah answered him first. "The troupe name, Silk Lotus, was the name of my business, when I first started teaching yoga, and mediation. When I added belly dance, I kept the name, and we became the Silk Lotus dancers. But our style is for the most part, classic Egyptian, so we chose dance names to reflect that."

"Interesting," he said.

"What he's too polite to ask," Latifah said, "Is whether this is cultural appropriation."

"Mm hmm," Nasheeta nodded. "I know that's right."

"Obviously I'm Chinese," Isis spoke up. "I chose my name, because I love the Isis statues, and when I dance, I'm envisioning myself to be dancing the dance of Isis. The dancer chooses who the dancer wishes her dance to represent."

"Though it may seem like all of our names are made

up," Farrah said. "Three of us are using our real names. Can you guess which ones?"

He grinned. He would guess, but was fairly sure of his answer.

"Latifah, Nasheeta, and Farrah," he said.

Zarifah clapped and laughed. "Very good."

"And what is your real name?" he asked. "Or is it a secret, for security reasons."

"Edith," she laughed. "Edith Smith. Which I'm hardly going to dance under. So I searched through a list of names, and picked the most unusual name I could find on the list, because it started with a 'Z', and now I am Zarifah!"

Everyone laughed, Cutter especially.

She's charming. Entertaining, charming, and fascinating.

"Since you brought up cultural appropriation, I will ask. Have you had any blowback, from your choice of names?"

"No, not really. There may be a rumbling here or there, but we're behaving in a way which is respectful of the cultures we are representing. We study the folkloric dances; the history, and we try to portray them in a good way. As long as we are showing honor toward them, most don't seen to mind. The custom of American's choosing Arabic dance names goes back to the 1980's, I believe, or maybe even further, and in Egypt dancers have stage names. So people are used to it."

"Besides, who doesn't love a belly dancer?" Saba said with a laugh. "Most people love us. Some love us a little bit too much."

Zarifah said, "Some of us need to keep our real names out of the public because of jobs, or family. And as you mentioned, there is a safety issue."

"I hope you are always safe," he said.

Watching him over her margarita glass, she sipped. "So, Cutter, what do you do?"

"I'm a Navy SEAL," he said.

"Really," her eyes widened, and she sat her glass down.

"Yes. Really." Ready to change the subject, he said, "Is dance your day job, or do you have another?"

"I teach gymnastics to children," she said.

"And I imagine you're quite good at that, after what I saw of your dancing tonight."

"A bit." She smiled.

"A bit?" Latifah laughed. "Don't let this girl fool you. She's an Olympic athlete."

"Excellent," he said. "Talented, and modest."

"Well, I didn't actually go to the Olympics, I was just in training for it."

"Why didn't you go?"

"Coaches told me I was too tall, and quit training me."

He frowned. "They don't sound like very good coaches."

"They were, and yet they weren't." She shrugged. "So now, I teach, and I dance for fun."

"Sounds like a good life," he said.

"It is," she agreed.

"Hey Amina, if we'd known a SEAL was in the audience, you wouldn't have had to have hired that bodyguard to protect Zarifa," Nasheeta said.

Cutter zeroed right in on Zarifah's face, which had paled, if it could pale, beneath all that makeup. Now he'd find out about those bruises.

"Why do you need a bodyguard?" He kept his facial expression and his voice calm, so as not to alarm her, but his alpha protective mode had kicked in. If there was a threat, he was ready.

"Because my ex fiancé decided to take a few swings at me," she said.

"A few swings," he said.

"But the police put him in jail, and now I have a restraining order against him," she added.

"That's like expecting a lock to keep a thief out." He shook his head. "Locks are for honest people. A determined thief will cut right through. It won't stop him. And a piece of paper won't stop a determined man."

"Well, it's all I have," she said.

"You don't carry?"

"A gun? I don't even know how to shoot." She gave a small shiver.

Obviously, a woman who is afraid of guns. And me going out of town. Great.

"But I bought some pepper spray," she smiled, and reached into her purse, pulling out her key ring from which dangled a pink plastic tube of pepper spray. She looked adorable with her little pink tube, and her hopeful sweet face, and he'd bet money she didn't know how to use it.

"Good," he said. "You keep that with you at all times, and practice with it."

"Practice?" She wrinkled up her forehead.

"Have you tried to use it?"

She shook her head no.

"When we get outside, I'll show you," he said.

The food came, and everyone dug in.

Too soon, dinner was over and it was time to go.

"I have to go out of town next week, but I'd like to call you, and make plans to get together, when I get home," Cutter said.

"Okay," Zarifah said. She held out her hand. "Give me your phone."

He handed it to her, and she put her number in.

"Thanks," he said.

"You're not going into danger, I hope," she said.

"Not next week," he said. "I've got to go visit my grandmother. She's eighty."

"Aw, that's sweet," she said.

"But danger goes with my job," he said.

She blinked, taking that in.

*Might as well be totally honest with her from the start. No
sugar coating anything. Only way to start a good relationship.*

"So this ex fiancé," he said. "Do you have a picture of
him?"

"Why?"

"So I know what he looks like. To protect you."

"Oh."

"That's what I do, sweetheart. Protect. Serve. Defend."

She reached for her phone, scrolled through it, and
found the pic. Thrusting it away from her, as if she couldn't
stand to look at it, she pointed it at him. "That's him."

He looked at the pic. An Arab most likely from the look
of him. Likely a wealthy one. He'd met many of that type.

"Got it." He nodded. "Thank you."

"Oh! No, thank you." She said. "For caring enough to
want to protect me."

"Always," he said.

They gazed into each other eyes, the attraction strong.

He saw hope, trust, and wariness, as well as attraction in
her eyes.

She didn't know him well enough yet. And that was all
right. This was a good start.

"Thanks for your number," he said.

"You're welcome," she said. "Safe travels, and enjoy your
grandma."

"Thank you. I intend to," he said. "Stay safe, Edith
Smith."

Surprised, she realized she'd wanted to thank him for

the flowers. He'd distracted her from that. "Thank you, for the flowers," she said.

"You're welcome. Thank you for your dance," he said, "and for inviting me to dinner with your friends."

Everyone stood to leave, and it got noisy as they all said their good nights.

When they came out of the restaurant, Cutter noted the black Mercedes again. This time, there were two men in the car, and they were watching the building. Cutter's senses went on immediate high alert.

There was no reason for the men to be sitting there watching them, unless their goal was to watch.

Someone is being followed. Neither of the two men fit the picture she'd just showed me.

He wondered who the men were, and who was being followed.

"Come over here," he said to Zarifah, and she moved toward him. He stood feeling the wind, so he could point her in the right direction, to spray her pepper spray.

She had it in her hand as if she didn't know how to hold it.

He showed her how to hold it, and how to spray it, and then said, "You'll want to note the wind, so that it doesn't blow back into your face."

"How can I do that if he's coming at me?" Her voice rose a bit with a degree of panic.

"You note it the minute you walk outside, then you're ready. Not the minute you see a guy coming at you. You're watching, being ready."

"Okay."

"Now try it."

After a couple sprays, he was satisfied that she at least knew how to shoot the spray.

He walked her to her car, and they said goodbye again.

Then he went to his car, got in and waited, until all the others had pulled away, and he continued watching, to see if the Mercedes would follow any of the ladies.

But none were followed.

Now the men were watching him.

He pulled out of the parking lot, and headed toward his home. Though he watched in his mirrors, the Mercedes didn't follow.

Though the men had done nothing to follow, he couldn't shake the feeling that something was off about those men, and that they were watching one of their party.

His intuition about such things had never been wrong.

6

Now that the Arabian Nights show was over, which was their big show of the year, the dancers could turn their full attentions to the new Shimmy Mob event. Amina had asked everyone to come to the studio five minutes early, before rehearsal if they could, so she could talk to them about Shimmy Mob.

"Team leaders have the music, and you'll get that from me. You'll need the edited version, which goes with the choreography, so don't go out and buy the other one. The correct one is five minutes long. I already have the edited version on my phone, if you'd like to listen to it now."

"Yes, I would," Zarifah said.

"Yes we want to hear it!" Latifah and Nasheeta chimed in together.

Amina found the song. "This is Shisha by Naked Rhythm." She hit play.

The music started and they all quietly listened to it.

"Oh I love it! So peppy," Bayda said.

"Yes, me too," Farrah said.

"Where are we going to dance?" Isis asked.

"I don't know yet," Amina said. "We have to line up a

place. I sent a few messages already, to get things started. One to the mall, which should have a lot of foot traffic. We need a place we can dance free, since we're not selling tickets to offset that cost, and because this is a fundraiser."

"The mall would be great!" Bayda said.

"Lot's of shoppers and people to see us there," Saba said.

"I'm not sure how to collect money either, beyond passing baskets around, after we dance." Amina said. "I've never put together a fund raiser of any kind."

"What about an online site?" Isis asked. "One of the fundraiser ones?"

"Or you could use your dance site for the studio where students sign up for classes," Latifah said. "Since that's already set up to take payments."

"No, I don't want to co-mingle the money," Amina said. "That doesn't help; it just creates something to detangle later. This has to be totally separate from my business. I don't want anyone thinking everything isn't transparent, and above board, with the money."

"Yes, that makes sense," Latifah said.

"But an online donation site sounds good," Amina said. "And we'll need PR. I'm hoping for coverage, so we can get the word out."

The next day, Amirah and Zarifah met for tea ,and planning for Shimmy Mob, at a coffee shop not far from where Zarifah worked. After quick hugs, they went straight to business.

"Today was the last date for dancers to sign up," Amina said.

"How many do we have?" Zarifah asked.

"Thirty five! Isn't that wonderful?"

"Yes it is! Wow, so many! I don't think I even know that many dancers in town."

"We don't have all the dancers in town signed up, but we do have a good number of them," Amina said. "Most are from Riverton, some are from cities right next to us, but we also have two dancers coming from three hours away!"

Zarifah's eyes widened. "That's quite a drive just to dance."

"They believe in the cause, and we're the closest Shimmy Mob city to them."

"I still think that is quite admirable. They're going to have to drive the three hours, dance, and then drive three hours to get home, so that's six hours in a car. I know troupe dancers who won't go that far, even to dance at a paid gig."

"Yes, I know." Amina nodded.

They shared a glance, as they both knew the two dancers being referred to. But neither of them was going to gossip about them.

"I love this whole Shimmy Mob," Zarifah said. "I get excited every time I think about it."

"It's going to be amazing," Amina said.

"Have we got a site to dance at yet?"

"No" Amina shook her head. "That's proving to be a lot harder than I thought it would."

"Do you want me to help with that?"

"Yes, I would love your help," Amina said.

"Okay, I'll need a list of places you've tried already, so I don't repeat what you've done."

Amina opened her spiral notebook, and opened it to her list of possible sites.

Zarifah took out her phone, and took a picture of that page.

"Oh what a good idea," Amina said. "That saves time spent rewriting everything."

"Thanks, but it's not my original idea. Hassan used to take photos of my planner all the time." She tapped on the blue planner in her purse. "He said it was to keep track of when I was free to see him."

"If that was the case, then why did he always call you, when he knew we were together, and you were busy?"

"I don't know. I used to wonder the same thing. Now, I believe he was checking up on me, to see if I was where I'd said I would be. I took the app off my phone, after he went to jail."

"What app?"

"There's an app parents can use to track their children by cell phone, to make sure they're safe. He put it on my phone, supposedly for the same reason."

"That is so not okay for a boyfriend to do," Amira said. "Even if he is your fiancé."

"I know that now," Zarifah said. "But at the time, I just thought he was being protective, and wanted me to be safe."

"Wow. Well, I don't see how that would keep you safe," Amina said. "All it would do is tell him where you are, not fend off an attacker for you!"

"Right." Zarifa nodded. "He was very controlling. I see that now. Back then, I just thought he was being concerned, and protective."

"I'm so glad you're away from him." Amina reached out for her hand, and gave it a squeeze, and then she let loose, and her face lit up with happiness. "I did connect with the shelter, and have that part set up. They're thrilled we are doing this. I've got an appointment tomorrow with the director, and will get to tour the safe house during the day, when the children are at school, and the mom's are at job training, or counseling."

"Oh, that's wonderful," Zarifah said.

"If you'd like to go with me, as my assistant, that could

be approved. But you have to promise never to reveal the location, not to write it down anywhere, or share it online. The location is a secret, and they're very careful who they tell about it."

"Wow. Yes, I'd love to take the tour," Zarifa said. "You know I'm discreet."

"Yes, I know you are, or I wouldn't have asked you." Amina nodded. "Okay, so I'll pick you up at eleven, and then we'll head there. Then lunch afterward, if you have the time."

"I have the time," Zarifah said.

~

Cutter texted Zarifah
How's rehearsal going? Have you practiced with your pepper spray?

She answered him.

Rehearsal hasn't started yet. And we haven't found a place to dance. Thanks for the reminder about the pepper spray. Got to dance now.

She put her phone away, and prepared to dance as the other dancers entered the studio's.

"Bad news. The mall is out," Amina said. "They want us to carry a million dollars worth of insurance, just to dance there for less than ten minutes."

"That's crazy," Latifah said.

"Whatever it is, I don't have that kind of money," Amina said.

"Oh no. So, we can't dance at the mall," Bayda said.

"What are our other options?" Saba asked. "Are there other places you've checked out?"

"But all we're trying to do is raise funds for the domestic abuse shelter," Nasheeta said. "Don't they understand that?"

"They do," Amina said. "But one of the problems is, it's a flash mob, and some flash mobs around the county have been destructive and disruptive. So their insurance company won't cover events like ours, in case something goes wrong. That throws everything on us."

They were back to the drawing board and still had to find a site.

~

The next day, Amina picked Zarifah up, and drove to the shelter.

The shelter didn't have a mailbox with numbers, or any numbers marking the house from the street. An older two-story building, it had an enclosed front porch, with high brick walls, over six foot tall, and screens across the top, between the porch walls, and the roof.

"Wow, they've done a good job hiding them away," Zarifah said.

"Yes, they have. I'm impressed," Amina said. She drove her small silver Honda up the drive, and stopped in front of a gated back yard. More brick walls, and a strong electric gate.

Rolling down her window, she went to press a button, but a voice came through the speakers beating her to it.

"Ms. Crandall?"

"Yes. I'm here with Edith Smith. We have an appointment with Margot Chadron, the director of your center."

"We're expecting you. Please park in the first spot by the back door." The gate door started to slowly swing open.

"Thank you."

Amina rolled her window back up, and drove through the gate that began to close behind her, once the car was through.

"It feels like they're watching us," Zarifah said.

"Because they are," Amina said. "They have to watch."

"I understand, I'm just not used to this."

"Me either, but I understand the need for it. That makes it easier. And knowing it keeps the women and children safe, and the women who work here, I feel safer, actually. No one's crazy ex is going to be able to come in here, and hurt people."

"That is a very good thing." Zarifah nodded her head emphatically.

Amina had parked, while they were talking, and now she turned off the car, and they got out to walk toward the back door.

The door opened, and a short black woman stood holding the door and smiling. "Welcome," she said. "We're all so excited for what you are doing for the shelter. Come on in."

They went up the concrete steps and followed her inside.

~

Saturday was the night before the big day. It was their final rehearsal, and everyone was excited to see what color the Shimmy Mob t-shirts were.

Amina, as the team leader knew, because the box was shipped to her, but she'd kept the secret, even from Zarifah.

"What can it be?" Bayda asked. "I can't wait to see them."

"You haven't even opened the box yet?" Zarifah was amazed.

"Oh, I peeked just a little," Amina, said, "I know what color they are, but I closed the box back up again."

Zarifah laughed.

"Sneaky," Bayda said. "I'd have peeked too."

"Help me hand them out?" Amina asked Zarifah.

"Yes, of course," Zarifah said.

Amina sat the box on the floor, pulled the tape off the top, and then reached her hand inside, her eyes twinkling, and her mouth turning up in a smile, as she teased. "Everyone ready?" she asked.

"Yes," the chorus of women replied.

She whisked out a red t-shirt, and held it up. "It's red!"

"Oh good," Zarifah said. "I love it!"

"Of course you do. Red is your color." Amina laughed.

The women had swarmed around them, to get their shirts, and as Amina read off each name and corresponding size, each dancer got her t-shirt.

Some of the dancers tried their t-shirts on right away, and some knew their-shirt would fit, so they tucked their shirts into their dance bags.

Latifah, stuck trying to put on a shirt, which was too small for her, ended up trading with Nasheeta, whose shirt was too big. Finally, each dancer had a shirt, which fit well enough, and they were happy.

"Okay ladies," Amina clapped her hands to get their attention again. "Ladies! Time to rehearse!"

Everyone lined up and she started the music.

With every Saturday scheduled as a Shimmy Mob rehearsal day, and two nights each week, Zarifah had less time for dating, than she ordinarily had. In between learning the dance, she was also trying to help Amina find a site for them to dance at.

Cutter was understanding and patient. Qualities she'd put on her wish list for the perfect man for her.

This time she was going to be picky, because she'd been

far too understanding, and forgiving before.

This time she wanted what she wanted.

And if she couldn't have the kind of man she wanted, she was far too busy anyway.

But even with everything going on, Zarifah and Cutter kept bumping into each other, as if fate was knocking them together, to make sure they connected.

The first time it happened, she'd just finished teaching one of her classes, and was coming out of her rental space, and heading to the Deli, a couple of stores down, when she saw him coming out of the barber shop, with a shorter, new haircut.

"Cutter, what are you doing here?" she asked.

He pointed to his head and grinned, then said, "I might ask you the same."

"I just finished teaching a class, and am on my dinner break," she said. "I'm heading to the Deli, would you like to join me?"

"I would," he said, with a grin. "Perfect timing."

"It is," she agreed. The butterflies in her stomach were now doing summersaults, and she was hungry. It was so nice to have company, and not be eating alone, and especially nice to be eating with him.

"So you teach here?" he asked. "I didn't know that. But I come here all the time to get my hair cut. I wonder why we've never bumped into each other before?"

"I don't know," she said. "It wasn't the right timing I guess."

"Timing is everything," he said. "Fate turns on a dime."

"True," she said. "I guess we just got lucky." She watched him open the door for her, and then she walked into the deli.

How did I get so lucky? What are the odds of me bumping into him like this?

The second time it happened, she was at the library returning books, when she heard a voice behind her, that gave her butterflies in her stomach.

"I'd say we have to stop meeting like this," he said.

She whirled around to see him, with a big smile. "Cutter!"

He continued. "But that's such a cliché, and whatever is making this happen, I hope it keeps up."

"It is kind of fun, isn't it?"

"Have time to go for a coffee?"

"I do. Your timing is good," she nodded.

"It's not me arranging it," he said. "But I'll happily take it."

The third time, she was pumping gas, when he pulled up at the pump next to her, got out, came around, and said, "Here, let me help you with that."

He was such a gentleman, and these little surprises were so nice, and becoming so frequent, that she found herself fussing with her hair and makeup, before she left her apartment to go anywhere.

Had he not been so surprised himself at these happenings, and they not been so random, she'd have thought he was following her, and setting the meetings up. But each time had felt so genuine, and the surprise and pleasure she saw in his face, made her think this was real. She didn't think he could've been faking it, or setting it up.

Besides, he was sometimes brutally honest. That had taken a little getting used to, but after the smooth moves of Hassan, she found that she actually liked his way much better.

Honesty was a solid foundation for any kind of relationship.

She would even bet that, if she asked him if a dress made her fat and it did, he'd tell her yes. It wasn't a bad thing to have someone in your life like that.

After the third time they bumped into each other, on the following day, she started looking for him everywhere she went. But she didn't bump into him then.

Maybe she was trying too hard.

Her phone did ring that night, however, and it was Cutter.

"Hello," she said.

"Let's put our schedules together, and schedule a real date," he said. "I want to take you to dinner somewhere nice, so you can relax."

"Oh that sounds nice," she said. "I'd like that."

"Have your planner handy?"

"Yes. It's right here in my purse."

They settled on a date, and she wrote it in her planner.

"Can we go somewhere that has steaks?" she asked. "I've been hungry for a big steak."

"I bet you're not getting enough protein. When was the last time you had steak?"

"I can't even remember," she said.

"Then a steakhouse it is. I know a good one. Pick you up at six."

"That's perfect."

When the day of their first official date came, she thought back over the get togethers, which had come before. It really didn't feel like a first date, as they'd been getting together a little bit here, and a little bit there.

He texted her every couple of days to see how she was doing. Partly he was making sure she was safe, which she appreciated.

He really is such a thoughtful man. It's good to know he cares.

She stared into her closet, wondering what to wear. Not one of her tight, skinny dresses, because she really was hungry. But not something loose and baggy, either.

Was there nothing in between?

She sighed and reached for the snug, royal blue dress, which everyone said brought out the blue in her eyes. Likely she'd have to get a doggie bag for half her steak.

By six she was ready, and Cutter was prompt on the dot. Her doorbell rang ,and she hurried to open it, stepping into her shoes just before.

When she open the door, his eyes widened in appreciation. He whistled a low, slow whistle, and she watched his lips.

She smiled up at him. "Hello," she said. "You look wonderful too."

He really did, in a dark suit, white shirt, and dark red tie. He could've stepped out of a movie, or a fashion catalog, he looked so good.

"Come on in," she said.

"It's a bit chilly. You may need a sweater, or wrap, but it's a shame having to cover you up, in that dress," he said.

"I'll just get my wrap," she said, and went back into the bedroom.

He watched her walk away, and he watched her walk back, pulling the wrap around her shoulders. He watched as if he'd like to unwrap her.

Holding her elbow, he escorted her to the car, and opened the door. He waited while she climbed in.

A single red rose sat on the dash, right in front of her.

"You like to spoil me with flowers," she said.

"Yes," he said. "That I do." Then he closed the door, and walked around to his side.

Once in the car, he turned soft violin music on, and then pulled out of the parking lot.

He was a romantic sort of man.

She glanced at him, and wondered how he would be in bed. If he would make love slow. She hoped he would.

7

She watched his hands as he drove.

After a while, he said, "You're very quiet."

"I'm just enjoying the music, and the ride," she said. "You were right. I do need a nice dinner, and to relax. I've been going nonstop."

"We're going to a small restaurant, where you should be able to do just that. It's less than an hour away, and worth the drive," he said. "They've converted a house into a restaurant, and the separate rooms created a small, cozier feeling, then most steakhouses."

"Oh that sounds nice," she said.

"I didn't see what was in your stack of books the other day," he said. "But it was quite a tall stack. What do you like to read?"

"Oh, a little bit of everything," she said. "Mystery, romance, romantic suspense, history. What do you like to read?"

"Fiction with action in it, history, nonfiction, military, biographies. Lots of things."

"Wow, you read a lot too."

"When I have time."

"It's probably hard to do, when they deploy you all over the world."

"I read when and where I can. It's relaxing for me. But if I get too caught up in a book, that could be a bad thing. So no, not so much during deployments. I'll tear through a stack, when I'm in the states though."

An image of the two of them, curled up on a couch or in bed, each with their books, reading, entered her mind.

One of the things on her list of qualities for a good boyfriend was, loves to read.

They reached the restaurant, and he pulled the car into the parking lot and parked. "This is it," he said.

She put her hand on the door handle.

"Stay put." He opened his door, got out, and came around to open her door.

It was so nice, the way he treated her like a lady, opening doors. He was always a gentleman, and tonight he looked so handsome.

Inside the steakhouse were small rooms, each with several tables covered with white tablecloths, and small vases of flowers with lit candles in the middle.

An intimate, romantic place was where he'd taken her on their first "official" date, and it was lovely.

After they were seated, and the waiter had poured water for them, and handed them their menus, she asked, "Do you have any suggestions? What is good?"

"Everything is good, madam," he said.

"Order anything you want," Cutter said. "If that's the Porterhouse, then get that."

"That is for two, sir," their waiter said.

"Yes," Cutter replied. "I know."

"That's two steaks," she said. "I can't eat two steaks."

"You said you were powerfully hungry for steak," Cutter

teased her. "I'm just letting you know to order as much as you want."

"I could never eat a New York strip and a tenderloin, even at my hungriest," she said with a laugh "But it says here, that it's for two, and we could share one. I've never done that before."

"Never? Well then, you're in for a treat. That's what we'll do."

"Porterhouse for two is a twenty two ounce, thick cut, served with roasted red potatoes, sautéed wild onions, vegetable of the day, and house rosemary demi glace. You may substitute a salad for the vegetable, or order a salad on the side," the waiter paused, waiting for them to speak.

"What is the vegetable?" she asked.

"Today vegetable is, roasted Brussels sprouts."

"Oh, I'm not a fan of Brussels sprouts," she said.

"You wish the salad instead?"

"Yes. Salad for me," she said. "Ranch dressing if you have it."

"We do." The waiter nodded. "And for you sir?"

"I'll have a salad as well," Cutter said. "Thousand Island."

"Very good sir." He left to put their order in.

"We can share part of each steak, and that way you'll have tried everything."

"Sounds good to me," she said.

The waiter returned with hot fresh bread and butter.

"Oh, this is one of my weaknesses," she said. "Fresh bread."

Cutter took the serrated knife, and cut slices of the bread for them. "Then enjoy," he said. "Tonight is all about treating you."

"It is?" That surprised her.

Usually, dates were about a man trying to impress her.

Watching Cutter, she realized he behaved as if he had no need to impress anyone.

I guess being a SEAL is impressive enough. They know what they can do, and don't have to prove anything to anybody.

He was the most truly confident male she'd ever met. It was a quiet confidence.

"So, if you hadn't gone into the SEAL's, or the Navy, what would you have done?" she asked, taking a piece of bread, and reaching for the butter.

He handed the small butter plate to her. "I might've ended up working in my grandfather's nursery, raising flowers," he said.

"That's why you know what you do about flowers."

"Yes." He nodded. "But as much as I enjoyed helping grandfather, I wanted to be a SEAL more than anything else. I thought about it night and day. Was obsessive about it, I wanted it so bad."

"Wow. Was your grandfather disappointed?"

"If he was, he never said. He did say that he was proud."

"Well I should think so," she said.

I don't dare ever tell him, that when I first met him, I thought he might be gay. I must've been out of my mind. He's the manliest man I've ever met. He just happens to like flowers and dancers.

"Penny for your thoughts," he said.

"Oh no," she said. "I can't."

"Now I'm even more intrigued."

"No, really, I can't," she laughed. "And anyway, it's ridiculous."

"And still you won't share it with me? Is it that bad?"

"I don't want to ruin our date."

"Nothing you say could ruin our date."

She raised an eyebrow.

"Okay now we are veering in a direction which concerns

me. Instead of the two of us having fun, there's a weird vibe moving in, which needs sorted out."

"If I tell you, you have to promise you won't get mad."

"I doubt anything you say would make me mad."

She raised her eyebrow again.

"Look, I'm not going to get angry at anything you say."

"Okay." She took a deep breath. "I thought, when we first met, you know, at the theater, and you liked dance and flowers..."

He started laughing, and said, "You thought I was gay."

She shrugged. "Well, flowers and dance."

He shook his head. "That's ridiculous. Before I met you, I dated lots of women. Mostly strippers."

"Oh."

"Yes, oh."

"What made you stop? Dating strippers."

"They never wanted to kiss."

"I like kissing." She smiled at him; glad he wasn't angry with her.

"I like long kissing sessions, the kind that steam the car up."

"Oh yes, I like those too."

The rest of their dinner went well, and soon they were back at her apartment.

He walked her to the door, and waited while he fished his keys out.

"Would you like to come in?" she asked. "And, stay for coffee?"

"I'd much rather stay for kisses," he said. "If you're offering kisses."

She turned to face him. "Oh yes," she said. "I'm definitely offering those."

Always ask for what you want, he thought. *That almost always pays off.*

He'd missed kisses, and long make out sessions, with a woman he cared about.

Since he'd met Zarifah, kissing her had been foremost on his mind.

Much can depend on a first kiss. It sets the tone for the relationship. And this first kiss has waited long enough.

Cutter bent to kiss her, not waiting for her to finish unlocking the door. His lips descended to meet hers, lightly brushing them at first, then he kissed her softly.

Her lips parted as she kissed him back, her arms reaching up around his neck.

He slid his hands around her waist, to her back, and pulled her closer. His tongue teased her lips, light and playful.

She opened her lips wider, her tongue coming to meet his, the tip teasing him back.

Their tongues met, touched, teased, danced.

He grew hungry for her, and she for him, and the kiss deepened, her breath coming shorter, her hands holding on tight.

Instead of breaking the kiss, he moved her back against the door, and finding the key in it, turned and opened the door, while still kissing her.

Cutter moved her into the apartment, closed the door behind them, and flipped the lock. Then he placed both hands on her hips, and guided her, as he kissed her, through the front room, into the bedroom behind it.

Still kissing her, he backed her up to the bed, until the backs of her knees met the bed.

When she felt the bed behind her knees, she gave way, sinking down onto the bed, and pulling Cutter down with her as they continued to kiss.

His hands left her hips, and moved slowly up her sides,

where he found a zipper on one side of her dress. She was now flat on the bed.

He raised his head, letting them both come up for air.

"Still too many clothes," she said.

"I agree," he said. "Let's lose them."

"My dress is not easy to get into, or out of," she said.

"I can help you with that," he said.

He unzipped her dress, kissed her neck, and then turned her around to kiss her lips.

Their first kiss had gone so well, he couldn't wait to see how their first long make out session would be. He intended to take things slow with her, and do no more than to kiss her as much as she wanted, and anywhere she wanted.

Kissing her was something he could do all day.

International Belly Dance Day was here, and the first Shimmy Mob flash mob event was happening. It was May first, 2011, and they would be making history.

Zarifah could hardly wait. She'd dressed an hour before she'd had to, and was dancing in her apartment, not caring if she bumped into anything, or knocked anything over.

She'd made her place danceable again, and reveled in that freedom.

While it might not be decorated as prettily, or as richly as it had been before, the space was hers, she was free, and she was dancing.

Turning on the music again, she danced, and laughed.

The joy was back in her soul, and dancing Shimmy Mob had given it back to her.

When the knock came on the door, it surprised her. She turned off the music, and went to the door and peeked out.

Cutter.

He stood holding one single red rose. Dressed all in black, he was the most handsome man she'd ever seen.

She felt like the luckiest woman in the world.

Though she'd been full of joy before, her heart now soared with happiness, as she opened the door.

"Hello," she said. "Just when I thought this day couldn't get any better."

"Brought you something," he said, handing her the rose.

"You spoil me," she said, her smile from ear to ear.

"You're worth spoiling," he said, giving her a warm smile.

She let him in, and went to put the rose in a vase with water.

Her happy face and sparking eyes greeted Cutter, when she opened the door.

Seeing her happy sent a smile across his face.

She took his breath away.

When she went to put the flower in her vase, he watched her move, her gracefulness, and strength. The careful way she put the flower in water, and set it on the table, that happy smile on her face.

He wanted to kiss her, but waited.

As if she'd read his mind, she set the flower on the table, and then came to him, putting her palms on his chest, looking up into his eyes, stretching up for a kiss.

Their lips met, and time slipped by, as they tasted and touched each other.

A beep made them break apart. It was followed by another beep.

His watch and her phone had gone off at the same time.

"Didn't want you to be late," he said.

"I set an alarm too," she said. "Oh, we need to go."

"There's time," he said. He knew there was no rush and she was just excited. They had plenty of time to get to the farmers market where the women would dance. "Are you ready?"

~

Next to the Riverton farmer's market, was an empty area, between a parking lot full of cars, and the fruit and vegetable stalls, where the local Shimmy Mob dancers would perform.

Cutter watched Zarifa, as she greeted the other dancers and they looked around the area they would be dancing. He loved seeing how excited she was, and how happy.

The excitement he'd seen building in her, the way she'd blossomed in the few weeks he'd known her, was a thing of beauty.

Zarifah had gone from being a victim, to being a survivor, to being a thriver.

He was so damn proud of her.

The dance group needed pictures and video of their dance, to be shared on social media, one of the things Shimmy Mob International had asked each team to send in, so each dancer had asked her family and friends to come out to watch them perform, and to take pictures and video.

Several of them had shown up, but there'd been no discussion of who was doing what, so Cutter opted for video. He had a good camera on his phone, and his hand was steady.

There would be at least one video they could count on.

Taking his cell phone, Cutter found a spot on the left side of the performance area, which was perfect for taking photos or video, and waited for them to go on.

He spotted Zarifah in the crowd, waited for her to see him, and then nodded to her.

She smiled, and waved back, clearly exited, as joy shone in her face and movements.

He returned a smile, happy to see her enjoying herself. Then he turned his head to scan the area, taking in the venders, the shoppers and browsers, and the occasional man standing by himself, likely waiting on his woman, as Cutter was. The farmer's market was busier than he'd expected, but then he didn't shop at farmer's markets. Instead, he went to the grocery.

Other than a few curious glances at the dancers, who were gathering together, wearing red Shimmy Mob t-shirts, which were eye catching red with white lettering, most shoppers were busy shopping.

It was a peaceful crowd.

Cutter's habit of scanning a crowd was momentarily interrupted, when Zarifah and the other dancers, moved into the open area, to begin their five-minute dance.

Amina, the Shimmy Mob team leader, spoke into a microphone, getting everyone's attention, and explained why they were there to dance, what Shimmy Mob was, and the local shelter they were raising funds for.

Cutter listened to her as he scanned the crowd again.

People were moving near to the dance area, and had turned their attention to the dancers.

Done speaking, the director signaled someone, who turned the music on.

The dancers moved out into the center of the pavement, then turned as one, and went into the number.

Holding his cell phone steady, to video their dance, as he'd promised her, Cutter watched with his own eyes to see her fully, and to make eye contact if she looked his way.

He could've watched Zarifah for hours, the way she moved, her long arms and legs graceful, yet strong.

The smile she wore on her face today spoke of triumph and happiness. She had a glow.

Her eyes met his, and the heat between them sizzled.

He sent her a smile.

Her smile deepened, the joy spreading.

She was the most beautiful dancer he'd ever seen, dancing in her joy.

He watched her throughout the entire dance, and as she took her final pose, with all the other dancers, he ended the video, before he slipped his phone into his pocket.

Crack.

Horror filled her eyes, erasing everything good, as the loud crack of a bullet broke through the noise of many hands clapping.

Cutter jerked his head around, and his sharp gaze went toward the area where the gunman must be, his hand automatically reaching for his side arm, as women and children screamed and ran in all directions.

Pulling out his side arm, the gun was in his hand, a movement as natural to him as breathing, as all his training kicked in.

Where's the gunman?

8

Cutter searched for his mark, as men, women and children ran, right and left, screaming. Innocents.

The gunman wouldn't be running. He'd fired at the dancers, but none had fallen. With nothing but cars in the lot behind the dancers, he had to be shooting at the dancers.

Who is his target?

Cutter's gaze searched and locked, onto an olive skinned man, with a beard, who hadn't been there before.

The man turned his head, giving Cutter a glimpse.

Hassan.

His angry gaze was searching for Zarifah, who Cutter could still see in his peripheral vision, as he kept one eye on her, while he prepared to get his mark in the cross hairs. Protecting his woman, who'd shuffled in one direction, and then another, more to dodge dancers who were running past her, than out of any instinct to move, before freezing, with her eyes as wide as a deer frozen in bright headlights.

Neither flight nor fight, she froze.

Rage filled Cutter. But then he focused, still as a rock, as his vision kept an eye on her, while getting his mark in the cross hairs as his training kicked in.

Zero in on target. Mark. Aim. Shoot.

Crack.

Clear shot. Repeat. Mark. Aim. Shoot.

Crack.

The fast sequence of a double tap. *Over and done.*

Hassan's head jerked back, both shots true to target, and then he went down, his gun arm dropping down toward the ground, the gun no longer aiming toward anyone.

The echo of Cutters firearm had caused even more hysteria among the general population, as more women's high-pitched screams filled the air.

"Everyone stay calm!" he yelled.

With a quick glance to Zarifah, he saw she stood frozen, still.

The only one still in the dance area. She appeared not to have been hit, just scared.

He scanned the area again, looking for a second man.

Seeing no other threat to her, Cutter burst into a run.

He ran over to where the man fell; ready to shoot again, if needed.

Reaching Hassan, he kicked away the man's gun, to where Hassan couldn't reach it. Then he knelt, checking for other weapons, and checking to be sure the man was dead.

Confirmed. Dead.

Zarifah.

He looked back to where she'd been standing.

She's gone.

He stood, his eyes searching for her. From the last look he'd seen in her eyes, she'd been terrified. He needed to find her. Calm her. Let her know it was over, and she was safe now.

But he didn't see her.

Has she been hit?

He could've sworn she hadn't been. He ran toward the

space where she'd been standing, and his eyes searched for where she might've gone. Then he heard her.

Weeping. *Not far.*

She was behind the closest stall to where they'd been dancing.

He placed his gun in its holster, and moved her way. Moving into the stall, he saw her, curled up beneath the wooden stand, her knees folded in, her arms wrapped over her bent head, covering her ears, as she shook and cried.

"Don't kill me, please," she begged. "I'll go with you, I promise."

It hit him in the gut, seeing her like this and hearing her beg.

"Zarifah," he called her name. "It's Cutter." He squatted down next to her. "You're safe. He's dead."

Still shaking, she peered between her arms, but kept her arms still wrapped around her head.

She saw him, and then she whispered, "He's dead?"

"Yes, he's dead. He won't ever hurt you again."

Her arms fell slowly away from her head, as if completely exhausted, and tears came rushing out now, as she released what her fear had held back.

Knowing she needed to be grounded, to touch something solid, he took hold of her arm and pulled her nearer, as he sat on the ground, then wrapping his arms around her, he held her close.

She clutched onto him, still shaking and crying.

He kissed the top of her head as he continued to hold her. "I've got you, babe. You're all right. I've got you."

Her sobs turned to hiccups, which shook her diaphragm.

She leaned into him, seeking his warmth and strength, moving slightly, as if she'd burrow into his skin, as if she couldn't get close enough.

His arms tightened around her, tight as he could make them, without hurting her, letting her know, by the fierceness of the hug that she was safe and protected. Cared for.

Her hiccups slowed, and then stopped.

Taking one hand, he stroked her head, her silky hair, treating her with the tenderness she deserved.

He wanted to take away her fear, her pain, her bad memories, and was waiting for her to calm, and know it was over, and she was all right. He repeated the words. "You're all right, babe. It's over."

Taking a deep, jerking breath, she leaned her head back, to look up at him. "It really is over? He's gone?"

"Yes," keeping his voice firm and strong, to reinforce that one word, he answered her.

She took another deep breath, the remaining tension making it jerky.

He cupped the sides of her face with both hands, and their eyes connected like an intense lock.

"Breathe," he said.

She took a breath, but not a deep enough one, like he'd wanted her to take.

"Deep breath," he said. "Again."

She sucked in a deep breath, and without breaking their gaze, breathed.

"Again," he said.

Following his commands, she slowly calmed her breath, her heart rate, and her mind, until she reached a state of calm.

He saw it in her, felt it in her, and heard it in her.

They'd never been as close as they were in this moment.

And then, he kissed her.

His lips descended, his hands still holding her face in his palms, his lips soft upon her lips, the most gentle of kisses, letting her know she was loved, treasured and cared for.

With a soft sigh, she responded, her lips parting, her breath slowly escaping, her lips and tongue ready to follow his lead.

His tongue had just met hers, when he heard sirens nearing.

Police had arrived. Likely ambulance too.

The sirens startled her again. Her startle reflex was ramped up from her experience.

He pressed his lips against hers, once more, and then, ending the kiss said, "We'd better stand now. The police will need to take our statements."

Dazed by the kissing, and the events, her eyes now widened. "Oh, police. Right. He's not allowed to come near me. I have the restraining order, in my purse."

"He can't come near anyone. He's dead," he reminded her, since she'd spoken as if Hassan were still alive.

It hadn't fully sunk in yet.

"But I'm glad you have the document with you," he said. "That will help, when you give your statement to the police."

"You, you shot him, didn't you?" She asked, her tone not sure.

Good. She hadn't seen.

He'd been hoping she hadn't.

She'd had enough traumas, and didn't need to see that.

"Yes," he said. "I shot him."

"I'm glad," she said. "I'm so glad."

"Come on," he helped her to stand.

Once she was up, he slid one arm around her waist, keeping her close.

She leaned in toward him, still drawing from his strength. "I'm so glad you were here," she said, "If you hadn't been..." Her eyes gazing up at him, widened, at the thought of what might've happened.

"I'm glad I was here too." He gave her a squeeze.

She was soaking up the physical attention like a thirsty sponge. But she was also a distraction.

Police were moving around the farmers market, assessing the situation.

His guns were holstered, but he would need to declare them, and give his statement. He needed to redirect her thoughts now. "Do you have your purse?"

"No. I hope it's where I put it before we danced."

"Show me where." He had a pretty good idea where it was, but this would redirect her thoughts, giving her something to do.

"Okay."

Sticking by her side, he let loose of her, and took her by the hand.

She walked toward the tree, where the dancers had put their things, with a companion there to watch them.

No one was there now, but her purse was still where she'd left it.

She picked it up, and then looked at him, unsure what to do next.

"Come on," he said. "They'll want to take our statements."

All the dancers were gathered in one area, far away from the spot where the body lay sprawled on the concrete.

Police had taped off the area where the body lay, and officers were taking down names, and asking questions.

"We might be here for a while," he said, "Go with your friends, and tell the police what you know. They'll want to talk to me separately. Don't worry if they separate us. You're safe now." He squeezed her hand, before letting go.

A policeman walked up to them, one hand on his gun. "Sir, do you have weapons to declare?"

He raised his hands away from his weapons. "Yes sir, I do. Two guns. One my side arm, and one on my calf."

The officer started to remove Cutter's weapons, patting him down, as another officer watched, ready with his gun.

Once they'd removed his forty caliber Sig Sauer side arm, and the thirty-eight revolver on his calf, along with a six-inch blade folding Buck knife, and with a three-inch bladed knife, Officer Kelly said, "Those are a lot of weapons for a civilian to carry. You active duty?"

"Yes, sir."

Officer Kelly nodded. "Figured as much. They're singing your praises, over there." He nodded toward the group of women in the red t-shirts. "Everybody loves a SEAL. One of them got the whole thing on video. It's clear you saved many lives today. I'm still going to need your ID, and your statement. Step over here with me, and we'll sit in the privacy of the squad car, away from your new fan club."

"Yes sir." All of this was expected. He had after all, just killed a man. Even if he'd saved lives by doing it.

An hour later, the homicide detective cleared Cutter to go. They gave him all his weapons back, except for the gun he'd used, telling him that he could have it back after the investigation was over.

Cutter now knew a lot more than he had previously about Zarifah's ex fiancé, Hassan.

Like the fact that he wasn't a U.S. citizen. Perhaps that was one reason he'd been upset about Zarifah cancelling their engagement. He'd have been able to stay in the country longer, if he'd married her.

And he was a person of interest, on one of the watch lists, with a watch only status. They didn't tell him why. He wasn't going to ask.

The man was no longer a threat to anyone.

Vendors had given their information to police, and then had closed up for the day.

No one was going to be selling anything, right next to

the crime scene, and most likely everyone just wanted to go home to his, or her, comfortable familiar places where they'd feel safe.

Zarifah had been very shaken up by the events, and he needed to see her up close, and assess how she was dealing with it.

Hopefully she'd been checked for shock.

An EMT could treat her, there were plenty standing by.

She was sitting near a closed fruit stand, with one of her dance friends, waiting. Probably waiting on him. The other dancers had all gone home.

He was glad that at least one of them had stayed with her.

"Ready to go home?" he asked.

"I am," she said. "Cutter, this is my friend, Bayda."

"Pleased to meet you," he said.

The woman grasped his outstretched hand enthusiastically. "Thank you, for saving our lives," she said. "We owe so much to you."

"You don't owe me a thing," he said, as he finished shaking her hand, and then let go.

"I told everyone to go on home," Zarifah said. "Bayda wouldn't leave."

"You're not getting rid of me that easy," Bayda said. "And we weren't going to leave you here, by yourself. Especially after what almost happened. Belly dance sisters look out for each other. That's what sisters are supposed to do."

"Thanks for staying with Zarifah," Cutter said. "I'm glad she has a good friend like you."

Bayda beamed.

"I want to tell the officers something," Zarifah said.

"Sure honey," Cutter put his arm around her. "Come on. They won't mind."

She'd seemed hesitant about talking to them; he could hear it in her voice.

They walked over to the officers together.

"Excuse me," she said, not quite loud enough, and then she cleared her throat, and said it again. "Excuse me,"

The officers turned to look at her.

"It's why we were dancing today," she said. "Shimmy Mob raises funds for our local domestic abuse center."

"Never heard of it," officer Owens said.

"That's because it's brand new," she said. "This is our first year."

"Awesome," he said. "Next time though, you need to get a permit. Get permissions. We can't really condone mobs, even for a good reason."

As they turned to go, Officer Kelly came up to Zarifah. "Let us know when and where you're dancing, so we can come by, and keep an eye on the crowd. Keep you safe, while you're dancing." he winked at her.

"I've got my own SEAL right here," she said, looking up at Cutter. "He does a real good job protecting me."

"Yes, ma'am, he does," officer Kelly agreed. "More than you may know."

"Good night," she said with a smile, waving at the police officers.

Surprised, the officers waved back at her, smiling and said, "good night."

Zarifah and Bayda gave each other hugs, and then Cutter watched to be sure Bayda was safe in her car, before she drove away.

"You've had quite a day," he said to Zarifah, as he watched her friend, making sure she was safe.

"Quite a day, yes," she said. "I really just feel like curling up somewhere."

"Do you want to curl up at home, or do you want to curl

up at my place, and watch a movie? Just snuggle. Til you fall asleep," he said.

"That sounds wonderful," she breathed the words out, as if each word was releasing stress she'd held.

"Good," he said, putting his arm around her, and guiding her toward his car. "So home, or my place?"

She obviously wanted to snuggle, as she'd made no choice.

"Your place," she said. "Snuggling sounds really good."

"I thought it might," he said.

"The police officer who took my statement, took my order of protection, wrote down some stuff about it, and then handed it backing saying 'These don't always work. Sometimes they make matters worse,'" she said.

"No piece of paper is going to stop a man intent on doing harm."

"I'm glad you stopped him," Zarifah said. "If not for you, I'd be dead right now."

"How about we celebrate that. I remember you don't eat, before you dance, and you need to eat something. Want to order a pizza?" he asked. "Pizza and a movie, and snuggle?"

"That sounds really good," she smiled. "Especially the snuggle part. I don't care if we have pizza, or whatever you want. But can we have ice cream? I'm really wanting ice cream."

"Of course. What kind of ice cream do you want?"

Ice cream must be her comfort food, he thought. *I wonder what her favorite is?*

"Some kind with chocolate."

"We'll stop on the way to my place, and pick up whatever you want."

9

———

Back at his apartment, she went into his bathroom to freshen up, while he put the ice cream and other purchases away.

She came back out. "I need a shower," she said. "I'm sticky and stinky."

"Go ahead." He said. "I'm going to order the pizza. What would you like on it?"

"It doesn't matter," she said.

"What kind do you like, when you're hungry for pizza?"

"Mushroom, onion, olives."

"We can do that," he said, picking up the phone. "Go ahead and hop in. I want one too."

In the bathroom she found a clean thick towel and a washcloth. Peeling off her clothes, she turned on the shower. Warm water streaming, she stepped in.

When she stepped out again, she saw he'd placed one of his clean t-shirts on top of the sink for her. She was glad of it, as she hadn't brought clean clothes with her. She dried off, and pulled the t-shirt on, feeling how soft it was. It had seen many washings, and she wondered if it was one of his favorites.

It felt nice wearing his shirt. The shirt came just to the bottom of her buttocks, so she pulled her panties back on. She did feel a whole lot better, and now she'd smell better too.

Rubbing her hair with the towel, she walked back out, carrying the rest of her dance clothes.

He stood in the kitchen, pulling out two paper plates and some napkins. There were two water bottles on the counter.

He pointed to them and said, "Hydrate."

She went over to her bag, tossed her clothes down next to it, and then came back for the water bottle.

"Do you like hard boiled eggs?" he asked.

"Yes, why?"

He opened the fridge, reached in, and then pulled out an egg and offered it to her. "Because you need protein, and our pizza doesn't meet that need. Here," he said. "There's salt on the table if you need it."

She took the egg from him, and sat at the kitchen table, tapping it to crack the shell off. "Do you eat like this all the time?" she asked.

"What, eat protein?" He looked at her. "Of course, don't you?"

"I tend to just not eat, to keep my weight down. I can't eat before I dance."

"So what have you eaten today?"

"Piece of toast and jelly."

He shook his head at her. "That's nothing."

"I eat a lot, after I dance, to make up for it."

"So you need that protein now." He sat the water bottle on the table next to her, and then said, "I'm going to hop in the shower. Won't be long."

"Okay."

Five minutes later he was back, with a towel wrapped

around his waist. He saw she'd eaten the egg, and smiled at her.

She smiled back. "Wow, that was fast."

"I had to learn to be fast. And the pizza will be here any minute."

"I could've answered the door, and paid for it."

"Yeah but I didn't want you to have to."

The doorbell rang, and she jumped.

"Be there in a minute," he called. He went and pulled on elastic waist shorts, and his holster for his side arm, then came back out, and headed for the door.

"Do you always do that?" she asked.

"Do what?"

"Answer the door armed."

"Sweetheart, I'm usually armed. And when I'm not, it's never far away."

"Oh," she said.

That could take some getting used to. But she had to admit; it did make her feel very safe.

He paid for the pizza, and then took it, and closed the door. He carried the pizza in, and put it on the coffee table in front of the couch.

"You get to pick the movie," he said. "Bring the waters, and come on."

His couch was very comfy, and after she ate two pieces of pizza, and had cuddled up next to him, she smiled, as she felt safe and happy with him.

He said, "I'm glad to see you're doing better."

"I'm just happy to be alive," she said. "Really happy."

"Seeing you happy makes me happy," he said, then kissed the top of her head.

Curled beneath the soft warm throw blanket he'd had on the back of the couch, she fell asleep before the movie was over.

When his cell phone went off, he reached for it, and saw it was his grandmother.

Answering it right away, before it could wake Zarifah, he said, "Hello grandma."

"Tony," she said. "I saw on the news about the shooting. I had to call you, to see if you're all right."

"I'm fine grandma. You'll never guess what I'm doing."

"Now don't give your grandma a heart attack here. Are you in the hospital?"

"No, I'm unscratched," he said. "But I have to be quiet, because, I'm holding an angel right now."

"This one is not one of those strippers."

"No, she's far from that. She's a high value woman, and I'm going to take very good care of her."

"Well, it's about time. When do I get to meet this angel?"

"I'll talk to her about that, and see when she can take some time off, for a little vacation."

"Is this the girl you talked to on the phone, when you came to visit?"

"Yes, grandma."

"I thought you might have found a good one. I'm glad."

"When I bring her to visit, I want you to promise me something."

"What is it?"

"I want you to promise, no more talking about grand-babies. I don't want you to scare her away with it."

"Does this one not like children?"

"She loves children. She teaches them gymnastics."

"Then she is healthy enough to have her own?"

"Grandma." His voice was warning her.

"I'll promise not to say a word near her about it, until after the wedding."

"Slow down, grandma. This is what I mean about scaring her away."

"What, she has something against marriage?"

"There needs to be an engagement first. I have to get her to say yes."

"I promise you, if you bring her here, I'll show her everything good about this family," she said. "Then she will want to marry you! She will not say no. You bring her, we will make it happen."

"Okay grandma. We have a deal."

"I'm glad you have not one scratch. And I'm glad you saved that girl. Is she your sleeping angel?"

"Yes, grandma, she is."

"I like her. She has a good heart. This Shimmy Mob, I do not understand it, but they are showing film clips from all around the world. It is a good thing, Tony boy. I like her already."

"Thanks grandma. She's going to love you too."

"I love you, Tony boy."

"I love you too, grandma."

"Bye bye," she said.

"Bye bye," he said, and hung up the phone.

He placed it back on the table, and looked down at his sleeping angel, her eyelashes resting against her skin, no makeup, and those bruises nearly faded away.

She really is beautiful.

He could hardly believe she was here, in his arms.

His grandmother was right, she had a good heart.

Instead of staying in a victim mindset, which she could so easily have done, she'd stepped up to join Shimmy Mob, to help other women like herself, who'd been attacked.

She cares about others.

He wouldn't mind spending the rest of his life protecting her, if she'd have him. He didn't want to lose her. And for one brief moment today, he might have.

SEALs didn't miss, but if the shooter had gotten one

good shot off, before Cutter had known there was an immi-
nent threat, it could've gone the other way.

Thank God it hadn't.

She might be an angel, but he wanted her here on earth,
with him.

*Funny how near death could change you. Make everything
crystal clear. Speed up time, and make you see your priorities.*

For the first time in his life, he was actively thinking
about getting married. Meeting her had changed his life.

But he would take it slow.

*There's no rush. She deserves a slow courtship, and to be
wooed, like the high value woman she is.*

He'd make sure they were suited for marriage together,
and do the best thing, for both.

It isn't easy being married to a SEAL.

*A long engagement will be good. She'll need that, after that
jerk off she'd been engaged to. She might need other things, to sort
herself out. Maybe a counselor of some kind, to talk to.*

He would encourage that, and whatever else she might
need.

*That Friday flower thing, Mrs. Brown talked about. That
will be a good way to start this courtship. And I bet Mrs. Brown
will deliver them for me, when I'm deployed, so the pattern could
be kept while I'm away.*

Something steady that Zarifah could count on.

It wasn't long after that thought, that he too drifted off to
sleep. It had already been a very long day.

THE END

WHAT IS SHIMMY MOB?

The inaugural Shimmy Mob was held on May 1st, 2011. Shimmy Mob members support domestic abuse shelters worldwide, with an annual bellydance flash mob, to raise awareness of domestic abuse and shelter locations. Sabeya, the founder of Shimmy Mob, intended to hold the event one time only, as a fund raiser for local women's shelters. The response to the event was unanimous: do it again.

Each year, on International Bellydance Day, all around the world, Shimmy Mob members dance, wearing matching shirts, dancing our choreography for the year to the selected song as a fund raising event. To learn more, visit: https://shimmymob.com/

ACKNOWLEDGMENTS

Thank you to all who helped make this book happen, and who have helped me share this story, and Shimmy Mob, with the world.

Thank you, Francesca Sabeya Anastasi, for creating Shimmy Mob and for being such an inspirational leader.

To all my Memphis Shimmy Mob assistants, and all the Team Leaders, who came after me, to help our local domestic abuse shelter and to help the women and children who came through the shelter.

And to all my dance sisters throughout the world, from those who joined Shimmy Mob from the first year in 2011 and each year after.

You know the meaning of sisterhood and you know how to love your neighbor.

Though I no longer live in one location, as we move across the U.S. in our motorhome, my heart dances with you, even when my feet can't dance beside you.

Sabeya, you made me want to share a Shimmy Mob story with the world, and so I did, and we know what this one small ripple in the waters has already done, when the book was previously titled *Protecting Zarifah*. Thank you for sharing that story in the interview.

To all my Shimmy Mob Sisters, and those I met in my Shimmy Mob and Bellydance journeys.

To all who've supported the cause and my books.

Now as to the writing of the book and the production side, my thanks ...

To Bobby, who helped with the gun scene.

To my editors and early readers who wanted more of this story. You will have known it as, *Protecting Zarifah*, when it was part of Susan Stokers Operation Alpha series. When the rights were returned to me, in August 2022, I then revised the book to fit into a new setting as part of my new SEAL series world, The Green Brotherhood: SEA Team XII. There, the book will now stay.

To Sheri L. McGathy, my cover artist.

To retired Navy SEAL Bill Hellman, who advised me on the creation of my new SEAL Team series, The Green Brotherhood: SEAL Team XII as I incorporated this revised story into the series.

Thank you to my family, and especially my husband, for love and support through all these journeys and adventures we've been through.

Special thanks to all my readers. I've loved being able to share this story with you, to give you a glimpse into the world of Shimmy Mob Bellydance. To those who are new to Shimmy Mob, you will find a page with a link to learn more.

My infinite love and gratitude to you all.

- Debra Parmley

NOTE FROM THE AUTHOR

Thank you for taking the time to read *Finding Bryce, Real Movie Hero*, and *Saving the Bellydancer,* in this trilogy box set. If you enjoyed my stories, please consider telling your friends and or posting a review.

Word of mouth is an author's best friend and much appreciated. Reviews are so important for authors. If you would be so kind as to leave a review and a rating on any website, this is the best way to give back and encourage authors whose work you have enjoyed.

Please know that I appreciate and read every single review.

Infinite love and gratitude.

Debra Parmley

ABOUT THE AUTHOR

Author Debra Parmley believes "Every day we are alive is a beautiful day," and she likes to give her readers and her story people a story that ends happily.

An Air Force veteran's wife, Debra writes suspense, and military romantic suspense, contemporary romance, historical romance, urban fantasy romance, fairy tale romance, holiday romance, poetry, and memoir.

Debra married her high sweetheart, whom she asked out after a five-dollar bet. After living in five states with her husband and their two sons, and then living 23 years just outside Memphis, TN, she and her husband sold everything in 2020 and now live and travel the U.S. in their 43-foot motorhome.

Debra is an adventurous writer who has sold travel and has walked the plank of a pirate ship off the coast of Grand Cayman. She has gone swimming with dolphins in Moorea, French Polynesia, has escorted a bus full of people through Scotland, and has set foot in 13 countries. She climbs lighthouses because she is afraid of heights.

You can see read about her travels on her Beautiful Day Traveler blog. https://beautifuldaytraveler.wordpress.com/

As Debra Bishop, she writes fairy tales for all ages, fantasy, and children's books.

Visit www.debraparmley.com

ALSO BY DEBRA PARMLEY

Military Romantic Suspense:

Green Brotherhood SEAL Team XII:

Finding Bryce, book one - eBook, paperback

Real Movie Hero, book two - eBook, paperback

Saving the Bellydancer, book three - eBook, paperback

Green Brotherhood Trilogy #1 - ebook box set, paperback

Brotherhood Protectors series:

Montana Marine - eBook, paperback

Defensive Instructor - eBook, paperback

Marine Protector - eBook, paperback

Marine Protectors box set - ebook

Blind Trust - eBook, paperback

A Triple C Ranch Christmas Wedding - eBook, paperback

Montana Delta Rescue - eBook, paperback

Montana SEAL Protector - eBook, paperback

Montana Rodeo Protector - eBook, paperback – 2024

Montana White Horse Wedding - eBook, paperback - 2024

Bobbins Sisters Trilogy:

Check Out – book one, eBook, paperback, audiobook

Check In – book two, eBook, paperback

Check Mate – book three, 2024

Single Title:

Aboard the Wishing Star - eBook, paperback, audiobook

Jenna's Christmas Wish - eBook, paperback

Western Historical Romance:

Gone to Texas: A Desperate Journey - (original sweeter version) - Large Print Hardcover, eBook, paperback

Dangerous Ties - eBook, paperback, audiobook

Deadly Adversaries - eBook, paperback

Desperate, Dangerous, Deadly: A Western Collection – eBook box set

Isabella, Bride of Ohio: American Mail Order Bride – (original sweeter version) - Large Print Hardcover, eBook, paperback

Penny from Deadwood - 2024

1920's Romance:

Butterflies Fly Free series:

Trapping the Butterfly – book one, Large Print Hardcover, eBook, paperback, audiobook

Dancing Butterfly – book two, eBook, paperback

Exotic Butterfly – book three, 2024

Poetic Butterfly - book four, 2024

Fairy Tale Romance:

The Twelve Stitches of Christmas – (short story) – eBook

Futuristic/Dystopian Romance:

The Hunger Roads Trilogy:

Another Change of Scenery – 2024

Down a Back Road – 2024

Into the Convergence Zone – 2024

Urban Fantasy Romance:

Vague Directions - ebook, paperback - 2024

Poetry Anthology:

Twilight Dips – eBook, print

Nonfiction Memoir:

Anywhere But Here: Our First Year of Full-time RV Living on the Road - eBook, paperback - 2024

Out of Print:

Protecting Pippa

Split Screen Scream

Protecting Zarifah

Vague Directions – short story

A Desperate Journey

Isabella, Bride of Ohio

Tales of Deadwood - anthology

We Know the Truth, Do You? Area 51 – anthology (going to the moon/time capsule)

Wounded Heroes - anthology

Hansel & Gretel: Down the Rabbit Hole – anthology

More Monsters from Memphis – anthology

Writing as Debra Bishop:

YA Fantasy:

The Rolling House – YA time travel serial fiction eBook

Children's stories

The Purple Unicorn - 2024

Fairytales:

The Sweetest Day - fairytale Hansel and Gretel story, eBook, paperback

Fantasy:

Gatalop – 2024

Bellserie – 2024

www.ingramcontent.com/pod-product-compliance
Lightning Source LLC
Chambersburg PA
CBHW032007310726
48972CB00002B/312